KING OF VEGAS

CITY OF SINNERS BOOK 1

SIENNE VEGA

Blurb

From the moment he comes into the Dollhouse, he won't take his eyes off me. He might be just what I need. A big spender to help me with my money issues.

But there's just one problem.

This is no average man. This is Giovanni Sorrentino, the new King of Vegas. And when I stumble on something I shouldn't, I realize I'm in big trouble.

Now it's more than just money on the line. I'm a goner unless I accept his deal—vow to be his, and I get to live. But how long will it be before this savage King tires of his new toy?

This is a work of fiction. Names, characters, places, and incidents either are the product of the author's imagination or are used fictitiously. Any resemblance to actual persons, living or dead, events, or locales is entirely coincidental.

Copyright © 2022 Sienne Vega

All rights reserved. No part of this book may be reproduced or used in any manner without written permission of the copyright owner except for the use of quotations in a book review. For more information, visit: www.siennevega.com.

First paperback edition February 2022

CONTENT WARNING: King of Vegas contains situations of graphic sex and violence. Please be advised the content is inappropriate for readers under the age of eighteen.

1

Falynn
PLAYLIST: ♪ 6 INCH - BEYONCÉ
FEATURING THE WEEKND ♪

"AIN'T a thing on this earth free except the air we breathe," Tasha says, leaning closer to the mirror, penciling in her brows. "If you're hard up, do what you gotta do, girl."

"It's not like there's much choice." I sigh as I set my things down inside our dressing room at the Dollhouse. I'm running late after the bus showed up half an hour off schedule.

"A girl's gotta survive somehow. There's no shame in it." Tasha winks at me in the mirror, always good for a pre-stage pep talk. As one of the veteran dancers at the Dollhouse, she's seen girls come and go over the past couple of years. Some escaped our lifestyle. Others fell deeper into it.

But she's right. I have to survive somehow.

It's the story of my life. As far back as I can remember, I've been somebody flailing in water, fighting not to drown, just to stay afloat. Years later, standing in the dressing room at the Dollhouse, it's no different. Except now I survive on stage.

I look down at the two outfits I'm debating between. Both are about as much fabric to cover one ass cheek, but that's the idea—as little as possible covered, as much as possible showing. Basically, the more ass on display, the bigger the tips.

"You know Jerry's good for it, right?" Tasha asks when I don't say anything. She turns away from the mirror, full face of makeup done. It makes sense why she's one of the most popular girls at the club—her curves make men drool on sight. Unfortunately for them, she also has the smarts to finesse them out of their cash. "He only takes a cut of what you make. Better than a lot of managers in these clubs. They love making their girls work 'til there's nothing left, then they take most of it."

"I'm in. I won't be able to pay the bills otherwise."

"Doesn't look like it, with Enzo catching a charge. Look, Falynn, start off small. Only offer what you're comfortable doing. It's all up to you how far you're willing to go—and if some asshole gets out of pocket, security'll check them."

"Which one?" I hold up both outfits by the hanger. The one on the right is a bandeau top and thong bottom bedazzled with rhinestones. On the left is a sheer, iridescent one-piece with an obscenely deep cut down the front and back.

Tasha points at the one-piece. "It'll stand out more."

I toss the bandeau and thong set onto the nearby sofa and start slipping on the one-piece. Tonight I'm wearing my chin-length, blunt-cut, bubblegum pink wig. It not only pops against my honey-brown complexion, but the shorter length's cooler to dance in.

"I'm up in five. See you later." Tasha moves toward the door, but then stops for another glance at me. "Falynn, for real if you need somewhere to stay, you know you're always good sleeping on my couch."

I smile in thanks. Since my first shift at the Dollhouse,

Tasha has taken me under her wing. Unlike some of the other girls who saw me as new competition, Tasha showed me the ropes and taught me the game. She's the only one I trust.

But I can't take her up on her offer. I've already crashed on her sofa several times over the last few months. I can't keep making it a habit. With Enzo participating in a robbery at gunpoint, he'll likely get locked up for real this time. I have to figure out how to pay my own way. Whatever it takes.

I'm working the stage with Skye tonight. When she sees me approach backstage, she gives me the type of dirty look you save for someone who cuts you off in traffic. The feeling's more than mutual, but unlike Skye, I can behave myself and play nice. At least whenever money is involved, and working the stage is all about money.

Our music starts, a darkly seductive beat fills up the gentleman's club. It's like a switch flips inside of me as I go into performer mode. I strut onto stage in my towering heels, swinging around my pole as the announcer introduces me as Honey.

It wasn't my original stage name, but a regular once kept calling me it, so eventually it stuck.

As the beat builds, I swing a few more times around the pole. On the opposite side of the stage, Skye graduates to tricks, contorting her body around the pole, her long fiery hair swaying hypnotically.

The men are enamored with her. In the club's dim lighting, shadows cover half of their faces, but their heads are turned in her direction. She has dollar bills piling up on her side of the stage.

More nerves flood my stomach as I climb up the pole. It's not working the stage that has my nerves out of control. It's what comes after that has me uncertain—the time I said I'd work in the VIP rooms. For years I've worked as an exotic dancer, but I've never escorted before. It's going to be new territory for me.

Enzo won't be happy. But maybe he shouldn't have gotten himself locked up. He shouldn't have left me with the bills and the debt, now having to pull in double the income to stay afloat.

If you're hard up, do what you gotta do, girl.

Tasha's words echo in my ears louder than the music blasting from the stereos. A new spark of confidence surges through me as I wrap my body around the cool metal, sliding down the pole in a deft figure-eight shape. It's still not enough to compete with Skye, who's busted it open midair on the pole, her legs splayed apart.

As I climb again, giving a few quick butterfly kicks, a strange feeling washes over me. It's that weird feeling you get when you know you're being watched. Only this is different, because I'm on stage, and I'm *supposed* to be watched. It takes me only a second to figure out where in the audience the feeling is coming from.

Far in the back, where the VIP section is situated, is a group of men in dark suits. Even at a distance I can tell the suits they wear and the bottles they drink from are expensive. The biggest spenders in the club, and the perfect marks for the night. But there's only one man who gives me the strange feeling tingling down my spine.

He sits at the center of the group, a broad-shouldered mass of muscle even in his meticulously fitted suit. His posture is relaxed with an arm hanging on the back of the couch. It doesn't take away from his commanding presence. He's authoritative, in such control he can afford to be so cavalier, so *lax* in a room filled with other men. Though his face is half hidden by the deep shadows of the dark club, his attention is unmistakably on me.

Another shiver jolts down my spine, but I don't let it mess me up. I perform more tricks, seductively spinning around the pole to more bills tossed my way. As the next song starts, I throw another look in the watchful man's direction.

He's *still* watching me. He leans forward only to grab hold of a drink, thick fingers enclosing around a glass a quarter filled by amber liquid. The shadows catch his face, keeping him obscured except for a square jawline peppered with dark stubble.

It's official: he seems to only have eyes for me—and he likes what he sees.

Just the rich motherfucker I've been looking for.

The nerves pooled in my stomach melt away into nothing. Tonight isn't going to be so bad after all.

An hour later, I'm off the stage, mingling with tonight's guests. It's the easiest part of working at the Dollhouse. You saunter through the lounge area, hopping table to table. You chat them up, laugh at a joke or two. Make them feel adored. Make them feel *special*.

Easiest cash I've ever earned in my life.

After flirting with Sal, a regular with thinning white hair, I check the time. It's half past midnight, which means the night is still young. There's still plenty more cash to be made. I'm due for my time in the VIP rooms, though I'm not sure if anyone has picked me out from the roster.

Mr. Rich Motherfucker is gone. The VIP section in the lounge is still full of the men in suits he had come in with, but he's disappeared. The last time I saw him was right after my time on stage ended. Did he leave for the night since I'm done performing?

I didn't realize I had anonymous fans who visit only to see me dance…

But if he's gone now, I need a new mark for the night.

The Dollhouse is one of Vegas's most elite gentleman's clubs. Most of our customers already have cash to throw around—or are on a last bender before their life goes up in smoke. It doesn't make a difference to me so long as I get paid.

The club is huge, two floors with several private rooms. The private VIP rooms are where us girls offer our additional services. Different girls offer different things. Like Tasha says, it's all up to us how far we're willing to go. If a guy gets out of line, security is pretty good about snatching them up and tossing them out.

I square my shoulders back and strut toward the hall leading to the VIP rooms. It's cordoned off by velvet rope, with two bouncers outside the entrance, ensuring only performers and VIP guests are allowed through. The bouncers nod their heads, stepping to give me passage. The music from the main part of the club follows me, still loud in my ears, a bass thumping like a heartbeat.

The hall is dimly lit by neon blue lights, casting everything else in shadows. I'm heading toward the showcase room, where VIPs pick their girls, when somebody whistles for my attention. It's Jerry, our club manager.

He's shorter than I am when I'm wearing my heels, pigeon-chested with scraggly gray hair he ties into a ponytail. Some of the girls think of him like a father figure, but I've always found him more like the creepy, handsy uncle hidden away in every family. It's the way he leers. Somehow more lecherous than paying customers.

"Honey, you've got a special request tonight," he says. He places a cold hand on my shoulder, letting it slide generously down my bare back. "Lotta money to be made from this one."

"Who—?"

"Room five. He's waiting on you. Oh, and once you're done, come by my office. I've got an important message for you," he says, and then he shuffles off down the hall.

I stand there in the dark for a few more seconds, barely lit by the blue bulbs above. This is the moment I've been thinking about all night. If I keep walking, if I go into room five, there's no turning back. I'm doing this for real.

A shaky breath leaves me as my thoughts land on Enzo and what he'd think. Actually, I know *exactly* what he'd think. He'd see red. He'd be pissed beyond belief his girl—the one he'd been with for almost two years—was providing sexual services for cash. Even as I worked as an exotic dancer, he's never been happy with it. He's sulked in the corner of the club plenty of times, providing a close and jealous eye, and then making it known later that night in his bed I understood I was his.

"You left me alone with all the bills. *And* your debts to those damn loan sharks. I'm doing what I have to do," I whisper to no one. Another pep talk to keep my nerves solid.

VIP room five is like all the others. In the center of the room is a long metal pole stretching floor to ceiling. Along the back wall is a large leather sectional for guests to sit and enjoy their private show. At the front is space for dancing or tricks or whatever else we're getting up to. There's mirrors around the room, offering guests every angle possible of us performers.

The mystery of where Mr. Rich Motherfucker went is solved.

He's seated alone on the sectional. Instead of shadows, now his face is obscured by a haze of cigar smoke. But his presence is as dominating as ever, his large and muscular form intimidating as he puffs out another ring of smoke and reclines against the leather cushion.

I keep it strictly business, strutting inside with my performer mask on. Right now, I'm not Falynn Marie Carter. I'm Honey, the sexy dancer about to milk him for as much cash as possible.

Music plays, slower and deeper than the fast-paced synthesized stuff in the main lounge. I draw closer, eliminating the gap between us, almost near enough for a real look at him. I'm a dark silhouette outlined by the blue lights in the room as I start dancing for him. *Only* him.

My hips gyrate in an entrancing rhythm. With each move, I'm slinking closer, lips pouting sexily as I stare straight ahead at him. If there's one thing I've learned in my years of dancing, it's men love eye contact; it makes them feel like they're the only man in the world you want.

I spin around, legs splayed far apart, and bend over to touch the floor, offering him a front row view of my ass in the air. My hands slip behind me and I undo the top of my one-piece in a fluid motion. It drops to my waist, revealing my breasts as I stand up and rotate my hips more sensuously.

He gives no reaction, only shifts in his seat, smoke floating around us.

Part of me begins to wonder why he requested me. There are better dancers at the Dollhouse. Girls with more T&A than I have. Definitely girls who're willing to go further than I am servicing customers. What is it about me that captured his interest? Why is he so intent on choosing me?

When I'm least expecting it, he gives his first order.

"Touch your tits," he says in a cold, commanding voice.

It's like leather. Smooth but firm and tight, possessing a dark, authoritative feel.

He's not asking. He's telling me.

And, for an inexplicable reason, as I let my hips sway and my hands rise up to cup my breasts, I'm obeying without question.

He leans back in his seat, places his cigar back in his mouth. Another large cloud of smoke puffs out from the end of the cigar, but before it clouds around him, I'm treated to my first real glance of him.

His hair is dark, a little long but neatly smoothed away from his face. His beard is also neat and trimmed, jawline as square and strong as I'd imagined when up on the stage. He has a large, masculine nose that centers his face, but it's his eyes that send another shock jolting down my spine.

They're the color of electricity. A burst of lightning contained in his gaze.

Damn, he's hot as fuck. Which means I'm in trouble as fuck.

I manage to keep up my performance, still seductive, biting on my bottom lip. He shifts again in his seat, almost as if about to sit up straighter. There's a charge sparking to life, kindling in the air between us. I can feel it, and I think he can too.

My gaze drops to his lap. It could be the shadows and low blue lighting, but if I don't know any better, there's a bulge in his pants. I'm turning him on.

That only encourages me more as I glide closer, ready to climb on him for a proper lap dance. His phone goes off, disrupting the sexy, sensuous vibe in the room. He snaps out of his watchful trance, pulling a phone from the inside of his suit jacket.

I pretend nothing has changed and gyrate some more.

He reads something on the screen. His thick fingers fire off several messages in reply. Then he's standing up, rising to full, impressive height. He has to be six-four, six-five.

I'm not sure what to do, so I keep moving, keep my gaze on him.

He pushes a stack into my hand. "We're not done here."

Finally, I stop dancing. I catch a whiff of his scent through the cigar smoke, a powerful musky blend of leather and cognac. It's affecting enough to disorient me and make me foggy-brained. Is this really happening right now?

"Thirty minutes," he says, his dark voice bringing goosebumps to my skin. "Wait near the back entrance."

He's gone within the next second. The door swings shut, and I'm alone, half-naked with a wad of cash in my hands. What the hell just happened?

As I blink out of surprise, I glance down and my jaw drops. There's *at least* a grand in this stack. If not more.

His last words play back in my ear.

We're not done here. Thirty minutes. Wait near the back entrance.

Does he want to continue our time together? Finish what we've started? But why near the back entrance of the club?

"I'm not *leaving* with him," I say under my breath. "He could be some psycho serial killer for all I know."

But I can't take my eyes off the wad of cash. The roll of bills is so wide I can barely close my hand around it. He's paid me well over a grand just for a five-minute dance. *High roller* doesn't begin to describe him.

Mr. Rich Motherfucker is willing to spend and he wants to see me again.

I'd be a dumb fool not to go along with it. *Right?*

2

Giovanni
PLAYLIST: 🎵 BLINDING LIGHTS - THE WEEKND 🎵

"I GAVE EXPLICIT ORDERS!" I growl as I storm down the hall.

My men flank me at once, walking fast to keep up. We're in the VIP section of the Dollhouse, and instead of getting my cock sucked right now, I'm dealing with issues that should've been resolved.

"We got new information," Robby Greco says from my side. "Jerry's saying he's gonna spill on the Lovatos."

I grunt, unimpressed. "Now that his ass is on the line. Sounds more like he needs a bullet between the eyes."

We pivot left down the long corridor at the far back of the club. The bouncers attempt to stop us, but Robby's on it. They fall back immediately once they recognize who we are. Jerry's office is on the second floor. The *cazzo's* spared no expense filling the room with pricey furniture and pieces of art—money spent from my father's wallet, *my* wallet.

For that he must pay.

And he will. Tonight.

I nod my head, and my biggest enforcer, Louis Civella,

steps forward. He kicks in the door to Jerry's office and we charge inside. Jerry's sitting behind his desk on the phone, his legs propped up like a fucking king.

In my club. He's as good as dead.

When the door blows open, he jerks in his chair. He's halfway into cussing my guys out before he sees me and his phone drops from his hand. Then it's a different story. Words elude him as he stammers like a dum-dum. Unfortunately for him, I have no patience for niceties.

"You've been having quite the year." I move closer, my demeanor as calm as a surgeon with a scalpel. But Jerry Bilson shouldn't take it as a good sign.

It's anything but a good thing that I'm calm, *composed*. As a boy growing up in New York City, taken under my father's and uncle's wings, I've been taught from an early age the importance of a clear head. Foolish men let emotion drive them. It clouds the brain, makes smart decisions impossible.

In a world like this, in a business and operation like this, living the life I do, there's no bigger necessity than being smart. A smart man is one still breathing with an empire at his command.

An empire that'll belong to me someday soon. All I have to do is prove I'm the rightful heir to my father Giuliano Sorrentino's throne. I deserve the crown more than Giancarlo, my twin brother. My purpose in Las Vegas is to do just that—prove myself as prince of the Sorrentino family, and show I have what it takes to become king.

But first I must return our family to past glory days in the west. I must conquer Vegas.

"Listen, Gio," Jerry says with a nervous laugh. "I don't know what you've heard, but—"

"Quiet!" I snap, walking around his large executive-sized desk. Louis and another guy, C.J., tail me, looming behind as reminders this is no friendly visit.

Jerry gulps but says nothing else.

I pick up his iPhone and bring it to my ear. "Hello, who am I speaking to?"

An uncertain female voice answers. She sounds like another bimbo he's picked up on the Strip. "Where's Jer? Who're you?"

"Jer's unavailable," I say. My cold eyes land on the sweating, shaking manager. "I suggest you find a new sugar daddy to fuck."

Before she can protest, I drop the phone on the ground. Louis smashes it with his boot. Jerry lets out a cry of indignation, but promptly shuts up when I move closer. I hover over his chair, placing my hands on either armrest. Our gazes are locked on each other.

I've got such a close-up look at this ugly motherfucker I can see every pimple, every greasy line on his face. Even smell his sour whiskey breath.

"You've been disloyal, Jerry."

He shakes his head. "Gio, I'd never betray…not you… I haven't—"

"Quiet!" I stand up straighter, surveying him with an unblinking stare. "Don't lie to me when we've seen the paper trail. We know who you've been conducting business with. A year it's gone on."

"You're misunderstanding! I've been gathering intel. A…a sleeper agent for you guys."

"Oh, really? How thoughtful of you. What did you learn during your hours spying on the Lovatos for us?"

He shrinks under my hard stare, choking on a breath like the swine he is. Bullets of sweat have started dripping down the sides of his saggy mug. "Well…how do I know you won't still kill me?"

"It's a chance you'll have to take, Jerry."

"Okay, okay, hear me out! If I could get some reassurance, I'll tell you everything," Jerry says breathlessly, spittle flying. "You wanna hear the truth, don't you? You wanna know if Lovato's scheming to push you outta Vegas? How about if there's a traitor in your midst? Believe me I wasn't working alone! Do we have a deal?"

A moment passes where I glare at him. My men stand dutifully behind me, ready for whatever I command them to do. Jerry inhales and exhales ragged breaths, more sweat shining on his forehead. I've already made up my mind.

It was decided even before I set foot in the office, he would die. Though I do enjoy giving him hope, seeing his beady eyes brighten with possibility.

"Fat chance, fat fuck," I say, stepping back. I motion for Robby to handle the situation.

Robby's fluid with it. He's a pro at taking care of these matters. He glides forward with the silencer on his pistol, finger resting on the trigger. A silent bullet later, Jerry Bilson slumps in his desk chair with a hole between his eyes. Blood trickles down his crooked nose as Louis and the others swoop in to dispose of the body and any evidence.

I've moved on to fixing myself a drink at the mini bar in the corner. Though a sense of ease slides over me that this matter has been handled, I'm no more in a better mood than when I stormed inside. I'm supposed to be downstairs in the VIP room enjoying the services of the woman who captured my attention at a single glance.

I had no clue Jerry had hired a woman so exquisite.

And she is exquisite. Her beautiful body flowed like liquid on the pole tonight.

Honey is her stage name, but I've already had Robby look into her. Falynn Carter is a twenty-four-year-old full-time stripper, part-time college student. Even with those towering stripper heels, she only comes up to my chest, but though she is petite in stature, she has the kind of curves that should be considered a sin.

Enough tits, enough ass and hips to fill up your palms. I can already see myself smacking my hand onto that ass, making the soft skin jiggle, leaving a print. A supple, tight body like that can't be created with even the finest surgery.

Tutto naturale, as my uncle Claro would say.

Her skin is like the honey for which she's named, silky smooth in texture. Her eyes are dark and emotive, enough to entrance you as she holds your gaze. I hadn't been able to look away as she stared straight at me, swaying those hips of hers like a seductress leading me to the pits of hell.

I paid extra to have her alone for the night. I'm not a man who hears no often. Even before she entered the VIP room, I knew I was in for a taste of that sweet honey pussy of hers. Still am as far as I'm concerned.

Only now I'm pissed and need some pussy to relieve my anger. If she's obeyed, she'll be waiting for me at the back entrance. Then I can take her to my hotel and stick my cock in that pretty mouth of hers.

Something tells me she's the type to mouth off. But women will bitch and moan about men for eternity if you let them. They say all we want is pussy. I say all they want is money. It's a perfect tradeoff. Another business transaction.

Honey will be rewarded generously for her services. If she's good, I may continue hiring her during my time in Vegas.

I drain the last of my cognac as my men roll Jerry in a giant Persian rug and haul him out the door. I set down the empty glass and check updates on my phone, barely paying mind to the aftermath of losing the manager of the Dollhouse. Business can wait 'til tomorrow. The rest of tonight is about pleasure.

The woman's scream comes out of nowhere. Then the shuffling footsteps of my men. I whip around, alert at once. Louis has grabbed a hold of somebody, his gorilla arms wrapped around what looks like a small, hysterical woman.

It takes me a second before I realize who it is.

Honey.

Falynn Marie Carter has just stumbled upon our cleanup.

It's a shame, because we spare no witnesses when committing our deeds. There's only one word that comes to mind as my gaze meets hers.

Shit.

3

Falynn
PLAYLIST: 🎵 SAVAGES - MARINA AND THE DIAMONDS ♪

"GET YOUR HANDS OFF ME!" I scream at the top of my lungs. I'm still in my show outfit, half-naked as this André the Giant of an asshole holds me tight. The indignity of it pisses me off more. I bend my knee and jerk my foot back, hitting him right in his dick and balls. He howls in pain and lets me go immediately.

As I scramble free, the door slams shut. Mr. Rich Motherfucker stands before me. No more cigar smoke. No more shadows. In plain view, we're facing each other for the first time.

My earlier assessment is spot-on.

He's exceptionally built, so ripped that his muscles are defined even under the material of his suit. He pins me right away with the shock of his blue eyes. Never blinking, they don't stray from me as he stares in unnerving silence.

I take a hesitant step back, the severity of the situation weighing on me.

Oh, *crap*. Crap, crap, crap!

I'm a witness to a crime. Not just any crime—*murder*!

I saw it with my own two eyes. Some of the men with

Mr. Rich Motherfucker hauled Jerry's dead body rolled up in a carpet out his office and down the hall.

Why had I decided to come up to Jerry's office to see about his important message for me? Why couldn't I stay down in VIP room five with the stack I'd made from the lap dance?

"L-let me go," I stutter.

"No," he says simply.

"I...I didn't see anything." I take a step back.

He takes one toward me. "Louis, give us a second."

The André the Giant wannabe gives me a disgruntled look before he plods off out the room, mitten hands cupping his groin. The door snaps shut behind him. We're now alone, but I'm not fooled for one second; his men are probably outside guarding the door—the ones who aren't preoccupied *disposing of a body* anyway.

"Really, I didn't see anything. I don't know what happened. I don't want to know." I take another step backward.

Him another one forward. His presence is intimidating, even as he stands before me as calm and composed as humanly possible. I can't take my eyes off him. It's like he's put me under some type of spell, like I can't look away without his permission.

He takes yet another step toward me. He's close enough to touch me now. If I thought I couldn't breathe before, his scent now permeates the air around me. A strong trace of warm cognac and rich leather invades my senses and makes it difficult to think.

I don't notice I'm holding my breath, that I'm *shaking* 'til he mentions it.

"There's nothing to be afraid of," he says into the silence of the room. "I'm not going to hurt you...unless you want me to."

The corner of his lip lifts in the faintest smirk. Before I can process what he's said, he reaches out and runs his fingers along the curve of my cheek. His thumb caresses my bottom lip. He doesn't seem to care that he smudges my lipstick.

No, he's too busy studying me. The intensity with which he stares at me is possibly even more terrifying than the murder itself. This tall, muscular man standing in front of me, with his electric blue gaze, fine suit, and dark scruff, is like the monster in every storybook.

He's the beast. I'm the beauty…he's about to destroy.

I'm holding my breath as a pulse comes alive, not in my veins, but between my thighs. Somewhere deep inside me, the fear manifests into something else. Curious desire to know just what's on the other side of fear, what this beast is capable of.

No!

Logic pushes to the front of my brain, reminding me I already know. He's a murderer. He's a cold-blooded murderer who's likely about to murder me too.

"Can I go?" I whisper.

If possible, the blue in his eyes deepens into sapphire. He lets the smirk he'd fought seconds ago spread along his lips, and he shakes his head no.

"I've hired your services for the night," he says. "Have you forgotten?"

"Oh, that. Actually, you can have the stack back. I stuffed it in the sofa cushions downstairs. Let me go get that—"

His large hand snaps shut around my upper arm, holding me in place. It takes no effort for him, no exertion whatsoever as I tug and pull to try to free myself. His eyes still haven't left me, but neither has the smirk vanished from his steel-cut face.

"We've already established a transaction, Falynn." He speaks my name like it's poetry, like it's the most beautiful word he's ever heard. His fingers glide down my bare arm and then grab a hold of my hand. He pulls me into him so fast, I'm dizzy, pressed up against his chest, feeling a lot like I've collided with a brick wall. He bends his head, his lips grazing my ear. "I'm afraid I can't let you go free just yet. Not 'til you've satisfied your end of the bargain."

I'm speechless as his teeth nip at my earlobe and his scent continues wreaking havoc on my ability to think. But I know one thing for sure, even through the haze of fear and seduction that is the rich motherfucker taking me captive:

I'm screwed.

4

Giovanni
PLAYLIST: ♫ CATCH ME - DXVN. ♪

THE HEADACHES KEEP COMING. Instead of disposing of Jerry sight unseen, we're caught seconds in by a stripper escort wandering the hall. It's so sloppy and embarrassing, it's borderline hysterical.

We're usually more meticulous than this. More well thought out, more prepared.

Tonight has been a deviation from what I had planned. Now I'm paying for it. We have strict rules about involving outside parties in our indiscretions. The outcome is almost always silencing them.

And, by silencing, I mean disposing of them too. No exceptions.

Yet, as I step into the hall and shut the door to Jerry's office, locking Falynn inside, I'm breaking this cardinal rule. I'm making an exception for a beautiful, sensuous woman who makes my cock twitch in my pants.

I'm what my father has long warned me about—a man blinded by the prospect of pussy. It has been the downfall of many great but foolish men. If I'm not careful, I'll join that list of fools.

Robby is waiting on me. I can tell by the hunger in his expression he expects me to order him to finish Falynn off. He's numb to causing pain, bringing death on people. Raised by his father, Stefano Greco, another close associate of my family, he's been molded for this lifestyle. It's what he dreamed of in grade school when they went around and asked everybody what they wanted to be when they grew up; Robby wanted to be a stone-cold, expert killer and capo for the Sorrentino crime family.

"Should I?" he asks, jutting his chin toward the door.

"Don't hurt a hair on her head," I say. I pull my phone from my pocket. "Bring her down to the car. She's coming with me for the night."

"Gio, she saw—"

"I know what she saw, but I don't believe I stuttered. Unless you're telling me I'm wrong, Robby?"

He shakes his head. "I'm saying she's a liability."

"Bring her down to the car," I repeat. "I'm handling her myself."

I let it hang in the air what *handling* means. It's up for his interpretation. Frankly, I'm bored of debating with him about what I should and shouldn't do. His opinion might mean something to me during business matters, but in this case, my mind is made up.

At least for now.

I can't harm Falynn. I can't bring myself to have my men dispose of her.

She's managed to pique my interest too much. So much that it's impossible to imagine the rest of the night without finishing what we started from the moment she strut onto that stage.

Falynn's mine for the taking. For tonight I'll have her.

Then tomorrow, with a clearer head, both in my mind and in my pants, I'll do what needs to be done.

Robby sacrifices his suit jacket for Falynn. She's still wearing that sheer, skimpy one-piece with the plunging neckline and her ass out in the back so we needed something for her to wear. She asked to go back to her dressing room, but we refused; she's not to be let out of our sight for the night. Even make eye contact with anyone else in the Dollhouse.

There have been enough fuckups as it is.

Robby walks her to the car with his hand clamped on her shoulder. She has her arms wrapped around herself, his suit jacket comically big and long on her, like a dress. My eyes skim the short length of her, noticing she's barefoot. She's taken off the stripper heels.

"You couldn't get her shoes?" I mutter to Robby as he prods her into the back seat.

"Whose shoes, Boss?" Robby asks.

Good point.

I disregard the matter and slide into the back seat beside her. Robby shuts the door and moves around to the passenger side. We have a car in front of us and in back of us serving as cover. I don't anticipate any enemies to make a move tonight, but you can never be too careful.

Now that the Sorrentinos have returned to Vegas for the first time since the '80s, we have many enemies waiting to wage war. The biggest being the Lovato family. They've deluded themselves into believing they have claim over Vegas. With their trendy casino La Festa thriving and raking in millions, they've gone unchallenged.

That's about to change.

Casino mogul and owner of the Wild West Casino, Everett Johansson, has found himself fifty million deep with the Sorrentino name. His debt is so high, the interest has interest, the figure growing by the day. That's the unwise thing about falling into debt with the mob—once you owe us a dollar, you'll really owe us ten.

Since Johansson won't ever pay off his debt, we've become his silent business partners. The Wild West Casino went on hiatus. We knocked it down and remodeled it from its cheesy Western theme to the Vittoria Resort and Casino, an ode to Italian-American opulence. Once the Vittoria opens, it'll dethrone La Festa, and become the most profitable casino in Sin City.

The perfect cover for our crime operation. Through Vittoria, we'll be able to launder money, run gambling schemes, and traffic drugs and weapons. We're about to become the most powerful crime family not just in Sin City but the country.

And *I'm* going to be the one who leads us to the top. The future king of the Sorrentino syndicate.

The FBI won't suspect a thing. With the Mafia's perceived decline in the twenty-first century, they've redirected their attention elsewhere. Foreign and domestic terrorism. Drug cartels. Cybercrime and civil rights. It's an open door for us to discreetly rebuild a part of our empire lost decades ago.

The city and casino lights glitter among the night's darkness as we drive toward the Strip.

Falynn's tucked into the far left corner of the back seat like a frightened puppy dog you brought home on a whim. She won't look at me. Her eyes are set straight ahead at the back of Robby's seat. She's shivering again. I'm assuming out of fear.

It occurs to me how this must look to her. Not only did she come across me and my men disposing of her dead boss, but I've now taken her for the night. I'm sure all kinds of wild thoughts are running through her mind.

Probably that we're going to rape or kill her. Maybe both.

I'm not a man who does comfort. I don't know what to do with an upset woman. When one cries around me, I become more hardened. Even annoyed. If I don't do emotion with myself, how am I to deal with emotion from hysterical women?

That's not to say I do not care when one is upset. Just that I have my own method of handling the situation. In this case, as I stare at Falynn shivering in the corner, I turn my head forward.

"Robby, turn up the heat. Falynn is cold."

"N-no...that's...that's okay..." she manages.

"Yes, Boss." Robby does as asked, dialing up the heat.

Never mind that it's September, which means it's fucking eighty-five degrees at two in the morning in Vegas.

If it gets Falynn to stop the chihuahua shaking, I'll bear it.

In no time, we reach the Vittoria. The extravagant resort and casino is an architectural masterpiece—a sleek five-hundred-feet structure carved of black marble and trimmed with gold. It's the new statement piece of the city. The newest, finest gem.

Robby pulls up to the valet driveway on the resort side. The valet on shift rushes over to open the door and help us from the car. He's unable to hide the shock on his face from seeing Falynn, barefoot in nothing but a large men's suit jacket. If he ogles a second longer, I'll have to order Louis to snap his twiggy little neck.

We enter the luxury hotel through the back entrance and take the private elevator to the top floor. Every corner of the hotel drips with opulence—marble and gold anywhere you look. It's on record as the most expensive resort and casino in the country.

The elevator doors roll open on the penthouse floor. Each penthouse spans two thousand square feet, filled with expensive furnishings.

Louis escorts me and Falynn into my penthouse and performs a sweep for anything unusual. I take security very seriously. The Lovatos are already pissed we're in Vegas; they're going to be even more pissed when they find out we've killed Jerry and cut their business transactions short.

But I don't want to think about work anymore tonight. It's time to blow off steam.

I shrug off my suit jacket and unfasten my watch. I'm ready to taste the honey Falynn's named after…

She stands in the middle of the living area, again like a lost puppy. For a woman as chatty in Jerry's office, as seductive in the VIP room, she's frigid and timid now. It's as if the spark that lit her only hours ago has been extinguished.

A carnal need courses through me to reignite that spark. Help bring Falynn Carter—*Honey*—back to life.

I grab the bottle of champagne the resort staff have brought up, along with the two flutes. I don't ask as I pour a glass for myself and then her. She doesn't take the glass when I offer it to her. Her eyes are on her bare feet.

I stare at them too. Her toes are manicured and painted a light pink, but it doesn't take away from the fact that they are Flintstone toes. Something about this amuses me, and I bark out a low laugh. The sound startles her, because she jumps back.

"Here," I say, pushing the champagne into her grasp. "Drink. Relax. I've already said I won't hurt you."

My back is turned to her as I walk up to the wide window spanning wall to wall, offering a panoramic view of the city. It's nothing but a dark grid of sparkling lights in the nighttime. Thousands of different people all over, thousands of different stories happening all at once.

I'm trying to be patient, let her calm down from her frenzied state. But I'm also a man who's had a bad night, who is seeking a piece of the pussy I've paid for. I'm not going to be able to sleep until I get to fuck.

Falynn watches me. Her reflection in the window's glass shows me she's staring as intently at me as I've stared at her all night long. Finally, she seems to work up the courage to ask a question.

"Why am I here?"

"I've told you."

"No…why am I *really* here?"

"I've told you." I turn around and approach her.

Never before have I felt more like a predator. A lion stalking toward his dinner for the night as she stands there small and defenseless. I can smell the fear on her, but also something else—a feminine, heady scent that's unlike anything I've ever smelled before; no artificial perfume can create an aroma like this, so naturally sweet and unfiltered.

It's *her* I'm smelling. Pheromones or whatever the fuck. The idea this is what her pussy could smell like, infects my brain. Hardens my dick as it stirs in my pants.

Both of our gazes dip to my groin. It's an unavoidable, large bulge…which says a lot as I'm already larger than most down below.

When I look up at her again, her dark and emotive eyes fill with curiosity. Heat has flushed onto her marvelously honey-brown skin. She nibbles on her bottom lip and her brows push together. I can practically *see* her thinking. She's weighing her options.

Probably whether she should fuck me or not.

But what she doesn't know is the decision is already

made for her. No woman has ever said no to me before. Tonight will be no different.

"Drink," I order again. "This champagne is very expensive."

"Why didn't you just screw me in the VIP room?" she blurts out suddenly. She hasn't so much as sipped from the champagne. Something about this annoys me. "If this is about our 'transaction' or whatever you keep calling it, why not just receive my 'services' there?"

She does air quotes for the words *transaction* and *services*. My annoyance from her not drinking the champagne fades. I can't help feeling amused watching her curl her index and middle finger. This woman is so...so sexy, but also so...so irresistibly *different* than the ditz-for-brains I'm used to.

"Tell me, Falynn," I say with a tinge of humor, "would you rather me fuck you against the wall of a dirty VIP room in a strip club, or in a king-size bed at a luxury hotel? Has it not occurred to you I'm treating you with respect by offering a better experience?"

Again, she proves how different she is. She scoffs. Right in my face. It's a first as, when I rack my brain to think of other times this has happened, my memory draws blank. Nobody has ever scoffed at me before.

Probably because everybody is scared shitless of me.

It's bold. It's...*refreshing*.

"You respect me?" she repeats. She sets down the flute of champagne and folds her arms across her chest. "Is it possible to respect a woman you're paying to suck your dick?"

"You tell me. You're the escort."

"I'm not... I've never... I don't..." She fumbles for more words, but comes up short before trailing off. That spark of boldness she's mustered up is gone again. "Tonight would've been my first night."

For a second, I don't understand until I look into her eyes. The sensuous imagery of this woman swinging on the pole on stage and gyrating her hips in the VIP room vanishes from my mind. As does the blood pumping to my cock, making it hard. At least for the moment, my curiosity takes the lead.

I drain my champagne. "Why?"

She only stares.

"Why were you going to do it? For the first time, tonight...*why*?"

She sighs and pulls Robby's jacket tighter. "Times are hard, okay? I have to make money somehow. Working the stage isn't cutting it like before."

"Why?"

Her right brow ticks upward. "Because...wait, do you really want to know, or is this more bullshit?" More moxie. I'm surprised I like it so much.

"I promise I have not bullshitted you once tonight."

"My boyfriend's gone," she says fast. Almost as if the faster she speaks, the less humiliating the confession will be. She reaches for the flute of champagne she set down and tosses it back whole. "Not gone as in dead. But he's caught a case. It's looking like he's not getting off this time. We've got bills and plenty of debts to pay—*he* had lots of debts to pay."

A prickle of irritation pinches at me. I'm not able to hide the judgment from my face. The disgust that a man who is fortunate enough to have Falynn in his bed, to call her his, has left her with nothing but money troubles. He's gotten mixed up with the law and failed to ensure she is taken care of.

Such a failure would never happen if she were *mine*. A

woman of mine would never be on display, fucking strangers to get by, regardless what happens to me.

"This boyfriend you mention has failed to protect you."

"Protect me how? Not everyone is loaded like you," she snaps. "Which reminds me, what's your name anyway?"

"That's irrelevant."

"You know mine."

"I'm the customer. I'm *paying* for this."

She openly rolls her eyes and turns her back on me. "You know, you said you respect me, but you love to keep reminding me I'm some possession you've bought."

"It's a fact of our arrangement. Does it hurt your feelings?"

I discover a second too late that's the wrong question to ask. Her vibe has changed again, growing frostier as she wanders over to the huge window. She stares at the city for a brief moment before whipping around and stripping off Robby's suit jacket.

"Then let's get it over with," she says. Her voice is strained, her face tight. Any softness about her is gone. It's like she's putting on a mask to dissociate herself from what's about to happen. She unties the string holding the top of her one-piece up. "This is why you say I'm here. So let's get started because I want to leave."

I'm torn on how to react. The baser part of me allows my gaze to slide over her body. Those delicious soft curves that demand to be licked, sucked, *smacked*. Her pert breasts bounce free, round brown globes with nipples like sweet Hersey's Kisses. The third time I've seen her topless tonight, and still just as arousing as the first.

My cock responds immediately, twitching incessantly in my pants. My blood is hot in my veins, lust overpowering any sanity. I want to stride toward her, toss her over my shoulder, and throw her onto the bed, then fuck her 'til she's so pleased she can't even speak her name.

But another part of me nags me from the back of my mind. The sullen look she wears, her face still beautiful even now, is quite a turnoff. It's an undeniable sign she doesn't want this, and is only complying because she believes she has no other choice.

There's an angel and a devil on my broad shoulders, and I hesitate on listening to either. With a ragged breath, my conscience for once getting the better of me, I turn away from her. I cross the vast living area with the sleek furniture and crystal chandeliers, stopping at the coffee table. I pick up the room service menu and browse the selection.

"Are you hungry?" I ask.

I can sense her uncertainty. She doesn't know whether to cover herself or continue insisting we get the transaction over with. I make the decision for her.

"Do you like breakfast?"

"*Breakfast*? At 3 a.m.?"

"Why not? One call and it's done. Nobody can tell me no."

"Why? Is that a perk of being rich?"

Perk of owning the hotel. But I don't tell her that.

"Tell me what you want to eat, and we'll order it," I say.

She appears in front of me wearing Robby's jacket again. "You're feeding me now?"

"Why are you resistant to being cordial, Falynn?" I ask with an amused smirk. "I'm not a monster, contrary to popular belief, including yours. I don't want to hurt you… and I won't unless you disobey. But I do want you to enjoy yourself. Relax a little. Is that clear?"

"What's your name?"

"Why does it matter?"

"If I know your name, I'll...I'll feel more comfortable," she says, big brown expressive eyes on me. "Plus, I'm tired of calling you Mr. Rich Motherfucker in my head."

I laugh. "Mr. Rich Motherfucker?"

"You're loaded. You were my main customer for the night. It fits."

"Gio. You can call me Gio."

"Okay, *Gio*, then yes...I do like breakfast. Any breakfast. My meals have been mostly ramen noodles lately, so anything you order, I'll eat."

An hour later, we sit on the sofa with the big-screen TV blaring, eating bacon and fried eggs. Falynn was not kidding about eating anything. So far she's scarfed down two eggs, too many strips of bacon to count, and hash browns. She eats without apology, not graceful as she sits cross-legged and uses her fingers.

I watch in amusement. I'm not hungry, so I only sip more champagne, but the room service is worth it if it makes her feel more comfortable. It's also clear this is the first real meal she's had in quite a while.

"How did you come to work at the Dollhouse?" I ask.

She swallows another bite of bacon. "I got fired from my last job waiting tables. None of the casinos would hire me. I have dance experience. Jerry took me on. He said he liked my look."

"A lot of men would say the same."

She diverts her gaze almost bashfully. "It was never supposed to be permanent working at the club. Just something to help Enzo pay the bills."

"This Enzo doesn't sound like the man you should be with."

"No offense, but I barely know you, *Gio*. You'll forgive me if I don't take relationship advice from you."

"My uncle just finished serving fifteen years in the joint," I say, sipping from the champagne. "His wife never once had to worry about a bill. She was always taken care of. He made sure of it."

She scoffs at me. Second time in one night. I'm beginning to cherish these small, feisty moments; they make my cock hard.

"What if I told you I wasn't with Enzo for the money?"

"Then why were you with him?"

"You're kidding me? Maybe because I loved him?"

"A broke man, a broke criminal…the *worst* kind of criminal?" I release a dismissive laugh that gets under her skin.

She makes a sound of disgust. "Don't you say a bad word about him. You don't get to judge him. You're out of line."

"You're right. But it's still the truth."

"Speaking of the truth," she says hotly, now on the offensive, "*why* did you kill Jerry?"

The question, admittedly, throws me for a loop. The laughter dies on my face and I cast her a cold look of warning. The fun and games of our little sleepover, late-night breakfast are over as I'm reminded at once she's still a witness to our indiscretion.

She picks up on the change in my body language, because she lifts her chin and stares defiantly back. "Are you going to kill me, Gio? Is that why you brought me here?"

"Enough. Finish eating."

I stand up, seething at what feels like a betrayal.

Though I trust no one—certainly not a stripper who is moonlighting as an escort—I have softened to her. I have gone far out of my way to treat her with kindness when I could've much easier been a brute.

Only one person has been taken advantage of tonight, and that's me.

"You're sleeping here with me," I tell her, my glare intense. "You're going nowhere anytime soon. Not 'til I decide what I'm going to do with you."

5

Falynn
PLAYLIST: 🎵 HUMAN - SEVDALIZA♪

IF THERE'S one thing to know about me, it's that sometimes I put my foot in my mouth. Never intentionally, but usually whenever I'm pissed off. It's why Enzo always refused to involve me in his schemes; I don't make for a good criminal, because I tend to blurt out whatever comes to mind. I'm also a bad liar; it makes my skin itch and my palms sweaty.

A cleverer woman would've played into Gio's hands sitting on the sofa in his penthouse suite. She would've schmoozed her way into lowering his defenses.

I couldn't help thinking WWTD—what would Tasha do?

She's a master at the art of tricking men into doing what she wants. She says it's a lot like a performance on the stage. You use your feminine wiles, your body to your advantage, get a man to think with the wrong head. Then it's off with his head—*and* his wallet. Above all, play it smart, play it subtle. Even the most pussy-whipped man recognizes a con when there's no finesse to it.

Not that *I* was conning. More like trying to survive.

I have no clue who Gio is, but it's obvious he's someone with immense power and wealth. A man who can order other men to dispose of a guy like Jerry as if it were any other regular Friday night.

Once I asked about Jerry over our room service, something changed in Gio. Over the course of the last hour, he had smirked. He had even *laughed*. He sat on a cushion opposite mine and watched me scarf down food like we were a normal couple and my quirky habits endeared him more than anything.

As soon as I asked my question about Jerry, the twinkle in his shocking blue eyes vanished. They darkened into a stormier shade. His steel-cut jaw hardened, his lips tight. He rose from the sofa, an intimidating muscular mass of a man. It wasn't until that moment I noticed how much sexier he looked out of his suit jacket. His dress shirt strained against his broad chest, the sculpted definition of his pectorals and abdomen vague outlines underneath. For as wide as his shoulders and chest are, his waist is trim.

I couldn't resist imagining that V line, fit, muscular men normally have. The generous indentions that point down to what most women wonder about when picturing a man naked—what does his dick look like? How big? How thick? And does he know how to use it?

Another pulse thrums between my thighs. I squeeze them together and watch as Gio storms from the living area.

Even his walk's masculine and commanding. His gait reminds me of a lion, the fluid manner in which he stalks across a room. His posture even, shoulders straight, chest out, powerful thighs propelling him forward. I actually let out a sigh. I've never noticed a man's stride before, but now that I have taken note of his, I can't shake the image of him stalking toward me.

It takes me minutes to gather myself sitting alone in the living area. He makes no effort to be quiet in the bedroom and bathroom. He fixes himself a drink, the ice chinking in glass, and drawers rattle open. The shower starts up, filling the suite with staticky background noise.

"Get your shit together, Falynn," I whisper to myself. "Ball's in your court."

Needless to say, tonight has been a wild, unexpected one for sure. When I made the decision to work the VIP rooms, I had done so hoping I could start off slow—always with a hard limit as to how far I'd go. I wasn't offering anything more than a job that started with *hand* or *blow*.

I figured once 4 a.m. came, as the club closed, I'd be done with my first night. I'd carpool home with Tasha and another dancer, Amaryllis. The car Enzo and I drive stopped working weeks after he got caught up, and I don't have the funds to fix it. Real shit luck.

Thankfully, Tasha doesn't mind giving us lifts late at night.

But I was supposed to come home to the crappy one-bedroom apartment I share with Enzo in East Vegas, with our dryer that doesn't work, and the blinds that are always crooked no matter how often I fix them. At least it's home, though.

Safe. Familiar.

Instead I'm here, held captive by some transactional terms I wasn't aware of when Gio became my customer. He's killed a man, has an army of enforcers ready to do his bidding, and I'm stuck alone with him.

I should be more hysterical. I should be crying for my life.

Because that's how this ends—I'm a witness to a crime. Gio is going to use me, get himself off, and then he's going to kill me.

The only way to survive is by playing the game. I rise off the sofa and slink toward the bedroom. Gio's dress shirt is discarded carelessly on the bed. His shoes have been abandoned by the closet. The TV's playing some late-night rerun of an old show; not sure the name, but it must be '90s or earlier because a laugh track plays every other line.

I stop in the bathroom doorway. My breath is torn from my lungs. Gio is *naked*.

He stands in the glass shower in all his beefy, brawny glory. And it *is* glorious.

The man is more chiseled than any masterfully sculpted statue. Muscles stacked on muscles. Washboard abs that water takes an eternity to trickle down, as it glides along the defined lines like a current does a riverbank. The V shape I've pondered about is better than anything imagined, deep cuts along his pelvis pointing directly to his penis.

His dick that's basically an anaconda. Thick, lengthy, and deadly.

It's enough to kill me on the spot. His blue eyes flash as he looks over and discovers me standing in the doorway. His dark hair is wet and slicked back against his scalp, his beefy arms up as his hands wash shampoo from his strands. A slow grin forms on his lips as he rinses off the last of it and then beckons me with a single index finger.

The shock of the moment burns heat onto my cheeks and stops my heart. I'm flustered like a damn school girl who's never seen a dick before. So much for being super seductive and confident. I fumble my way out of the bathroom and put as much distance between us as possible. That's in the living area by the glass window of a wall, overlooking the Vegas cityscape.

To my horror, Gio follows. He strolls from the shower, out of the bathroom, and into the living area. His reflection shows up in the glass without a stitch of modesty. He hasn't even put a *towel* on! How am I supposed to think logically with that thing swinging at me?

I glance at him from over my shoulder. His dick practically touches the floor with its damn monstrous length.

"Gio," I groan, snapping my eyes shut. "Can you…uh, put a towel or pants or…?"

"What's the matter? You've never seen a cock before?"

He's toying with me! The humor is threaded in that normally smooth, hard voice of his. He sees how flustered I am, and he's loving every freaking minute of it. If only I can stop being so frazzled over a hot, Italian sculpture of a man, and think straight.

I've seen Enzo naked a thousand times. Plenty of other men before Enzo. None of them have ever had this effect on me. It's like fear has gripped me. An intense and scary feeling that's holding me tight because it knows the second it lets me go, I'm a goner.

It's beyond lust. It's a carnal, primitive need to surrender myself to this man. This *killer*.

And for him to do with me as he wants. For him to wreck me, *destroy* me for the night. What the fuck is wrong with me?

I'm practically leaking, I'm so wet. Both my inner and outer folds are a slippery mess. I can feel how slick I am for every step I take. Even as I stand still by the window. My pussy is pulsating, throbbing as fast as the heart in my chest. The aching need becomes so strong it's painful.

"Are you going to join me?" he asks.

"Are you going to put a towel on?"

He chuckles. It's a rich and smooth sound, much like the cognac he smells of. "For being a stripper and an escort, you're a little bit prude."

"I'm *not* a prude!" I snap, folding my arms indignantly.

"Did you forget I just showed you my tits, like, twenty minutes ago?"

"I saw them—beautiful. I also saw everything else on stage. But now you're uncomfortable. Seeing me like this makes you blush. You may think you're fooling me, but I can see the glow on your skin." He starts toward me, slow and purposeful, giving me enough time to move if I wish. But I don't. Because my brain is blank. So much for my sexy femme fatale plan. Once within reach, he touches my cheek.

His hand travels lower, down the arc of my throat. His fingers brush my collarbone. His gaze is on my chest, as if seeing through me. *Inside* of me.

A tingle shocks its way down my spine.

I step back. "If we're going to complete the transaction, then fine. But only hand and blow jobs are on the table. You have to wear a condom. I don't do gagging. And I will not lick your hairy balls."

He glances down at his package, then looks up at me with a brow raised. "This is what you call hairy balls?"

It's true Gio is trimmed and neater than most guys. Actually, it's obvious he takes great care of his physique and hygiene. I'm bullshitting, looking for stupid reasons to make this encounter as unpleasant as possible for him.

Because I'm stubborn and I refuse to give in to the desire threatening to consume me.

I swallow hard and drop to my knees. "I hope you like teeth."

His gaze holds mine, him standing above me. His dick inches from my face. He laughs and shakes his head. "Is that a threat, Falynn? You're going to bite my cock off?"

Before I can answer, he turns and walks away, his laughter still alive. I watch him go, on my knees, noting how even his ass is a well-defined curve of muscle.

As the water starts again in the shower, I release a frustrated growl. I've got to do better. I've *got* to step my game up.

Gio lets me have the bed. I hold on for as long as I can, but as dawn bleeds onto the sky and the sun rises, exhaustion claims me. I end up falling asleep staging a protest in an armchair only to wake as he lifts me into his arms and places me onto the bed.

My heart panics into a quicker beat until I realize he's putting me to bed without the intention of lying with me. Too drowsy to fight off sleep, I drift off seconds later.

I wake up to find I'm alone. It's 10 a.m. and the TV is playing *The Price Is Right*. For a moment I lie still in the gigantic king-size bed and squint around the equally gigantic suite bedroom. The events of last night trickle in. I spring up with my face in my hands.

If it were possible, I'd pretend it hadn't happened. I'd act like I never met Gio and his henchmen. I definitely never saw them haul Jerry out of his office rolled up in an ugly carpet rug. I could go back to life before last night's shift at the Dollhouse. Pretend I'm not being held captive.

With a groan, I lift my face and notice a wicker basket at the foot of the humongous bed. I scramble over on my hands and knees and dump the basket upside down. Neatly folded clothes spill out along with bottles of shampoo, conditioner, all kinds of makeup. Hell, even *tampons*.

I snort out a laugh. It's a basket left for me, including any feminine product I might need at the moment.

Did Gio put this together for me? And where *is* Gio anyway?

Hopping off the bed, I explore the penthouse suite in a

way I hadn't bothered last night. This place must cost at least a grand a night, with exquisite art on the walls and perfectly polished furniture everywhere you look. The carpet beneath my bare feet is lush and chandeliers sparkle above my head.

First, I check the bathroom and then wander into the living area and kitchen. The curtains have been drawn, blocking out the desert sunshine. Gio must've closed them at sunrise when I'd fallen asleep and he'd placed me in the bed.

I stop in my tracks as I come across the front door. With no Gio around, was I free to go?

I sure as hell am going to try. I rush toward the door, undoing the bolts and latch. The second I yank it open and move to run into the hall, I collide with well over two hundred pounds of brawn.

It's the André the Giant lookalike. The one Gio called Louis. He's standing right outside the door. Probably by Gio's orders to make sure I don't escape while he's away.

"Do you need something, Miss Falynn?" he asks in a testy tone.

"Uh…no. By the way, sorry about hitting you in the groin. I was kind of panicking."

The corner of his lip quirks. "Just make sure you control your knee next time."

"Right. Won't happen again. Sorry to disturb you."

I step back inside like a child in a timeout and close the door.

Just grrrrreat. I'm trapped. Gio really has no intention of letting me go. My stomach sinks as I come to terms with the fact I'm a dead woman walking.

It's official: he's going to kill me.

I plod back into the bedroom and collapse in the

armchair by the glass wall. I'm not sure how long I sit and stew in my thoughts, but *The Price Is Right* ends and *The Young and the Restless* comes on. Ironically enough, both shows have titles that describe my life in the last twenty-four hours.

The lock in the front door clicks and someone walks in. I don't budge an inch as a second later Gio strolls into the bedroom in another well-tailored ensemble. He's forgone the suit jacket and is wearing a crisp black dress shirt and slate-gray pants. His *GQ* vibe is disrupted by his disturbingly bloody knuckles. Fresh blood too.

He cocks a brow at the sight of me, like I'm the weird one with fresh blood on my knuckles. "How's this morning been? Did you get some sleep?"

"Is there a reason you have blood on your hands?"

"None that concern you," he answers. His bright blue eyes gleam looking at me. He really does enjoy driving me crazy. "What can I say? This morning has been a rough day at work."

"I bet someone's face paid for it."

"Sounds like you're a gambling woman."

He unfastens his watch. Also different from last night. It's smooth and stainless, making a heavy chinking noise when he drops it onto the dresser. Something tells me it costs more than I make in several paychecks like everything else he wears.

When he realizes I'm not going to say anything else, he switches topics as if it's no consequence at all. "I'll be in the shower."

As my brows scrunch together and I move to protest, he disappears into the bathroom. For the next fifteen minutes, I sit and stew about the fact that not only am I held captive, any protests don't faze him at all! Last night when I'd staged my first one, refusing to go to sleep, he'd simply sat down in the living area and made phone calls 'til I eventually *did* doze off.

Bastard.

The instant the shower stops, I march into the bathroom. He's left the door open. Steam floats around me, fogging up the mirror.

"Blood all washed off now that you've showered?" I ask as he towels off. Then I lift my arm and sniff myself. "Speaking of, I should probably shower…if that's allowed."

He wraps the towel around his waist. "It's allowed, Falynn. You're not a hostage."

"No, I just can't go anywhere or do anything."

"That's in your best interest."

"How so?"

His muscles tense as he plants his palms flat on the bathroom counter. "'Til I figure out what to do with you."

"I thought you weren't going to kill me."

"I'm not."

"*Or* hurt me."

"I'm not. Unless you mean the *good* kind of hurt." His gaze finds me in the mirror, so intense even as a reflection my stomach flutters.

"Y-you know what I mean, Gio," I stutter, putting on a tough front. "Then why am I here? Why have you kept me?"

"Take a shower. Wash that sweet honey pussy of yours. Enjoy the lotions and perfumes and things I've brought you. Pamper yourself."

"You picked out those products yourself?"

He nods.

"Even the hair care stuff?"

"You sound so surprised."

"That's because you picked products for Black women," I say skeptically.

A low chuckle accompanies his smirk. "Do you think you're the only Black woman I've been involved with?"

"Your ex-girlfriend is *Black*?"

His blue eyes glisten out of amusement. "I like all colors of the rainbow, Falynn. Black being one of the sweetest."

With that, he strolls past me out of the bathroom as if the discussion is over. I follow him into the bedroom.

"You bought me those things? Why?"

"Why are you suspicious? I believe a thank you is the proper reaction."

"*Thank* the man holding me hostage?" I scoff defiantly, glaring.

"For the last time, I'm not holding you hostage. You're free to go anytime you like…once our transaction is over."

"Unless you've forgotten, I've tried to get it over with! *You* keep walking away!"

He chuckles and pulls open the closet. It's filled to the brim with a diverse selection of luxury men's clothing. He chooses another dress shirt and pair of slacks.

"Cut the crap, Gio. I'm not stupid. This isn't about me servicing you. This is about you disposing of me, isn't it?"

He peeks at me from over his broad, defined shoulder. "No, Falynn, it's about being able to tell you are faking. For a performer, you've failed to create that illusion. The fantasy."

I don't even understand what the hell he means as he quickly dresses. Again without an ounce of modesty as he drops his towel, and I try not to become a dick-obsessed thot ready to spread it low and wide.

"I have business to attend to," he says, buckling his

belt. Next he attaches his gun holster. "I'll be back in a few hours. Stay put. Treat yourself."

When he leaves, the door snicking shut, I sigh. I wait a while before I try my luck at the front door of the penthouse again. Louis still waits outside like the loyal watchdog he is for Gio. His brows jump in question the second he sees me.

"Um," I say, flashing a nervous smile, "I know I can't go anywhere. But...but I was hoping I could have my phone back. A girl's got to stay preoccupied somehow, and I have a *ton* of apps to keep me busy. It'll help the time go by."

"Sorry, Miss Falynn," he says in a surprisingly gentle tone. "I have orders to limit your access to the outside world. That includes all communication devices with internet access."

"Oh, okay. That sucks."

"Orders are orders." He gives an apologetic shrug.

I'm not mad at him. He's just doing what he's told. My smile shifts into a more sincere one, and I thank him anyway. I return to the confines of the penthouse and look around the lavish space. The stuff from the wicker basket catches my eye. If I'm going to be stuck here for the foreseeable future, I might as well make the best of it. I put the toiletry products and designer clothes back into the basket and carry it into the bathroom.

For the first time since last night when I got dressed backstage at the Dollhouse, I look at myself in the mirror.

Really look at myself.

Damn, I'm kinda rough. My brown skin has lost its usual luster, and my hair is limp and flat from a night spent sweating under a wig and cap. I can practically feel dirt particles collecting all over me the longer I go without a shower.

I'm normally a hygiene freak; something Gio and I seem to have in common. For once, I take his advice.

Robby's suit jacket falls to my feet and then my sheer, shimmery one-piece follows. The water is steaming hot as I step into the glass case and bask in its heat underneath the showerhead. Dirt and grime washes away and my natural curls feel nourished even before I've applied any product.

I spend a gluttonous amount of time in the shower, washing, exfoliating, *deep conditioning*. After I moisturize all over my body, I spritz on some perfume—Gio's brought me several from brands like Dior and Dolce & Gabbana. I go with the one I like best, which is Viktor & Rolf's Flowerbomb.

As I return to the basket to dig some more, I notice the designer labels on the clothes. There's all sorts of outfits included. Everything from a pretty backless sundress to a pair of satin women's pajamas. But it's the lingerie that holds my attention.

It's from La Perla, and it's an intricately embroidered bustier with balconette style cups and a thong and garter to match. My fingers run over the luxurious silky black satin. This might be the most expensive piece of lingerie I'll wear in my life.

Some of Gio's parting words come back to me.

It's about being able to tell you are faking. For a performer, you've failed to create that illusion. The fantasy.

A shrewd smirk crosses my lips. If it's a fantasy Gio wants, it's a fantasy Gio'll get.

I'm waiting for Gio in the dimly lit penthouse when he returns. The sun set half an hour ago. The Vegas city lights have already twinkled on. As he's done before when walking inside, he unclasps his watch and sets it down. The clink is loud in the otherwise silent suite.

He calls my name. He makes it to the bedroom before I reveal myself. I'm wearing the expensive La Perla lingerie, paired with my stripper heels. I've skipped on the wig, though. Instead my natural chocolate curls are out, free and wild, framing my face. I've applied a touch of makeup: mascara, eyeliner, and sinfully red lipstick. I strut out from the shadows, looking sexy as fuck, *feeling* sexy as fuck.

He stops in his tracks. His electric blue eyes skim over me head to toe. For once, I've thrown Gio off his game. His normally stoic expression slips for a split second before he cocks a brow.

"You've been busy," he murmurs.

"So have you," I purr, using the same sultry tone when on shift at the Dollhouse. It's the tone that gets guests hard and stupid enough to hand over their cash. Except tonight I'm hoping Gio hands me my freedom. I start toward him, an extra sway in my hips. "Let me help you relax."

In this moment, I'm not Falynn Carter. I'm *Honey*, putting on a performance just like I do when on stage.

Gio doesn't move as I approach. He lets me take his hand and lead him toward the chair. He lowers himself into it with eyes still trained on me. They're darker than an ocean storm, his expression back to being unreadable. But it doesn't matter. This is what he asked for. I'm giving him what he wants—the seductress who entranced him on that stage last night. In the VIP room afterward.

I press play on a sexy and sensual playlist I found off the TV's music app. As soon as the slow, lush beat starts, I'm surrendering to the music, gyrating to the sound. My hands slide along the curves of my body, seductive in how my fingers skim the cups of my bustier. They outline the cinch in my waist, the flare in my hips, then slip to the apex of my thighs. I trail my fingertips over my pussy lips, simulating touching myself.

His shirt tightens against his broad chest, the next breath he inhales slightly more audible.

My hips sway in smooth figure eights, hypnotizing him as I draw nearer. Though this is a show I'm putting on for him, I'm slick again. My thong is damp from the idea of where this ends—not with my escape but with Gio fucking my brains out.

I kick one leg up and then drop to the floor in a split, bouncing up and down. The imagery evokes what I want it to—the idea of me bouncing up and down on his dick. I can see the subtle reaction in his features, how his cheek twitches and his jaw tightens. I'm getting to him.

I put my all into this lap dance, channeling my inner Beyoncé the time she snatched Terrence Howard's whole soul.

Back on my feet, I sashay closer, planting my hands on either armrest. I toss my head back, whipping my curls around. Chest pushed out, the arc of my neck exposed, I rotate my hips in another wide circle. When my gaze meets his again, they're lust-filled and half-lidded.

I slide into his lap, curl my hands on his shoulders. They're as hard as any rock, straight shredded muscle. I come in close, running fingers through his slicked-back hair. Lips to his ear, my tongue darts out and licks the shell. I let my thong-clad pussy grind against the fast-growing bulge in his slacks. The friction is tantalizing for us both, an unbearable tease as only thin fabric separates us.

His big ass dick is ready to go, ready to fuck me right here and now. His ragged breathing, and dark sapphires for eyes, tells me he's a moment from doing it; from grabbing me and slamming me down on his length, lap dance long forgotten. My head fills with thoughts of how good he feels, how thick and fat his dick is, how he'll stretch me beyond my limits.

I breathe in his musky scent as I move on to tease his lips with mine. I graze his lips, fingers still playing in his hair, my ass still grinding into him. He releases a surprise growl and his hand wraps around my throat. He wrenches me closer, smashing our lips together in a bruising kiss.

His tongue plunges into my mouth with no hesitation. He hasn't let go of my throat, applying light pressure as his other hand grips my ass. In response my pussy throbs harder, begging for more.

Our tongues slide together in a duel. We're fighting each other in our own way. His hand on my throat. Him palming my bare ass. Me with my fingers twisted in his hair and hips rotating against his in an ever-torturous motion. He squeezes the flesh of my ass so hard it'll probably leave a mark. I moan into his mouth, whispering, "Fuck me, Gio. Right now."

His answer comes in the form of a strangled groan, and if possible, he squeezes my ass harder. He's unraveling before me as I hoped he would. As most men do when seduced by a sexy woman.

Now's my chance. I let my hand drop down his chiseled chest and then in a bold Hail Mary move, I rip his gun from the holster attached to his waist. Before he notices what I've done, I knock him over the face with the barrel, using as much strength as possible. Then I'm out of there. I hop off him, modesty be damned in my bustier and thong, and run for it, gun in hand.

The craziest risk I've ever taken in my life.

6

Giovanni
PLAYLIST: ♬ LOYALTY - KENDRICK
LAMAR FEATURING RIHANNA ♪

THE FUCKING bitch tried to knock me out! The cold metal of my Glock collides with my cheekbone in a crushing blow. It takes a second for my nerve endings to catch up, but when they do, searing pain erupts across the side of my face. I howl like a monster defied and leap to my feet.

She's already off. Her petite form scurries across the bedroom in those impossibly high heels. I'll give it to her, she maneuvers in them well. Most would break their necks.

But I'm not sure where the fuck she thinks she's going half-naked with no money, a gun in hand, and my men standing guard outside the room. Her escape attempt is futile. She has nowhere to run, nowhere to hide.

The disrespect is too blatant. My temper roars to life. I dart after her, using my size and power to my advantage. I blow past her with little to no effort. As she grapples for the doorknob, I slam my hand against the door, keeping it shut despite her desperate attempts to pull it open. She gives up with a strangled cry and beats her fist against my chest.

I can tell she's really trying to hurt me, but unfortunately for her, she's weak and I'm built like steel.

Not once in my life have I ever hit a woman. In that moment, I have never wanted to more as I grab a hold of her, wrenching the Glock from her. My fingers dig into the flesh of her upper arms. It's almost an involuntary reaction to raise a hand and strike, but as soon as our eyes meet, the terror is clear in hers. She's afraid of me.

Disgust coils inside me, a sour taste in my mouth. I throw her onto the sofa and walk away. I need a moment to cool off.

My cheek is bleeding. I wipe the blood off on my sleeve and pour myself a glass of cognac. Something to cool my nerves. In the next room, she breaks into anguished sobs. So she thought she could seduce me, distract me, then run off.

I should've known the change in demeanor from earlier today was a red flag. Someone as fiery and stubborn as Falynn doesn't go from resentful and resistant to willing in a few hours. She's the type to formulate a plan—albeit, a poor one.

Still, this more than anything raises the point I've been avoiding for almost twenty-four hours. I cannot let her go. But I cannot kill her. Even bring harm to her. For as cold-blooded, methodical and emotionless of a man I am, I'm drawn to her for a reason I cannot explain. She's hit me in the face with my own weapon, and still I want her.

I pinch the bridge of my nose and close my eyes. This is a fucking disaster.

My iPhone vibrates and the word *Papa* pops up on my screen. I cuss under my breath and answer on the third ring.

"Giovanni, my boy," Papa wheezes. Fatigue and illness

soften his normally raspy baritone. "How's the City of Sin been treating you?"

"Good, Pa. How're you feeling?"

"The treatments have me feeling better. I'll be back to my old self in no time."

It's delusions of former glory. The doctors have already made it clear it's not a matter of if but when. I don't say this to him. No use bringing down his spirits. Nothing to be gained from dashing his hopes.

It's more important to focus on who takes over his empire once he passes. Both Giancarlo and I believe it's our birthright.

"That's great, Pa. Continue following doctor's orders."

He makes an impatient sound then changes the topic. "Robby has briefed me regarding Jerry at the Dollhouse."

"Oh, that. It's been handled."

Though the statement is vague, Papa understands what it means. Jerry's body has already been cut up into dozens of pieces and then turned into mush. The remains have been disposed of in various locations to ensure no part of him is ever to be found.

"And management of the club?"

"No need to worry. Hiring someone else will be simple."

"Always a step ahead. It's what makes you so skilled. You're fit for my throne."

"Thank you, Papa."

"If you succeed with Vittoria."

"I will."

"And if you carry on the bloodline," Papa continues in another wheeze. "The Sorrentino name can't end with you and your brother."

I chug the entirety of my cognac and fix a second glass. "It won't end with me. I've told you this."

"And you have not taken a step to prove me wrong. You won't be a thirty-one-year-old stallion forever. The mistake I made was marrying late, breeding late. You sons were not born 'til I was *forty-four*, Gio."

"Age doesn't matter for men."

"You'd think so—" He coughs over the phone. "But it does. You can't be a fearsome leader the older you are. Look at me, still leading the family when I can't go without an oxygen tank. I barely had a chance to mold you boys, to show you the ropes for you to take over. Prepare you to rule the family."

He has a point. I know he does. For decades, Papa bucked tradition by remaining his own man. He never wed and started a family like most men in our lifestyle. That didn't come until much further down the line when he realized he'd have no heir.

Nicola was a woman he'd met and liked enough to finally take the plunge. Our mama, she was fifteen years his junior, willing and waiting to pop out children for him. Giancarlo and I were born fraternal twins, two baby boys destined to be his heir whoever he should choose. Thirty-one years later, he's still yet to do so.

"Don't forget, we're expecting to see you for Claro's homecoming celebration," Papa says.

I nod to no one but myself. "Of course, I'll be there."

"It would be pleasing to see a woman on your arm. Giancarlo's already speaking of *proposing* to Fiona."

We hang up without me making any promises. I'm acutely aware my father is judging me. He's comparing Giancarlo and me in all measures of life. Both involving our family organization and other metrics he believes his heir should have. One of those things is an heir to his heir. Something I have not produced; something Giancarlo will before me.

It's not lost on me I could lose my chance at heir over this. But what can I say?

Love and romance have never been a desire. Women have only occupied brief spaces in my life for entertainment and gratification purposes. I've never seen myself as the family man.

Though for families involved in this lifestyle, love is rarely the main motivator. Those relationships and marriages are transactional like everything else in the world. Tit for tat. Give and take and vice versa. Nothing in this world is pure no matter what anyone wants to believe. There is no such thing as selflessness. Sacrifice is an idea in our heads, not a reality.

Even if and when I do wed, it'll be just another transaction. Just a woman to have my sons. For that, she'll be rewarded a comfortable existence for the rest of her life. Love won't have a thing to do with it—it never had for my parents. Pa barely attended Ma's funeral…

I shake these musings away as I down my second glass. The problems I put on the back burner when Papa called come back to me. Falynn's stopped sobbing in the next room; the only sound coming from her is the occasional sniffle. Before I can even entertain the prospect of attending Uncle Claro's homecoming celebration with a woman on my arm, I'll have to deal with her.

And then it hits me. The crazy notion comes so suddenly, I question my sanity. It's possibly the craziest idea I've ever had, but it might work. It solves my problem. It gives Falynn an out.

Third drink in hand, and another fixed for Falynn, I go into the living area. She's curled up into a little ball on the sofa. Her stripper heels are on the floor. Any makeup she was wearing has been rubbed off her face, leaving mascara marks down her cheeks. Despite this, lips puffy and eyes red, she's still beautiful.

I hold out the drink for her to take. "Cry any more and you'll give yourself a headache."

She turns her cheek to the drink. "Please…please just do it already."

"Do what?" I set her drink onto the coffee table and sit down on the sofa opposite her.

"Kill me. Dispose of me. Whatever your type calls it."

"How many times have I told you? I'm not going to—"

"Hurt me," she finishes for me. "And yet you won't let me go."

"That's because I need some insurance first. That you can be trusted," I say smoothly, leaning back into the sofa. I nurse my drink in one hand and stretch my other arm out along the sofa's spine. "After the little stunt you just pulled, you can imagine my trust in you is as low as ever. But I'm a forgiving man—and I want this to be beneficial for both of us."

She groans. "I have no clue what you're talking about! Please, just stop. My head hurts."

"I can promise you I'll let you go…but not now."

"Then when? After I fuck you? Let's get it over with!"

"After you've been useful to me, and I can be assured you won't go back on our deal," I interrupt with a cavalier air. I swallow some of my cognac and take my time continuing. She needs to calm the fuck down if we're going to have a civilized conversation. "I will let you go with a handsome reward…and a ticket out of the country."

"Out of the country?" Her gorgeous face screws up in distaste.

"That's right. You can never return. But first you have to help me."

"I'm not committing any crimes for you! If you think I'm going to be your little henchwoman, then—"

I laugh despite the serious look on her face. "You, a henchwoman? Falynn, honey, I don't hire women for such dangerous jobs. And if I did, there are more capable and deadly women than you out there. If you believe nothing else I've said, believe that."

"Then *what*?"

"I need the assistance of a beautiful woman," I say, eying her with humor. "One who is willing to pretend to be mine for a few weeks. You complete the job to my satisfaction, you can go about your way."

She stares at me for what comes to be a full sixty seconds. "I'm sorry, but…are you asking to hire me as your girlfriend?"

"If that language makes you feel better, then you may call it that."

"But you can hire any woman off the street. Women more willing than me."

"I want you."

My statement is basic, said plainly with zero room for doubt. She spends another few seconds staring long and hard at me. I can practically see the gears in that stubborn mind of hers as they twist and turn. She's weighing her options.

"Am I required to have sex with you?"

"You're not required to do anything you don't want to. Your body is yours to give away when you choose."

"*If* I choose," she says haughtily. "And I *won't*. Not to you."

A dismissive grin shows itself on my face. "That's what you say now. But I believe differently."

She rolls her eyes. "How much money?"

"How much would you like? I can cut you a check for

several million. Enough to live off of in many other countries."

Her brows jump. "Who are you?"

"I've told you, I'm Gio."

"Yeah, but Gio *who?*"

"That's information for another day. Is this a yes or a no to my proposal?"

"Will you kill me if it's a no?"

"You'll live regardless. But I can't promise my next offer will be as good as this, whatever it may be."

She exhales a deep breath and slaps hands to her cheeks. Fingers pressed into her skin, she stares at me as if concerned this is some kind of trap. Finally, she gives up and reaches for the drink I've fixed her. She downs it in one sloppy swallow, droplets spilling onto her satin-encased breasts.

"Fine," she whispers. Her eyes meet mine. "I'll do it."

7

Falynn
PLAYLIST: ♫ IN TIME - FKA TWIGS ♪

LAST NIGHT, I made a deal with the devil. I agreed to be Gio's girlfriend for an indeterminate amount of time in exchange for freedom and a handsome payoff. But what other choice did I have?

Gio said it himself, the other options weren't going to be as generous. An inkling told me, no matter what he said, one of those options was ending up at the bottom of the Hoover Dam with cement blocks chained to my feet. The other options probably weren't the greatest either.

It doesn't matter, though, because as I wake the next morning, I can't help wondering what I've gotten myself into. For a second night, I drifted off alone in the king-size bed with Gio smoking a cigar in the living area. Now minutes before 9 a.m., not much has changed, as I catch snippets of his voice from the next room. He's on the phone, ordering somebody to take care of something important.

I rub my eyes and slide off the bed. I'm wearing the satiny pajama short set from the basket. As I enter the living area, the fried scent of bacon hits my nose. There's a whole cart of room service waiting to be gorged on. My first thought?

Damn, it's impossible having a backbone when food's involved.

My second thought? I better not dare touch that blueberry muffin. This could be a manipulation tactic.

Gio ends the call and greets me. "I ordered the works since you seemed to like everything the other night."

"You mean when I stuffed my face with three pancakes at once?"

"It was five, but who's counting? Sit down and eat."

I'm astonished. Was that humor? An actual joke from the cold, mysterious man who is holding me captive? I stand there, staging yet another impromptu protest. He uncovers the different plates on the cart and gestures to the food.

"You're not going to let all this go to waste, are you?"

I shrug, pretending I don't care. In reality, I really, really want some of that feta spinach omelet.

"Must everything be a protest for you?" he asks with a shake of his head.

The resolve I'm holding on to melts away as my stomach chooses now to growl. It's been a day and a half, and I've eaten exactly one full meal. Yesterday, when Gio was gone for hours, his enforcer Louis had popped in a few times to check if I wanted anything. Too stubborn for my own good, I'd turned him down each time.

I reach for one of the buttery croissants on the cart and tear off a chunk.

"Force of habit," I mumble.

His top lip lifts in a slight smirk. "Believe me, Falynn, I've already learned that about you."

"Are you sure I'm the one you want? I bet a man of your means has so many options."

"Yes, I'm sure."

"In that case, you might want to consider you won't be fooling anyone. You dress in designers." I drop onto the sofa and set the croissant down for the plate with the omelet. "I dress mall bargain bin, if that's a style. You know I color in the scuffs on my leather boots with a Sharpie marker?"

He joins me for breakfast, using a fork to pick up a piece of cantaloupe. "And your boyfriend never bought you nicer things?"

"Enzo? Buy nice things? With what money?" It's hard not to laugh at the question. Enzo is the furthest thing from financially stable as can be; he and I are matched in that sense. Except he uses petty crime to get by. I dance. "Enzo can barely afford the shirt on his back. Hence the petty crime. Not that I'm looking down on him. We're the same."

"You're not the same." Gio gives me a look I can't place, rising up from the sofa and smoothing out his tie. "Now shower and get ready. One of the dresses I picked out for you. And make it reasonably quick. I know women will take an eternity if you let them."

"You mean I *actually* get to breathe fresh air today?"

"If you behave yourself. Leave the escape attempts for another day."

Gio is already out the door by the time I catch on that he was teasing me. Kinda like how a school boy will tug on a girl's pigtails in class, just to get her attention. This thought brings a smile to my face. One I'm glad no one else is around to see.

I grub on the platters of breakfast with zero shame. By the time I'm done, there's only crumbs left. Then I hit the bathroom for a shower and some grooming. I guess if I'm going to pretend to be Gio's girl, I should look halfway decent.

After my shower, I change into the summery, backless sundress I had eyed yesterday. The breezy tangerine fabric complements my warm skin tone well. I leave my ringlet curls out and do a more natural bronze glow makeup look.

When I emerge from the bathroom, Gio's back. He's pacing by the humongous bedroom window as he talks on the phone. He stops mid-sentence, his electric blue gaze landing on me. Though it's room temperature in the suite, a shiver courses through me.

Since meeting Gio, I've discovered there's nothing quite like being on the receiving end of his stare. It's paralyzing and penetrating all at the same time, like he possesses the power to pierce straight through me, past the exterior, into parts of me otherwise unknown.

Unsure of what to do with myself, I stand in mock confidence, thrusting my chest out and putting a hand to my hip. Maybe I can distract him with sexy cleavage while I pretend his piercing stare doesn't make my vagina dance. "Do you like what you see?"

He licks his lips and hangs up on whoever is on the phone. Striding past me, tearing his gaze off me with what I sense is difficulty, he says, "Come. There's a car waiting on us."

I don't know what to expect as I slide into the back seat of Gio's luxury town car. Several of his men give me funny looks, as if questioning what the hell I'm still doing alive. Funnily enough, I'm wondering that myself, but I tamp down those thoughts for the time being.

It's a warm September day with no shortage of

sunshine anywhere you look; the crowds are out and about all over the Vegas Strip as the driver pulls out of the Vittoria's valet parkway.

Our drive is a short one. I haven't even acclimated to the car ride by the time we're pulling into another valet entrance for Caesars Palace. From the generous tip Gio slips the valet to the VIP treatment we receive as soon as we set foot inside the opulent bright and gold atrium, we're treated like royalty. A concierge leads us down past the many columns and statues carved of marble, listing off all the preparations he's taken for Gio's arrival. On our left and right, Gio's men flank us, our own private security detail.

People stop and stare. Some snap photos, probably thinking we're celebrities or something. Hell, even I look over my shoulder a couple times to double-check Mariah Carey isn't anywhere in the vicinity.

We end up in the Forum Shops. It dawns on me as we enter Jimmy Choo, the store has been closed for us. Another concierge is on us at once, offering to bring over champagne and strawberries. Unsure of how to respond, I bite the inside of my cheek, and let Gio answer. To my surprise, and slight horror, he defers to me.

"Show the lady whatever she likes."

I almost choke on air. "Me?"

He raises a brow. "Yes, *Honey*. Don't you remember I promised to buy you anything you desire? What do you think this shopping trip is for?"

Definitely not to buy *me* shit. I fidget out of instant discomfort. I glance at the nosy, grinning concierge, then to Gio's men, who are stone-faced and quiet, and lastly, to Gio himself.

"Can we talk alone?"

He looks at the others. "You heard the lady. Give us a moment."

The others scatter. The concierge announces she's going to fetch us our champagne and a few items she thinks might look good on me. His henchmen disperse to the outer edges of the high-end boutique. Even though we're now alone, I still keep my tone low.

"You're being serious? I'm supposed to pick something out?"

"Pick out whatever you like."

"But...*why*?"

The flat expression on his face is condescending, like the answer is obvious. "If you're to be my woman for the next few weeks, you'll only be dressed in the best. You said it yourself: it has to be believable."

I stare at him. "But I can't afford any of this. Did you miss the part about scribbling Sharpie marker on my boots?"

"Pick out whatever you like," he repeats. "Money is no object."

As if on cue, the concierge returns with an even brighter smile. She eases a flute of champagne into my hand and then steals me away. The next thing I know, I'm strutting across the boutique floor in a $2,000 pair of crystal-encrusted Jimmy Choos. I pivot with ease on the stiletto heel, hand on my hip like a model on the runway. The concierge eggs me on with an impressed nod and claps.

It's the first pair of many. For the next hour, I try on so many shoes, I lose count. Every time I like a pair, I glance in Gio's direction. He's sitting in the lounge area, sipping his champagne. For each look I give him, he gives back a nod.

We leave Jimmy Choo's with an armful of bags—bags one of his henchmen carries for us. It's on to Versace and

Valentino next. In both we're met by another overeager concierge more than willing to dote on me like I'm the Queen of England.

"I want you to put my woman in a dress as beautiful as she is," Gio says in Valentino.

My cheeks heat up. Though I'm aware Gio's attracted to me, it's different hearing it out loud. Spoken in front of everyone in the store. Before I can gather my bearings, he surprises me a second time, placing his smooth hand on the small of my back. He drops a kiss on my cheek that further sends me into a tailspin. Not only am I flushing on my face, but I'm attacked by a dramatic increase in heart rate.

At that point, the concierge shows mercy and takes my hand. She already has racks upon racks of different dresses waiting for me in the dressing room—a dress for literally every occasion you can think of. I make sure to model each in the lounge area for Gio's approval.

I get the feeling he *likes* watching me try on these different outfits. He sits back, relaxed with one arm along the back of the accent chair and his right foot at rest on his left knee. The last dress I model in Valentino's is a dress I'm pretty sure the devil himself would say is too damn sexy.

It's black and strapless, with a plunging neckline that accentuates my décolletage. The super sexy top half transitions into a long skirt that flows dreamily as I strut out of the dressing room. The mood in the boutique shifts as everyone sets eyes on me. I spin in a slow circle.

"Keeper or nah?" I ask when no one says anything.

Gio rises from his seat, his blue gaze intense and dark. He speaks only to the concierge. "You've accomplished the impossible. Box it up."

Minutes later, as we move onto Cartier and shop

jewelry, his words are spinning in my head. Did Gio pay me yet another high—and very public—compliment?

On top of that, he put his hand on my back, and *kissed* me! Sure, it was my cheek and only the small of my back, but compared to twelve hours ago, it was a startling turn of events. Twelve hours ago, I had whacked him in the face with his gun and he'd tossed me on the sofa like a rag doll.

It's not how I saw things playing out after my failed escape attempt. Nerves flutter inside of me as we browse Cartier and expensive jewelry I've only dreamed of is hung around my neck and clasped onto my wrist.

While this *Pretty Woman*-esque shopping spree with my criminal fake boyfriend is fun, in the back of my mind, I'm wondering how long can it possibly last? Once Gio grows sick of me for good, and the novelty of dressing me up like a doll wears off, *then* what?

Call me paranoid, but a real part of me still feels like my days are numbered.

We shop into the evening, building me an entire wardrobe that'll last a month if not longer. Gio's dropped at least a cool twenty g's on me in one afternoon. I have to sleep with him now, don't I? I'm just saying, I've screwed plenty of guys for way, way less. Including Enzo.

Again, my thoughts land on WWTD—what would Tasha do?

I think about calling her, but then I remember I don't have a phone. That, along with my wallet, purse, and keys, are all still at the Dollhouse. What must the girls be thinking? I never showed up for my shift last night. Have they already alerted the authorities?

After shopping, Gio takes me to Nobu for dinner. His

guards escort us every step of the way. An entire section is cordoned off for us and his henchmen. We sit down to our waiter promising to return with sake. Gio unfurls his napkin, a mystery across the table from me. He hasn't said much, nor has he looked at me since my fashion show in Valentino.

More nerves quake in my stomach. I stumble over my words. "I…I didn't know you like Japanese."

"Is Japanese cuisine fine for you?"

"Are you kidding? I love sushi! And sake. And sashimi. And food in general. I'm starving," I ramble. I run a finger along the glass candle holder sitting between us on the table. "Surprisingly enough, you work up a huge appetite trying on clothes."

"They looked good on you. All of them."

"And you paid for all of them without breaking a sweat."

"I told you money is no object."

The waiter returns with the most expensive sake Nobu carries and takes our order. Since we're at such a nice restaurant, I decide to be ladylike and order only a spicy tuna roll and some sashimi. We take our first sips of sake as I remind him yet again he can have his pick of women.

"I can," he admits, blasé. His gaze travels onto me from across the table, never leaving. "And I've chosen you, Falynn. You accepted that last night when you agreed to our deal."

The sake slides down my throat, smooth and sweet. I hold the choko cup with my palm and say, "I just…I hope I don't disappoint you. You're clearly used to the finer things in life. I'm not."

"Don't worry about that. Your job is to look beautiful on my arm. That's all."

I tease him with a small smile. "I'm still not sleeping with you."

Who am I kidding? This is almost certainly a lie.

He takes the bait, and releases a chuckle. He surprises me with a sexy smile of his own, his stoic, bearded face lighting up just slightly. "That's what you say now," he tells me, a flash of the lust from last night in his eyes. "But we'll see how long you keep that promise."

I don't do well when I'm flustered. Nerves fluttering, skin hot, I change the subject. "About last night…I should probably apologize for hitting you in the face."

"I've told you. A little pain is good. You'll find that out soon."

"And you say you're not going to—" I say, pantomiming a knife slicing my throat.

"Falynn, that's not the type of pain I'm talking about, and you know it. It's why your skin is glowing right now. You're *flushed*."

I am. And hot. And bothered. And, damn, I really wish my pussy would stop aching in want. I squeeze my thighs together and clear my throat.

"What's on the agenda for the rest of tonight?"

"Business."

"What *do* you do anyway?"

"It's none of your concern."

"That seems to be your default answer for just about everything."

It occurs to me I still don't know jack shit about him. Not what he does for a living. Not how he's so sickeningly wealthy. Not even his freaking last name.

Yet his crew hover on the sidelines keeping us protected at all times.

He's a mystery I'm desperate to solve. If only I was given the clues needed to have a fighting chance.

But one thing I've learned about him is he's cool, calm, and composed. He's calculated and cold, though that veneer slips when prodded hard enough, like last night when I tried running away. Before that as I danced for him and lust sparked in those electric eyes.

Suddenly, a desire rises up in me to be the one to make him lose control. To be the woman who unleashes whatever darkness he's containing, for better or for worse.

Our dinner arrives, and we dine in mostly silence. I'm not good with silence…or awkward pauses. It's killing me as I masterfully pick up a piece of sashimi with my chopsticks. If Gio won't talk, I will. Even if it's to myself.

"So, what do you do for fun?" I ask conversationally, like we're two strangers stuck on a plane together.

"Fun?" He cocks a brow.

"Yeah…fun. You've heard of that, right? It's when you let loose, live a little."

"What do *you* do for fun?"

"Nice try turning the question back on me, but I'll bite. I like dancing, which is probably pretty obvious. I enjoy cooking and traveling. Music and movies."

He scoffs. "Music and movies don't count. Anyone can like those."

"Including you? Tell me, Gio, what's on your 'recently watched' on Netflix?"

Given how elusive he is, I don't expect an answer. Instead he rubs his scruffy jaw and a slight smirk materializes on his mouth. "I don't have much time for Netflix, but…if I have to guess, probably *Pulp Fiction*."

I gasp so loudly, the waiter passing us by glances over. "I love *Pulp Fiction*! Well…most of Tarantino's work. Say what you want about him and his assholeness, he's a great director. Except *Once Upon a Time in Hollywood*. That was trash."

Gio gives a low chuckle. "Strong opinions on his films. What's your favorite?"

"Easy. *Kill Bill 1* and *2*. Yours?"

"I told you. *Pulp Fiction*. But I'll gladly watch any of his films."

"We should have a movie night," I blurt out without thinking. I rush to correct myself. "Um, you know…I just meant…if we're pretending to be a couple. But you said it's just an appearance thing, so…probably not."

Humor gleams in his eyes as he stares at me. "Falynn, you must really learn to filter your thoughts more and not say anything at any time."

"Force of habit. Blame yourself for choosing me."

"Movie night," he repeats with some thought. He wipes his mouth with his dinner napkin. "That might be your best idea yet."

My eyes widen. "Excuse me? You mean you want to?"

He smirks and winks at me. "Perhaps tonight. *After* I handle my business."

Oh, shit. I think I might be on my way to solving the mystery after all.

8

Giovanni
PLAYLIST: 🎵 PYRAMIDS - FRANK OCEAN 🎵

"BOSS, CAN WE TALK?" Robby asks when we settle on the sofa of the suite he's sharing with C.J. Falynn has been returned to the suite I've been keeping her in, closely guarded by Dominico, another soldier I've brought along to Vegas.

I gesture for Robby to continue, a glass of whiskey in my other hand. "You've already rehearsed a speech. I can tell by the twitch in your beady eye."

He chortles. "I don't have beady eyes."

"What is it, Robby? What's so time sensitive you've requested we speak?"

"It concerns the stripper."

"Falynn," I correct without hesitation.

Robby's eye twitches. "Yeah, her."

"What about her?"

"The broad is deadweight, Boss."

"Don't mince words on my account, *cazzo*," I snipe. The ice in my glass chinks as I take a sip. "I expected a lot more diplomatic language. Not for you to be so…blunt."

"There's no time for diplomacy with a black-and-white

situation. She is a liability, a waste of time and resources. The girl needs to go."

"Go where, *cazzo*? Tell me."

The pasty fuck's face glowers. "You know where. I'll handle it. Make it quick. She won't even suffer."

Papa has always said I have a poker face that can win me the world championship if it were ever on the line. Most people are unable to separate their emotions from their physical reactions. Their brows arch or their nostrils flare. They smile and frown. The rest of their body movements give them away, fidgeting or tapping feet.

I'm able to separate myself from such basic human tendencies. Emotion is my mortal enemy, which is why it's kept locked away inside of me. Occasional spats of anger or agitation may rise to the surface, but even then, I'm able to keep my cool. I'm able to be methodical and use my head. I'm always in control.

As Robby suggests we dispose of Falynn, my heart ticks faster. My pulse spikes. I can feel it grow warmer in the room, though I sit as casually as if nothing has changed. I sip from my whiskey and study Robby with a heavy stare, my silence an answer in itself.

What he's asking is out of the question. I've told Falynn she lives, and I'm a man of my word. Even if I weren't, the idea of disposing of her is an unsavory one. It leaves a sour taste in my mouth when I should taste the warmth of the whiskey.

Foolish as it may be, as detached and heartless as I am, I have begun to like the girl. In no serious, no real consequential way—meaning, should it become necessary, she's expendable. More so in a way that amuses me. In a way I find refreshing.

She doesn't realize this. She doesn't understand her unfiltered behavior and stubborn streak have caught my attention in the manner it has. I'd prefer she doesn't figure this out. The less she knows the better.

It's dangerous, messing with a woman like her. Not only is she gorgeous, but she's charming and smart. Men have ruined their lives over less worthy women. But I'm not one of these foolish men. I'll keep her alive, indulge in her company for a few weeks, and then cut ties forever.

"Boss, we don't have time," Robby says after the silence goes on. His pale skin gleams with sweat. I've talked to him about his perspiration issue, but the *stronzo* continues to sweat like a piglet. "C.J. found out word on the street is that Lovato's unhappy with what happened with Jerry. He's taking it as a slight against him."

"It was a slight against him."

"But we need to figure out how we'll address any future issues with him. It's going to happen. And you still haven't found a new manager at the Dollhouse—"

"Your point seems to be I'm slacking off from my duties as *capo*. Is that what you're suggesting?"

The cold steel in my tone causes him to falter. He stutters, more sweat leaking from his pores. I ease up on the intensity in my stare; Robby is my right hand, a loyal companion, and whose concern is earnest. There's no need to humiliate him for contradicting me.

He dabs at his brow with a cocktail napkin from the minibar. "What I'm saying is, Boss, we've been in Vegas for a couple weeks now, and have not established stability in our operation. The casino's grand opening is almost here. Today's shopping spree at the Forum put us behind."

At the bottom of my glass, I drink the last of the watered-down whiskey, and then take an ice cube into my mouth. The cold cube crunches between my teeth as I stare down Robby some more. He makes excellent points, but his solution is a non-negotiable.

"Your concern is noted," I say calmly. "We'll double our efforts to stabilize our territory here. We'll find a new guy to manage the Dollhouse. We'll put the finishing touches on the casino's opening. Get in contact with Lovato's crew. Arrange a meeting between us. Ensure you make it known it's on friendly grounds."

Robby nods along, eager I've taken his advice to heart. "Yes, Boss. That can all be done."

"But understand, Robby," I continue, the chill returning in my tone, "she stays alive. You are not to hurt a hair on her head. You will treat her respectfully...as one of my personal guests."

Robby doesn't agree. His sweaty face flickers with quick distaste before he forces it away. A sneer replaces it as he says, "That must be some tail. I need to find one to blow some steam off."

I don't bother correcting him. He doesn't need to know the truth. I haven't had a taste of the pussy. Yet.

It's almost midnight by the time Robby and I finish discussing business. I return to the penthouse suite Falynn is in, expecting her to be in bed already. Possibly staging another one of her hunger or sleep strikes like the last two nights. Both have failed, but it doesn't seem to deter her stubborn ass from trying.

But I'm wrong. I enter the suite and find her parked on the sofa in the living area. She's wearing one of my gym shirts. An ugly, old Yankees T-shirt that has faded over time —perhaps the oldest piece of clothing I have. On her svelte curves, though, it looks anything but old and ugly; she's breathing new, sexy life into the thing.

Does she have anything on underneath? *Fuck*.

Just her panties. As she sits curled up on the sofa, her shapely bare legs are in full view. Those creamy, smooth, golden-brown legs of hers as my shirt cuts off midthigh. Her curls are free and wild, inviting imagery of being tousled in bed. She hugs a throw pillow with a casual air, like she doesn't look sexy as fuck sprawled on my sofa, half-naked.

This is a trap. Another one like last night, where she danced for me. She shook that fine ass of hers, got me under her trance, and then stole my gun and whacked me with it.

I stand by the door, unclasping my watch. While habit, it also buys me a few seconds to compose myself. My gaze travels over to the movie playing on the big screen.

"You're up," I say. "And you're watching *Reservoir Dogs*."

"When I agreed to a Quentin Tarantino movie night, I meant it. With or without you."

I cross the room and lower myself onto the larger sofa. "I was handling—"

"Business, yada, yada, yada. I know," she huffs, sitting up. She criss-crosses her legs, the pillow in her lap. I'm half distracted by the flash of pink from underneath *my* T-shirt.

Pink panties. Satiny ones.

"I had no idea you would raid my closet." I gesture to the T-shirt.

She glances down the front, staring at the faded letters. "Oh, this? I found it by accident. The negligees from Agent Provocateur are gorgeous, but this is comfier. I would've asked, but then I remembered you were not to be interrupted." She mimics my stern tone, wagging a finger. "Conducting vital, world-changing business or whatever. So I put it on anyway. Do you mind?"

"I do if it means you'll strip it off right here."

"Nice try, it stays on." She crosses her arms decidedly.

"I always watch a movie before bed. It helps me unwind. Which reminds me, speaking of bed, *when* have you been sleeping?"

"I don't sleep much."

"Sleep is a basic human function. Of course you sleep."

"Two to four hours. At most."

"Are you kidding? No wonder you're so cranky!"

I cock a brow. "I am not *cranky*."

The face she makes is the definition of *if you say so*. It's bothersome and amusing and endearing all at once. I want to kiss it off of her. Then do other things to make her squirm and punish her for such boldness.

"The past two nights, I've fallen asleep and you're awake. I wake up and you're awake," she goes on with an incredulous head shake. "You must be a vampire or something."

"Not a vampire. Just an insomniac."

"Enzo's an insomniac. He became one after his mom passed."

"Forgive me if I'm not interested in hearing about your poor, street thug boyfriend."

I don't like when she mentions him, but upon seeing her reaction, I regret my rudeness. She gives me the silent treatment, glaring at the screen. Her grip on the throw pillow gives her away; her fingers dig into the edges, a sign of agitation.

"What I mean is, insomnia doesn't bother me. Sleep is an overindulgence for the weak. I have business—"

"To conduct," she finishes for me. "Just what kind of business? The world will never know!"

"Are you going to mouth off the whole movie?" I ask in another effort to lighten the air. "It'll be over by the time you finish talking."

"Oh, I wasn't aware you were watching *with* me."

"That was the agreement, was it not? Turn up the volume."

She obliges, reaching for the remote. I settle against the sofa cushions. In seconds I'm engrossed in a movie I've seen a thousand and one times. She may have me beat on number of viewings by how often she quotes lines along with the movie.

The first time, I glanced at her in mild surprise. By the fourth or fifth time, I'm joining her. It becomes a test of who knows the next line better, earning a laugh from us. When *Reservoir Dogs* finishes, she asks if I'd like to watch *Pulp Fiction*.

I check the time. "You're not ready to overindulge in eight hours of sleep?"

"You call it overindulge, I call it beauty rest."

"You have enough beauty as is."

That throws her off. It's not the first time I've said such a thing today, but so far, she's been shocked each time. I've learned her tells for when she's flustered—she blinks many times, her lips part, and her honey complexion flushes with a reddish undertone. Right now, she runs a finger through a loopy curl and then puts *Pulp Fiction* on.

As the movie begins, I'm thinking of what Robby said earlier. Is it true what he implied? Am I pussy-whipped? Am I thinking with my cock like a *stronzo*?

I glance at Falynn. It's true I want a taste of that delicious honey between those thighs. I want to run my hands down that delectable fat ass and watch it jiggle when I smack my palm to it. I want to grip her throat and push my tongue into her mouth, kissing her hard, forcing a soft little moan from her mouth. I want…to do so many things to her. The list goes on for miles.

I feel a tug in my pants, my cock twitching to remind

me it's been five whole days without satisfaction. For a man who has pussy lined up coast to coast, five days is a long time. Too long to go. I can always find a bimbo on the casino floor, or even one at the Dollhouse, but…

Falynn. She's the one I crave. No one else will do 'til I have a taste of her.

The movie plays, and once again, we are immersed. We laugh along with a few of the scenes, sit on the edge of our seats at the thrilling parts, and share fun trivia about the movie. At one point, I undo the top buttons of my shirt and roll up the sleeves. I make us drinks. Falynn orders dessert from room service.

During the infamous dance scene between John Travolta and Uma Thurman, Falynn shares it's her favorite scene.

"I just love the bad dancing," she gushes, brown eyes bright. "Neither of them take themselves too seriously."

I nod along, letting a question slip. "Have you always been a dancer? Is it something you've always liked?"

"Dancing is in my blood," she says, shrugging. "My mom was a dancer. So was my grandmother. I wanted to be a lawyer."

"You still can."

"Doubtful. As you can see, my life is a hot mess."

"And you think no lawyers have hot messes for lives? Do you think lawyers are perfect?"

"I think most lawyers don't strip for money. Most don't escort on the side. Most don't get mixed up with men on the other side of the law."

"Am I the man on the other side of the law?" I'm half amused by the inclusion.

"Actually, I meant Enzo. But thanks for admitting you're a lawbreaker."

I smirk. "We all break the law sometimes."

"Speak for yourself! I don't so much as jay walk."

"No, you just date felons."

Her eyes narrow and she folds her arms. "Touché, but also kinda a low blow."

"No disrespect. What I'm saying is, you can still become a lawyer."

"Yeah, right. That dream's pretty much done. Have you forgotten you told me I have to leave the country? For good, I'm assuming."

"That's the deal, yes."

Another pause comes between us. I return my attention to the movie, but in my periphery, Falynn is staring at me. I give up on pretending I don't notice and gesture for her to speak.

"Can I ask you a question? You have to promise you'll answer."

"I can promise you I will not lie, but not that I'll answer."

She inhales a breath as Samuel L. Jackson and John Travolta argue the difference between American and European McDonald's on the TV screen. "Are you a mobster?"

I stare at her with a straight face, figuring there is no use in avoiding the answer.

"Yes."

9

Falynn
PLAYLIST: ♫ DREAMERS - K.FLAY ♪

GIOVANNI SORRENTINO, son of Giuliano Sorrentino, renowned mobster and businessman. The news slams into me and leaves me breathless. Though I've suspected, hearing it from Gio's lips is a whole new level of shock altogether. I don't know how to process the information, so I spend a ridiculous amount of time gaping at him.

He picks up his drink and takes a sip. "You understand why I've been reluctant to let you go."

"Because you're the mob and the mob *whacks* people!"

"You've been watching too much *Sopranos*."

"Are you kidding me? I witnessed you and your men murder a guy!"

"You should scream it louder—the other half of Las Vegas didn't hear you."

"I'm...I'm going to be sick."

I stumble onto unsteady legs and beeline through the penthouse, straight for the bathroom. The sugary alcoholic contents of my stomach are in the toilet seconds later when the knob on the door jiggles. Gio is standing outside.

"Open the door," he says calmly.

Curled against the toilet bowl, butt on the tile, I heave some more. "No," I croak feebly afterward.

"Falynn, you're being ridiculous." The tone he uses is that of an exasperated husband when his wife whines about something he deems frivolous. "Open up."

"Go away. I didn't ask to be in *Goodfellas* the sequel!"

"Anyone who would make a sequel to a classic like that deserves to be *whacked*."

"Now, you're fucking with me!"

I'm not sure what it is about the moment that's churning my stomach. It could be the truth. It could be the pint of double fudge brownie and strawberry cheesecake ice cream I consumed. Or the whiskey sours during *Pulp Fiction*. Maybe a vengeful combination of all three. All I know is I hug the porcelain toilet 'til Gio's footsteps fade, and the only sound left is me puking my guts out.

To my surprise, I wake up in the king-size bed. I twist and turn, tangled in the sheets. The morning light spills into the room without consideration for its brightness. Retinas burned, brain a muddled mess, I push myself off the bed. Problem is, my foot's still caught on the sheet. Down I go, smacking face-first into the floor like a cartoon character.

SPLAT!

Gio laughs. I'm shocked, because a) I didn't notice him in the room, b) I haven't ever heard his laugh sound so uncontrolled, so *unfiltered*, c) I don't remember how I got to bed, or d) all of the above.

All of the above.

"Oh, it's you again?" I mumble as he stands over me. I begrudgingly accept the hand he offers. He hoists me to my feet in an easy flex of power. "How did I get to bed?"

"I put you to bed...*again*. It seems to be a habit of yours."

That's true. Third night running.

I rub my kneecap, which sustained carpet burn during my fall. "Did I pass out in the bathroom?"

"You did."

"Then how did you—you know what, never mind."

"I'm a crazy mobster and you don't think I have the means to get into a hotel bathroom?"

He's in a playful mood today as he gives me a shoulder squeeze and then strolls out of the bedroom. He's in another crisp white button-down, sleeves rolled to the elbows. It might be only 9 a.m., but apparently it's never too early for a smoke—Gio sticks a cigar between his lips and lights up. I follow him like a curious puppy.

"Breakfast as usual," he says, gesturing to the cart. "Eat up. You emptied your entire stomach last night."

"Mmm...sexy. Still want me as your pretend girlfriend?"

"Unfortunately for you, yes. Rest up today. I need you well tonight."

My brows draw close. "What's tonight?"

"Dinner with a work associate."

"Another mobster?" I gasp. The wave of nausea from last night returns and I clutch my stomach.

"Your boyfriend was in a street gang...and Mafia talk makes you sick?"

"First of all, the Mafia is on a whole different level of crime. That much is obvious. Huge difference between some guys off the street hitting up a liquor store. Second, how did you know Enzo was in a gang?"

"Wild guess," he answers, more humor infusing his smooth tone. "But thank you for confirming. You'll be on my arm tonight, so I need you to look good. *And* to behave yourself."

I fold my arms with distinct indignation. "I know how to act!"

"That remains to be seen. Eat. Relax. Be ready by six."

"And where are you going—?"

Before I can even get the full question out, he's strolling out of the suite. The door swinging shut is my only answer. I huff out a petulant breath and then turn around to the room service cart. There's no use letting another morning's delicious breakfast go to waste.

The day *drags*. Who would've known being a Mafia girlfriend would be so damn boring? After breakfast, I convince my security guard, Louis, to escort me to the resort's gym. I'm not trusted anywhere by myself, so every machine I use, Louis stands no more than five feet away. Always close enough to yoke my ass should I try to run for it.

But at this point, I'm beyond trying to run away. I've pretty much given up on that idea. It's no use when I have no money, no phone, no real friends or family except Tasha. Even if I do get away, then what? Go back to my crappy apartment and wait for them to track me down? Work another night on stage at the Dollhouse…which Gio and his family own?

Nope. At this point, I'm trapped. I know I'm trapped. I *accept* I'm trapped.

So far, Gio has kept his word. He's treated me, more or less, with respect. He hasn't hurt me, hasn't even tried to force me to provide my "services" when he can easily make me. Instead, he's taken me on a $20,000 shopping spree, tucked me into bed when I've fallen asleep in chairs or slumped over toilets, and he's kept me well-fed. What's there to complain about *really*?

Aside from lack of freedom. Aside from the fact that he's a dangerous, deadly man at heart. And sexy, which only makes him more deadly and dangerous. The confidence he exudes is so effortless, so natural it's infused with who he is as a man.

Ever look at a man and just know he can fuck? That was the first thought coming to mind when I laid eyes on Gio at the Dollhouse. I can tell in how he acts, sense it in how he moves. Now that I've seen his trim, cut body naked as the day he was born and the appendage swinging between his legs, I'm hungry.

I kinda wanna ride his huge dick into orgasmic oblivion. *At least once.*

If my days are numbered, why not go out with a bang…as in Gio banging the fuck out of me?

As I towel off from the stair machine, I decide I'm changing my mindset. The insane predicament I've found myself in isn't changing. But why continue to fight it when this could be the escape from my shitty old life I've been looking for?

What am I clinging to, really? I'm a stripper with an assload of bills and college debt piling up. My boyfriend's about to be locked up for the next three to five years. His debts to the loan sharks remain unpaid. My mom disowned me a long time ago, and my boss is dead. I have nothing.

"You remind me of my little sister," Louis says out of nowhere. He hands me another towel.

I hesitantly accept. "Me? Your little sister?"

"She's about your age, your vibe."

"My vibe? What's that mean?" I wipe my brow and suck down some water from my hydro flask.

"Young, silly, very into what's hip."

We leave behind the machines and move toward the resort gym's exit. As I fall into step beside him, giving him a furtive glance, any sense of caution leaves me. He looks like a big teddy bear more than anything, dressed up in an all-black suit. His expression is easygoing and his tone conversational. He's just like any other regular guy off the street...except maybe sometimes he kills people.

"Not sure what you mean by silly, but I'll take it as a compliment."

"It is one, Miss Falynn," he replies. We move down a wide corridor with plush diamond-patterned carpeting and artistic sconces lighting up the walls. "That might be why Boss is keeping you around."

"Excuse me?"

"You lighten things up. Make him laugh."

Louis ushers me into the elevator and presses the top floor, taking us to our penthouse. I let a small smile form as I replay his words back for every ding the elevator makes.

You lighten things up. Make him laugh.

I'm ready and waiting for Gio when he arrives to pick me up. I've straightened my hair, donned a sexy cocktail dress with a deep, plunging neckline, and slipped into stilettos that make my legs and ass look amazing.

Gio takes one look at me, eye-fucking me head to toe with a cock of his brow. He offers me his arm and guides me down to his shiny red luxury car—a Rolls-Royce convertible.

He opens the passenger-side door for me.

"You're driving us?"

"It's a nice evening to go for a drive ourselves," he says, waiting for me to get in. "Of course, we'll still have coverage."

My gaze lifts to the side mirror, where a sleek black car waits behind us. Louis sits at the wheel.

Gio slams on the gas a second later. Gravity shoves me against the seat belt as the scenery of the Vittoria falls behind us. He turns onto a narrow street behind the resort and casino and then onto the Strip. Traffic is jammed this time of evening, but he navigates the crowded lanes with careless ease, slipping between cars with barely a look.

Before I can orient myself, we're speeding onto the freeway. I check the side mirror. Louis is on our tail, apparently accustomed to his boss's speed demon driving. Hot September air whips around us, messing our hair.

He doesn't seem to care. He steers with one arm, sliding into the next lane when the mood strikes him. I gather my long, flat-ironed hair as if my hand is a ponytail holder. My heart is thumping in my rib cage, and I'm not so sure it's just because of Gio's fast driving.

A sense of thrill sparks through my body. When Gio swerves into the fast lane and guns it, jetting by any other car on the freeway, the sound of laughter fills my ears—*my* laughter.

It catches Gio off guard. He swaps his gaze between me and the road ahead several times. Then one of his rare, slight smirks touches his lips, framed by his dark beard. If possible, the convertible shoots even faster. I stick my arms up and feel the air kissing my skin.

Las Vegas melts away and steep desert canyons materialize in every direction. We have the road to ourselves as we speed toward the golden horizon. I have no clue where we're going, but I've never been more excited for a dinner party. Even if there's a possibility of bloodshed tonight.

What the hell has gotten into me? Another delirious laugh slips past my lips. I have no idea, but I'm finally living life the way it was meant to be lived—indulging in the finer things, flirting with the edge of danger, letting go with reckless abandon.

We come up along a wide bend and a huge mansion in the desert hills pops up. Gio slows the closer we get to the wrought-iron gate. It spreads open for us, allowing us entrance. The driveway winds along the front of the massive house. The Spanish-style architecture of the red roofing and clean, white stucco walls stand out against the desert landscape.

He shifts the gear into park and turns to look at me. His bright blue eyes only stoke the fire of adventure burning inside me. "We're here."

10

Giovanni
PLAYLIST: ♫ THRONE - SAINT MESA ♪

TONIGHT IS ABOUT CONDUCTING BUSINESS.

I arrive at Lovato's Vegas compound with ten of my men in tow. With a sinfully gorgeous and sexy Falynn on my arm. The night's festivities have already kicked off. Music blasts from the many open windows, shaking the Spanish-style mansion on its foundation. Guests hang around the large veranda, blowing smoke and sipping drinks.

The night feels as long as the dark stretching into the desert hills. A bottomless void with no end. But one way or another, come dawn, a path forward will be set. Either an understanding will be reached, or we'll be at war.

We enter the mansion to bright lights and a double grand staircase in the foyer. Businessman and entertainment mogul, Johnny Goldman, strolls up to me with a big, fat grin and his hand held out. He's old as dirt—looks and smells like it, with tufts of hair sticking out his ears and a face that puts the cryptkeeper to shame. In years past, he did business with Uncle Claro when he worked the west coast side of the family's interests.

In the present times, he's knocking at death's door with a surgery-enhanced wife a third his age. We shake hands and trade quick pleasantries.

"Good to see the Sorrentinos return to Vegas," he says, flashing dentures at me. "Claro regretted having to scale back operations those years ago. How is he?"

I pull back my hand from his Skeletor grip. "Claro's surviving like the rest of us. I'll send him your regards."

"Please do, and remember," he wheezes, moving closer, "if you ever need a cover, Goldman Entertainment is open to a partnership."

New business prospects are the least of my concerns. My focus is solely on launching the Vittoria and quelling this potential feud with Lovato.

I bring Falynn with me to the open bar. My men are my shadow, drifting along, going where I go. So far Falynn's been obedient; she's played the role I hired her to play, and looked distractingly sexy doing so. Even as a man of composure, with the ability to be as cold as steel, I admit she's difficult to resist.

Those eyes are a deep and alluring abyss. Her lips, lush and plump. Her skin, bronze silk. Her body, a work of art with womanly curves flowing and dipping in all the right places. Even her smell intoxicates me—fresh and sweet, like spring.

It's what draws me in whenever I look at her. The light amid the dark. The spark of life that lives inside her in a world where blood and violence reigns supreme.

Falynn Carter has become an escape. If only a temporary one.

"How am I doing?" she asks, eyes twinkling. She takes a delicate sip of her drink, so close I catch an inhale of her sweetness. "I've been behaving myself."

"Good girl. Keep it up, I might reward you later," I

tell her, arm slipping around her waist. I'm not pretending to care about being handsy. I couldn't care less. Falynn is mine for the duration of our arrangement. So long as she is, I will touch her however I please when I please.

Now is one of those times as my hand rides along the swell of her supple ass. It's one of the most delectable asses I've seen, cheeks rounder than a globe of the world.

Falynn is in a good mood, because she giggles and leans closer. She playfully tucks her face into my neck. Her breath skims over my skin like the night air as she whispers, "Why wait 'til later? Why not now?"

My grip on her ass tightens, a full squeeze of ass meat in my palm. Before I can properly answer her, a *cazzo* with a hook nose and cheap suit approaches. Louis is a buffer between us in case he tries anything, but in a second, he reveals his intention.

"Mr. Tony would like to sit down to a drink if you are available."

I leave Falynn with two of my guys, making sure they'll keep her close, and then I proceed to go meet Antonio Lovato.

Tony and I have a lot in common. Both sons of the don. Both *capos*. Both early thirties with career aspirations as bloodthirsty as our fathers. Both with brothers vying for a throne we believe is ours.

But Antonio Lovato is a hothead. He's sloppy and unfocused, easily distracted. He's like a dog let loose from his leash; he'll chase after every fucking car in traffic if you let him.

He's seated in a den decorated with gaudy NYC artwork along the walls and rich mahogany furniture. Neither match the flavorful style of the Spanish architecture mansion, but the Lovatos aren't known for taste;

they're known as fucking thorns in the side. We sit down at either end of a long table.

"It's good you were able to make it, Gio," Tony says, his gaudy gold watch glinting under the lighting. He's decked out in gold everywhere—the chains around his neck, the flashy rings on his fingers, even the cap in his tooth. "It's always a benefit to meet like this, talk face-to-face. Otherwise, there's communication issues. You agree?"

"We're busy men, Tony. It's no hard feelings. *You agree?*"

The corner of Tony's mouth twitches. He's an unremarkable man, average height and pudgy build with sunken eyes. He'd be nothing if it weren't for his father.

His guys are lined up behind him, a wall of enforcers ready to defend their *capo* at the slightest notice. Behind me are my guys, equally alert and ready for disruption. But, for now, we sit like the civil gentlemen we pretend to be and sip our whiskey.

"I heard there's been some issues over at the Dollhouse. A misunderstanding, I'm sure. Nevertheless, I'd appreciate it if you don't interfere with the people I do business with. Jerry's passing is a tragedy."

I lean back in my chair, cavalier in how I stare across the table at him. "You've been misinformed, Tony. There was no misunderstanding. Jerry was disloyal, so he had to be taken care of."

"But is it disloyalty when he's working with the family who owns this territory?"

"Maybe in the past. Time's are changing. It's true the Sorrentino name has been absent in this city in recent years, but we're here to stake our claim. Tell your papa he's mistaken."

"My father's never mistaken." He leans forward, elbows on the table and fingers steepled. "You're asking for bloodshed by challenging us. Is that what you want?"

A slow grin spreads onto my face. "We've never been afraid of bloodshed. A little blood's a *good* thing."

"Is that a threat?" Tony pops out of his chair.

Weapons are drawn before he's on his feet. His guys and my guys have their guns trained on each other with me and Tony in the middle. For as calm as I am, my reflexes are anything but. As soon as Tony jerked in his chair, I was rising to meet his challenge. A second passes where everybody fumes, glaring at one another.

Tony sneers like somebody's told a joke. "We're done here. You'll regret this, Gio."

"I'm not a man of regret, Tony. I'm a man of action."

I storm out of the den with my men swarming behind me. I'm normally in control, but Tony pushed the right buttons. If it's war he wants, it's what he'll get. Violence is my friend. Death is my family. I'll have that *stronzo's* head on a motherfucking pike before he can take his next breath.

Tony doesn't know the beast he's just awakened. The bloodlust he's stirred in me. A current of rage burns in my chest. A flame that will torch his whole world and leave nothing but ash in the aftermath.

I seek out Falynn, blowing through the huge mansion like a tornado. I find her where I left her. Except some *cazzo* fuckhead is speaking to her. Where the hell is Dominico? He was supposed to be guarding her!

To make matters worse, the fuckhead leers. He reaches out and glides his knuckles down the length of her bare arm. I catch only a snippet, "Sweetheart, everyone's got a price."

His cranium bounces against plaster as I slam him into the wall. My knuckles are white and tight, twisted up in his shirt, my teeth bared and gaze dark. My bloodlust sets in.

"She's spoken for," I tell him in my calmest tone. A warning sign of all warning signs.

"Hey, whoa, calm down. I was just—*ARGHHH!*"

He weeps like a little bitch when I twist his hand, bending it so far back you'd think he was double-jointed. I'm barely aware everybody in the vicinity is watching, including my men, who edge closer, waiting their turn to take over for me. It's not every day their boss loses his cool.

"There is no price for this one," I say.

Crack.

I pull his index finger out its socket and then move onto the next finger. His middle finger rips right out with a merciless yank. He howls and his knees wobble on the verge of collapse.

"You want pussy? Find one of the whores selling it for a hundred a night. You touch her with these grubby little fingers again, I'm chopping them off and mailing them to your mother."

The fuckhead drops to his knees cradling his hand. My men and I are out of there. Falynn is hauled off along with us. We make it out to the driveway before I give my next order. I'm fuming more than ever, the burn in my chest affecting my breathing.

"Dominico was supposed to be watching her," I growl to Robby. He's by my side as we come up on the cars. "He needs to learn a lesson about leaving his post."

"Got it, Boss. The water buckets?"

"Tonight. Right now. Take him out and do it."

"Louis'll follow you back—"

"Don't. I'll return my own way."

"But, Boss—"

I hop into my convertible. Falynn is already buckled in. She hasn't said a peep throughout my fury. The engine revs up with a bold roar into the warm night. We're off in a matter of seconds, zipping down the desert highway.

Falynn yelps in surprise when I slam on the gas even harder. The Rolls-Royce darts forward, curving along the steep canyons. The moon tries to chase us from up above, failing as we fly into the darkness.

My hands shake on the wheel, but I grip it tighter. I'm out of control, reckless in the moment. The hold I have over my temper is gone. Instead it's burning me up with a heat hotter than the fucking sun.

This is why I keep emotion at bay. This is why I shut it down at all costs. Why I'm composed and calculated. If I were to truly unleash the firestorm raging inside me, I'd burn the world down.

As we speed through the black canyons, it becomes too much. I can't drive when I'm blinded by fury. I'm seconds away from doing some dumb shit like flipping the car and killing us both. I'm reminded of the best piece of advice Papa gave me. Many, many years ago…

Emotion is a weakness. Stupid people are emotional. Smart people know better.

I hit the brakes as abruptly as I smashed on the gas. The Rolls-Royce convertible whips out of control for a couple seconds. Tires screeching fills the quiet air. We come to a jerky halt amid dust and cacti and no other soul for miles.

Falynn sits in shock. Her fingers are gripping the overhead handle. Her breath is audible. Her hair a windswept, albeit sexy, mess about her shoulders.

My breathing's worse. It's ragged and animalistic. I suck in some air and expel it from my lungs a second later. Then I scrub a hand over my face.

"Is everything okay?" she asks softly.

I grunt like a beast. It's the best I can do at the moment.

Her hand slides into my lap. It catches my attention, distracting me enough from the flame of anger burning in my chest. I look over at her.

Fucking hell.

She's biting her lip. She has those round, alluring eyes on me, framed by thick lashes. I recognize the look immediately—it has *fuck me* written all over it. It's the look she had when she gave me that trap of a lap dance. Is this another fucking ploy of hers?

"Thank you for what you did," she says.

"I did a lot of shit tonight…including almost breaking some fucktard's hand."

"Dominico was getting me a drink. Then he came up. He thought I was a…a, *you know*."

I scoff. "A prostitute? Probably because every other girl there has a price on her pussy."

"It doesn't matter. You didn't have to get involved, but you did. Thank you."

"Let's get it straight—you're my woman. You're *mine*. Just like my businesses, like my territory. I will not tolerate another man touching my—"

"Property?" Her tone is almost amused.

Yeah, she's fucking with me.

My gaze darkens. "You agreed to this. You knew what you were signing up for."

"You're right," she whispers. She holds my gaze and slides her hand up my thigh, near my groin. "And I don't regret it. Not for one second. I'm yours, so do it. *Make* me yours."

A beat passes as her words linger in the air. Then we're launching ourselves at each other, crushing our lips together in a bruising kiss. I grip her arms by the elbows, dragging her across her seat and the gears, into my lap. A moan slips out of her as I part her lips with my tongue and taste her mouth.

So sweet. So delicious.

But I'm an impatient man. As I kiss her hard, I push away the low neckline of her dress. Her breasts spill into my palms, soft and a delectable weight with pebbled nipples. I break away from her mouth to kiss a path down the column of her neck and then breasts. She arches into me, perched in my lap, her head tilting back. I flick my tongue over her hardened nipples, at first fast, and then slowing up for torturous circles.

A strangled moan leaves her, and she grinds against me. Her own little tease, she reminds me how close that sweet pussy of hers is to my hardening cock. Just a couple layers of fabric separates us.

Pieces of clothing that need to be done away with immediately.

I suck and tease her nipples some more while sliding a hand under her dress. I shove aside her thong and sink two fingers into her. She groans and rocks her hips, fucking herself on my digits, coating them in her slick cream. Her pussy walls pull at my fingers, silky, hot, and tight.

My hard-on twitches as I imagine it's my dick, not my fingers, she's milking.

Fuck. I need to be inside her right now.

We work on my pants too, freeing my heavy cock with some maneuvering in the driver's seat. Our mouths meet again as I waste no time pulling her down on me. The instant I enter her, velvety heat engulfs me. I groan into her mouth and kiss her harder, fingers twisting in her hair to hold her against me.

Our movements are frantic and desperate. I thrust my hips up and plunge deep inside her. She whimpers and clenches around me, her skin flushed warm, her breaths shallow.

She feels too good. Too wet. Too hot. Too tight. I let go of control and become the animal I am in my basest element. I grunt and slam up into her, gripping her arms tightly, bouncing her on my dick.

Every last muscle in my body is tense. I'm on the edge, so close to busting a nut, I can almost taste the mind-numbing release. The feeling is what I seek as my rage dissipates for pleasure. For the heaven fucking this sweet pussy feels like. There's no going back. She's mine now. For as long as I want her.

It excites me, the thrill of corrupting her, molding her to fit this sinful world of mine.

She comes undone with a deep shudder, pulsing around me. Still I don't let her go. I only fuck her harder. Each second is pure animal desire. I drive into her without mercy 'til I hit the glass wall and it shatters around me.

The convertible might as well be floating in the dark canyon. I spill inside her, my body tense and rigid, my adrenaline soaring through my bloodstream. She rides out my climax and rocks those supple hips of hers. I brush stray hairs from her face and capture her lips with mine, cementing what we've just done.

What she is to me now—*mine*.

"Back to the penthouse," I growl when we pull apart. She crawls into the passenger seat and I tuck my dick into my pants. I turn the Rolls-Royce on, and in seconds we're speeding along the dark desert highways again.

Time to finish what we started.

11

Falynn
PLAYLIST: 🎵 BURNING DESIRE - LANA DEL REY♪

I WAKE Gio up the next morning with his thick cock in my mouth. I flick the fat tip with my tongue before enveloping him whole. His generous length easily reaches the back of my throat. I fight my gag reflex, breathing through my nose, and suck like my life depends on it.

Drowsiness quickly fades as his electric blue eyes darken into sapphires. He lies back against the pillows and headboard, muscular arms folded behind his head. He's so damn sexy, a Mafia king carved and chiseled of marble, lying among the thousand thread count sheets like it's his throne.

Blow jobs have never been my favorite. Enzo loves them. I've tolerated them for his sake.

But as my tongue chases a thick, protruding vein along Gio's shaft, a deep soul-burning desire wakes in me. A fire that sparks in my belly, one that I've never felt before, that only his dick deep inside me can put out. My pussy aches in jealousy at the thought.

I reach between my legs for some relief and touch myself. My fingers rub my clit as my moan vibrates on his cock. His answer is a rumble deeper than thunder. It rolls from his broad, sculpted chest, his fingers digging into my hair. He guides me.

Up. Down. Up. Down. Faster. *Sloppier*.

My eyes water. I'm slobbering all over his cock. The messier the better. His grip in my hair tightens, forcing me down 'til his fat tip bruises the back of my throat. I make the most of it—this is a performance like any other, and I'm a performer. I give my all.

Suck the fucking soul out of him.

The room fills with nothing but the sloppy, wet noises of me taking him to the hilt. I'm swallowing his cock whole, mouth open as wide as possible to take his thick length in full. Every muscle of his trim, shredded body tenses. His breathing more ragged than ever. He's close.

I come up and swirl my tongue along his tip and alternate my technique. Let my tongue ride the length of him. When I reach his balls, I take one into my mouth, and suck on the sac filled with what I want shooting down my throat.

His head lolls back against the pillows. His low, husky groan is its own reward. Encouraged and determined, I sink back down onto his cock, if possible deeper than before, gagging as I take every last inch. Without warning, Gio comes.

He holds me in position, filling my mouth with every drop of his seed. I do my best to swallow it all as it floods my mouth. Some dribbles down my chin and onto the sheets. I waste no time, scooping it up with my finger, sucking it into my mouth. He groans and fists his cock. His broad chest rises and falls for every breath. The dark glisten in his eyes elicits a tingle down my spine. He's getting hard again, his cock rising in all its monstrous glory.

Before either of us can make a move, his phone goes off. Irritation flashes across his stony features as he stretches an arm out to the nightstand. He answers with a grunt. I drop down among the many pillows and watch him, the strap of my negligee low on my shoulder. I make no attempt to hide the fact that my hand is back between my thighs. They're spread wide enough to offer him a prime view as I toy with my pussy, fingers drawing circles on my clit and slick folds. My stomach may be full with his cum, but this pussy needs to be too.

ASAP.

I watch him as his impatience builds. Whoever's on the other end speaks fast and with a thick New Yorker type of accent. His gaze lands on me playing with myself. I can see the exact moment his lids hood and eyes darken with carnal lust. His jaw clenches down harder, as if fighting it with every fiber of his being. He gets off the bed and turns his back on me.

"All right, I'll handle it," he says in a growl. "There's no need. It'll get done."

When he hangs up, he moves over to the closet and slides a leg into the first pair of boxer briefs in the drawer. Not his usual finessed, composed self, he puts on dark gray slacks and grapples with buckling his belt. I sit up among the pillows with a pout, hand still selfishly between my legs. If he doesn't get back here and blow my back out! Ugh!

"Don't tell me you're leaving!" I whine.

"Important business to handle. A lot happened last night before I almost broke that *cazzo's* hand over you." He moves on to the accent chair in the corner to put on his leather wingtip shoes.

"But can't it wait? Five minutes for a quickie."

"It's time sensitive. I get back in that bed with you, I'm

not coming out for at least an hour. That pretty pussy of yours is too delectable to give up in five minutes."

Warmth flushes over my skin hearing his smooth accent talk about my pussy. I pet her some more, still unabashedly offering him a primetime viewing. If I tease him enough, how can he turn me down? My essence is slippery on my fingers as I play with my folds.

It distracts him for a moment as good as any hypnosis before he forces his gaze away. He finishes putting on his shoes and then rises.

"You keep playing with that pretty pussy like that, trying to sabotage me, and I'll have to punish you later."

I moan obscenely and lick my own juices off my fingers.

Lust flashes in his blue orbs. He strides over and drops a kiss on my lips. His hand travels between my legs, cupping my wet, warm pussy in his palm. He massages my little disappointed nub with his thumb and sinks two fingers inside me. His digits are immediately coated, considering I'm soaking wet. I bite down on my lip and attempt to squeeze my thighs together to trap his hand. Yes, I am that shameless. No, I do not give a fuck.

"Later," he promises as he stands up and takes his hand away. He breathes in my scent from his fingers like it's his favorite scent in the world then begrudgingly returns to getting dressed. "I want you facedown, ass up when I get back."

"That's only who knows how many hours from now. Another day trapped in this suite. You could at least leave me with a bathroom that has a decent showerhead." I'm still pouting when he throws me a look over his shoulder, his brow cocked. I shrug. "What? A girl's been lonely in this penthouse these past few days. The showerhead in the bathroom doesn't have enough pressure to get me off."

He comes over and kisses me again, this time more passionately. His hand slides over my cheek. "Go out today. Wherever you want. Take yourself shopping if it makes you happy. Louis will escort you."

"I think I'm all shopped out after our little high roller spree the other day. I wish it were possible to…" I trail off with a hesitant sigh.

"What is it? Possible to what?"

"I *miss* my friends, Gio. My friend Tasha—"

"The one from the Dollhouse with the fake ass?" he asks in mild amusement.

I choke out a surprised laugh. "Is it that obviously a BBL? I'll have you know she paid thousands for it in the DR!"

"Didn't say it was bad work—just that it was undeniable." He pauses to think a second, fastening his luxury watch. "If it will make you feel better to see Tasha, see her. Go out to lunch. But Louis still comes along. And if you say a word to her about—"

"I know, I know. You don't have to worry. I won't utter a word about anything that's gone on," I tell him, rising onto my knees. My hands glide up his massive chest now finely adorned in a crisp designer dress shirt, and I smirk at him. "One thing you don't realize, Gio, is that I'm no snitch. Enzo stayed involved in some foolishness. Never once have I said a word."

He nods slowly, my words enough to reassure him. He gives me a goodbye peck that feels nice and leaves a pleasant tingle on my lips. "I'll make it up to you. All this time cooped up in this room. You're coming with me to my uncle's homecoming celebration. We'll have some off time then."

There's something endearingly tender about the promise. It makes my heart flutter, but I don't dare think about why. But even vaguely, somewhere in the back of my mind, it occurs to me that Giovanni Sorrentino, while a cold, calculated, ruthless Mafia boss, is also kinda…sweet? Caring? Thoughtful? When he *wants* to be.

The door thuds shut after him. I fall back against the pillows and sigh dreamily. The more time I spend with Gio, immersed in his world and all things him, the more I can't help thinking a girl could get used to this lifestyle after all.

Louis drives me to Mastro's Ocean Club, where I'm meeting Tasha for lunch. Like with everything else as of late, it's on Gio's dime. Though she doesn't know that. When calling her up to invite her out, I only mentioned it was my treat. No details on who was really footing the bill at such a pricey spot.

It's the first thing she asks once the maître d' seats us. "Girl, you must've bagged yourself a sugar daddy."

"It's definitely been an…*interesting* few days."

I pause, glancing at the portly gentleman in black seated at the table next to us. Louis is studying the menu, but for as engrossed as he appears in the day's fish selections, make no mistake he's listening to every word spoken.

I'm not stupid enough to tell Tasha the full details of what's going on. I don't even *want* to. What's going on between me and Gio is for us only. Everything from the deal we made, to the secrets I'm keeping for him. None of it is anyone's business except ours.

Last night when he came out of nowhere and shoved that greasy sleazeball propositioning me against the wall, thrill pulsated in my veins. There was something unspeakably, erotically powerful about watching a man as cool and composed as Gio flip his shit over you. My panties were drenched the second he proved in a room full of people I'm not just his, I'm so valuable he'll fuck somebody's world up for me.

The moment he parked in the dark canyon after minutes of whipping down desert roads, I pounced on him. Welcomed that fat dick into me like I had been imagining, agonizing for, for days. Even if sometimes I hadn't let myself admit it. I'd wanted to fuck Gio from the first second I laid eyes on him among the blue neon lights at the Dollhouse.

I've never been this reckless. I've never been this checked out of reality. Because when I'm with Gio, it's another world altogether—a sinful, darker world that beckons me like a moth to a flame. I don't begin trying to understand what the fuck has come over me, but the Falynn Carter I was a week ago isn't who I am today.

We order our meals and sit back with rum and pineapple cocktails. We're seated outside in the September sunshine, misters keeping it cool and pleasant enough.

"So?" Tasha asks when I say nothing.

"So what?"

"So you're not gonna tell me what the fuck's been up with you? Girl, you've dropped off the grid for how many days now? You know your shit's still at the Dollhouse? Amaryllis was saying you up and quit."

"I'm…I'm taking a break," I say mysteriously. I sip more from my cocktail. The sweetness from the pineapple and rum blend is perfect for a day like this. "I'm not sure when I'll be back, Tash. If ever."

One of her perfectly penciled brows hikes up. "What you mean 'if ever'? Falynn, you need a job. Thought you said those loans Enzo took out—"

"Can kiss my ass," I joke with an easy laugh. "I'll get to them when I get to them."

"Girl, do you hear yourself? Your rent—"

"I don't live there anymore."

A bold statement. But true. Once this deal with Gio is over, I'm starting a new life…*somewhere*. A vision of a vivid, tropical paradise forms in my mind.

"Is that code for the sugar daddy's moving you in?" Tasha asks, unimpressed. She's normally not one to pass judgment; it's the first time I've heard it in her tone. She catches herself a second later and sighs. "Look, do what you've gotta do, baby girl. You know that's my life motto. I just…I hope you're safe about it. Women like us, we come up missing all the time. Nobody gives a fuck. I'd hate for you to get in over your head."

"Don't worry about me." I offer her a smile before my lips touch the straw in my glass.

"Well…remember I'm always here for you. We're ride or die bitches, okay?"

Guilt gnaws at me. It catches me by surprise, but I hadn't considered if I'd ever see Tasha again once Gio pays me off and I leave for good. Maybe there's a way I can send for her, have her visit me…

"Did you know Jerry's MIA too?" Tasha asks. "Nobody knows where the sleaze has gone. He hasn't shown up to the Dollhouse in days. He's not even answering his phone."

More gnawing guilt. I push through and feign confusion. "Jerry? Miss out on the cash to be made at the club? That's surprising."

"That's what I said."

The rest of lunch goes by fast. I'm careful about navigating the topics we discuss. We stick to casual, fun stuff, like laughing about funny club stories and chatting about the latest *Real Housewives of Atlanta* episode.

Afterward, we hug each other goodbye. The way Tasha eyes me, I know she suspects something's off. But I keep up my role. I pretend nothing's different.

"Don't forget…if you need me…" she says before she goes.

Once she's gone, Louis comes out from his lurking nearby. He looks so intimidating, larger and taller than everyone in the restaurant, dressed in black head to toe with shades covering his eyes. If I didn't already know he was kinda a softie, I would be intimidated.

"Hot friend," he says conversationally. "Maybe you should hook her up with me. If Boss gets a girlfriend for hire, I get one too."

All I can do is laugh.

When evening time rolls around, I pace the penthouse waiting for Gio. After Louis took me to lunch, I returned to the penthouse and changed into gym clothes. A workout later, I was no less antsy. Gio's dick is so good, he has me thinking about it 24/7.

Fuck. I'm dickmatized, aren't I? I'm a goner. More and more addicted to him.

I shower and dress in a silky blouse and skirt he bought me at the Forum. Both amount to months' worth of rent, but as far as Gio is concerned, money is no object. Instead of wearing a beautiful and expensive bra and panty set that was also bought during our shopping spree, I forgo undergarments. What's the point? Easy access to my goodies matters most.

I'm at the huge wall-to-wall window in the living area when he finally returns.

Nerves knot in my stomach when our eyes connect. He

stalks across the room toward me without a word. I stand still and wait for him to give direction. From his pants pocket, he withdraws a long and thin jewelry box. My smile is a confused one as I accept the gift and peek inside.

I gasp. It's a diamond-encrusted tennis bracelet. The diamonds glisten up at me, joined by a delicate clasp.

"Gio…you didn't have to…" I murmur.

"Pretty things for a pretty girl," he says, kissing me. His tongue flicks against mine for a brief moment before he withdraws. He takes the jewelry box and tosses it onto the sofa. By the way his gaze skims over my petite, curvy body, I can tell what's most important on his mind. "Tell me about your day. Did you see Tasha?"

I nod. Another flutter of nerves. "We had lunch at Mastro's Ocean Club. It was good. Ask Louis."

"Already did. Wanted to hear it from those full lips of yours. But you didn't follow my directions."

"Huh? I didn't mention a thing to Tasha about—"

"Facedown, ass up, Falynn," he interrupts coolly. He takes a step toward me and I take one back. "Instead you're dressed looking out the fucking window."

"No panties," I whisper in a tease. I'm smirking as I watch comprehension dawn on his face.

His hands are fast. In the next second, one grips my arm as he pulls me into him. The other dives under my skirt to feel me up. "You are so fucking wet. A fucking ocean down there." He grips the fatty folds of my pussy, the pinching sensation drawing a moan out of me. Two fingers plunge into me, circling along my slick walls in an agonizing slow fashion. "Keep your eyes on me. Understand?" he orders.

I moan again. He pinches my pussy lips again, harder.
"Is that a yes or a no?"
"Y-yes," I choke out.

"Did you touch yourself today?"

"Hmm?"

Another pinch. *Ouch!*

"Did you touch yourself today?" He enunciates each word, his accent sexier and thicker than ever. "Did you fuck this pussy—*my* pussy today?"

"Mm-hmm...yes." My eyes have closed and my lips are pressed together as I concentrate on the feeling of his thick fingers and pretend it's his even thicker cock.

He gives me another unexpected pinch. The sharpest one yet. My pussy aches and creams all at once. His other hand clamps on my throat and he brings our faces close enough for our noses to touch. His breath tickles my lips as he growls, "Didn't I tell you to keep your eyes open? On me."

"Yes...ahh...yes."

"Then fucking do it." His fingers slide inside me, still rubbing circles along my clenching walls. "Tell me how. I want to know how you fucked yourself."

"Ooh," I moan, shuddering as he inserts a third finger, opening me up wider. The stretch feels so magnificent I begin to feel like I'm floating. My walls tremble with me, gripping at each finger in a wanton beg for more. "I...I was in the shower."

"And what did you do in the shower?"

"I sat on the bench and put the showerhead to my p-p-pussy."

His pace goes from slow to fast and forceful. His thumb strums my clit and his fingers pump into me, making it impossible to concentrate on anything else. It's harder and harder to form a sentence. Even a thought. I rock my hips against him, hoping for mercy. For him to put me out of my misery and make me come.

"Did you get off?" He kisses me tenderly on the throat.

The exact opposite of the fingers working into me. The contrast has my brain even more muddled. I almost close my eyes but remember his rules.

Wanting to be his good girl, I don't take my eyes off him and moan like the shameless putty I am when we're fucking. A quick smirk flitters across his hardened features, and he kisses me again. This time open-mouthed with tongue.

"I...I worked my pussy with the showerhead...but it didn't...it couldn't...ahhh."

"It couldn't what?"

"Get me off!" I shriek, riding his hand. I'm so damn close. Sooo close to pleasure exploding from my core.

But before I can be rewarded, his hand is gone. I'm thrown for a second by the sudden absence in my aching pussy. Even keep rocking against air for a whole extra second. His gaze smolders as he brings his hand up and tastes me on his fingertip.

"Mmm...delectable. Like honey."

He sticks his juice-coated fingers past my lips. I take them into my mouth, sucking on them, and savoring my sweet taste. He's right—I *do* taste like honey.

"Gio, please," I whine. I'm on the brink of fucking sobbing. "Please just…"

"What? Just what, Falynn?" he growls.

"*Fuckkk meee!*" I yelp as he grants my wish in record time.

What happens next is a blur. His belt clanging. His hand clenching around my arm. He spins me around back to front, flips my skirt up over my bare ass, and slams into my pussy from behind. The brute force of his body crashing into mine knocks me against the humongous window. I'm pressed against the glass, helpless and delirious as he begins his assault on my body.

His hands clench either hip, fingers digging into my flesh as he holds me in position. The room fills with our skin slapping against each other. I treasure every second of the moment I've been waiting all day for. The fullness he brings me after a long, grueling day spent empty.

"Take off that shirt. Take your tits out," he pants. His hips slap against my ass for every hard thrust he gives.

I keep one flattened along the glass for some leverage. The other I use to strip off my blouse. When he discovers I'm not wearing a bra—just like how I didn't wear panties today—another thunderous growl rumbles from his throat.

He ruts into me so hard, my body wobbles unsteadily. But his grip on me is as stable as ever. My body matches him thrust for thrust.

I have no choice but to gaze out at the glittering city lights that is Vegas at night. Down below thousands of tourists wander the world-famous street. All it takes is for one of them to glance up to the Vittoria's penthouse floor. We're in plain sight up against the massive window as Gio spears into me and I flash my breasts to the city.

Anyone can look up at any second and see us fucking. The thrill excites me, eliciting a shiver down my spine. My pussy tingles too, still squeezing Gio's cock with its viselike grip. I know it drives him just as wild. I can hear it in his ragged breaths as he fucks me.

One hand remains on my waist while the other grips my shoulder. He slams into me harder than ever, tapping new depths in my pussy. We're a couple of loose cannons on a short fuse as we pant and moan and rock.

My orgasm explodes from within. I release a scream and buck against him. Orgasmic shocks shoot off from the thousand nerve endings in my pussy, sparking through the rest of my body. I toss my head back and I scream at the top of my lungs loud enough for every person in the Vegas metropolitan area to hear. For them to know I've been fucked, and I've been fucked well.

Gio follows me, finally sating my pussy. His cum pours into me, coating my walls. He continues his thrusts until they grow shallower and shallower, and he pulls out. My folds are still tingling, dripping with his cum. He whirls me around again in another dizzying spin, squeezing my breasts in his large hands. The glass is cool against my bare spine as he crushes his lips to mine.

"Get in the bedroom," he says in a low, commanding tone. "Facedown, ass up."

It's official. I'm a goner for real.

12

Giovanni
PLAYLIST: 🎵 THE BEACH - THE NEIGHBOURHOOD 🎵

"YOU'VE BEEN RECKLESS, SON," Papa says over the phone. His oxygen tank hisses in the background. "You've risked our reemergence in the west. It was supposed to be focused on opening the Vittoria and making it a success. Instead you've involved yourself in a turf war with Lovato's kid."

I grit my teeth listening to Papa scold me. I don't dare back talk. Once Papa gets going, there's no stopping him. It's a smarter call to let him air his grievances, pretend to listen to each word, and then go about my day.

This is a lesson I learned long ago. My twin brother, Giancarlo? Not so much. He's too hot-headed to listen. He's like Tony Lovato—they fly off the handle and mouth off. It's short-sighted and lacks strategy.

But it's things like this that make me the superior *capo*. I'm smart and calculated. Most importantly, I know when to shut my fucking mouth, and when to strike. On the phone with my sick and ailing seventy-five-year-old father is not the time to rebel.

"There's nothing to worry about, Pa," I say calmly. It's

midday, and I'm seated in the office of the Vittoria casino. Robby's lingering nearby, my sounding board as we map out our strategy for expansion. "Tony's a little bitch. He's a bug that's easy to crush. I *will* crush him myself. No doubt about it."

"You've strained relations all the way back here in our Queens territory. This day and age, it's bad for business. It makes partners nervous to be caught up in the middle of a war."

I pick up a model figurine of the Vittoria Resort and Casino and toy with it. "The Lovatos don't have the influence they've had in the past, Pa. Nobody will pull out if we challenge them. Our deals are solid. I ran into Johnny Goldman the other night—he's interested in working together again."

Papa makes a sound of disgust. "Not interested in dealing with that cheat."

"Pa, get some rest. Do some soothing meditation. Feed the ducks at a park. Whatever it is that will set your worries at ease. Everything on the west coast is under control."

"I expect results, Giovanni. When I next see you for Claro's homecoming, I expect a smoking-hot bimbo on your arm and some profits."

We hang up with nothing more said. I tuck my phone into my pocket and recline in my giant executive chair. Robby plays with a stress ball, tossing it up and snatching it out of the air.

"Not so pleasant chat?" he asks.

It's in that moment I realize I'm scowling like a grumpy fuck. "He's old. Senile. He doesn't understand how the dynamics have changed on this coast."

"Boss, you know I'm backing you through and through, but your father—he's seen and done it all. If he's not interested in a turf war with the Lovatos, we should tread carefully."

"What do we have to lose? We have more soldiers, more connections, more money to throw around. Tony Lovato and his crew are weak. If there's any time to take them out and eliminate their threat, it's now. I don't do rash decisions, and this is no rash decision. I've thought this through in every scenario."

Robby shakes his head, tossing up the stress ball. "I dunno, Boss. You had us rough Dominico up for a simple oversight."

"It was no simple oversight!" I growl suddenly. "He was given a task to watch over Falynn. He failed to do so. He suffered the consequences."

"Falynn who is a liability."

"We've been over this. Falynn's presence is not up for debate."

"The girl's some bitch off the street. Wasn't she advertising that night to anybody who paid? She's not worth the trouble, Boss! You said you'd handle her, but it's been over a week now. I'm sure the pussy is A1, but you've gotta cut your losses and dispose of her."

I'm on my feet, swooping over to where Robby reclines on the office sofa. My glare is dangerous as I hold up a warning finger. "I'm not going to tell you again. It is not a matter up for discussion. Choose to defy me, and there'll be a consequence that makes Dominico's look like ice cream on a Sunday stroll. Are we clear?"

Robby intakes a breath, then nods. "Of course. Falynn's yours. She's here to stay. I won't bring it up again."

"Now go make yourself useful. We need to check on the Dollhouse."

Once Robby's gone, I wait another second or two.

Then a flame of anger engulfs me and I'm a firestorm destroying everything around me. The anger I've worked so hard to keep at bay is no longer something I can easily keep under control. Now that the hold has been broken, I'm a torrent of years of pent-up rage and fury.

My fist smashes into a portrait hanging on the wall. It's an old-timey photograph of my grandpops and Ricky Gunn outside the Flamingo. I move on to shoving shit off the table, sending the vases and figurines careening to the floor. I grip the sides of the bookshelf against the wall and knock that over too. The heavy wooden piece shakes the ground. Books spill out in a heap.

I don't give a fuck. My tirade is only beginning as I move on and punch the big-screen TV. More blood trickles from my open knuckles, but the burning pain eggs me on. I howl destroying every corner of the office. I break the legs of chairs and tear into documents. I smash liquor bottles and rip artwork off the wall. I don't stop 'til there's nothing left but the wreckage of my explosive anger.

I'm a beast and I've been unleashed. After I tried so fucking hard to contain myself. After I spent years practicing how to stay cool and composed. I breathe erratically as my back hits the wall and I sink down, bloodied hands and all.

Robby's words triggered something in me—a reminder that this thing between me and Falynn boils down to another transaction. Give and take. Cash and pussy. Has there ever been a more fitting pair?

I can't get attached. I have greatness in my blood. I'm destined to rule this city, this coast, this whole fucking country.

No more losing control. If I'm to rule, become the Mafia king that's my title by birthright, I need control. I need to stay the calm and collected, emotionally removed ruler I'm capable of being.

I know what's driving my outbursts. I've tapped into too much emotion dealing with Falynn. It's making me unstable in more ways than one. I should take this as a warning sign to pull back. My future as king of not only Vegas, but the Sorrentino syndicate depends on it.

Falynn is curled up on the sofa when I return to the penthouse. Over the past couple of nights, we've developed a routine. Fuck, then dinner, then fuck again, then shower and bed…where we end up fucking some more.

I'm an insatiable man as far as she's concerned. I've stopped trying to figure out what it is about her that drives me to the brink of insanity, that comes over me as soon as I catch a whiff of that sweet scent of hers. As soon as our gazes connect and I see that gorgeous face with her banging little body. Her pussy is like nothing I've had before. I've fucked so many bitches I've lost count, but Falynn…

She's a euphoric drug. She leaves me high and in need of another hit. She's dangerous for a man of my lifestyle. No woman should have this much power, this much influence.

As I walk into the suite, still in a sour mood from my shitty day, she doesn't utter a peep. She's wearing another slinky negligee from La Perla. Her attention is on the TV. An episode of some *Housewives* reality show plays. I undo the top few buttons on my shirt and turn off the TV.

She gives no reaction. I hover over her prepared to give her a kiss, but she turns her head and gives me her cheek instead. Wondering if she's feeling extra rebellious tonight,

King of Vegas

I slide a hand between her thighs. She jerks away, scooting that fat ass of hers in the opposite direction.

Now I'm pissed. Another bump in the road of my shit day.

"What's wrong now?" I snap.

"You said you'd be here by seven."

"Yeah, so?"

"It's after *nine*, Gio."

My reaction is laughter. I stand up straight and bark out a laugh. This only pisses her off more. She sits up, glaring with a throw pillow in her lap.

"Oh, thanks for once again showing me I mean nothing."

"What the fuck is your problem?" I turn my back to her and stride over to the minibar. After this shit day, I need a few drinks. I'm in no mood to have my buttons pushed, and that seems to be all Falynn wants tonight. I would've much preferred one of her amazingly nasty blow jobs. The window on that seems to be closing.

"I waited for over two hours for you. But thanks for finding it funny."

"I had business! You think I sit around on my ass all day?"

"A call would've been nice!"

"Listen here, girly, you work for me!" I spin around, drink in hand. The anger contorts my face. I can tell by the way she's looking at me, it also burns dangerously in my eyes. "You do what I say when I say! If I come home and want a blow job, you'll drop to your fucking knees and open your fucking mouth."

"Oh, is that how it works? Then go ahead, Gio…fuck me! Since my feelings don't matter. I exist for you and your fucking dick. Go ahead and get your nut!"

I scrub a hand over my face. Women are so infuriating

during arguments like these. It's like having two separate conversations. There's no rationalizing when she's in such a headspace.

"When the fuck did I say that?"

"When you called me your *employee*." Tears gloss in her eyes and she looks away. "But I don't know why I'm surprised. You told me what it was from the beginning. I'm just some…some toy for you. You'll throw some cash at me and discard me when you're done."

It's at this second I know with certainty—I'm a fucking dumbass. Not for how I've acted tonight. But for falling for this tearful woman. I know because as her voice breaks and she clutches the pillow, there's a tug in my heart like a little bitch. I feel bad for her, want to comfort her even…

How did I let these feelings develop? How have they gotten so far so soon? It hasn't even been two weeks since the night at the Dollhouse!

With a sigh, I chug my cognac. Then I glide over to the sofa where she's curled up. I put my arm around her and pull her close against me. She doesn't fight it, lets her body press into mine. Her head falls onto my chest. I kiss her brow.

"It matters how you feel," I confess. "How many times have I told you, Falynn? It's important you are comfortable and happy. *Tell me* what makes you feel this way."

"You do," she whispers. Her hand comes up and stops on my chest. Right above my heartbeat.

We sit in silence for a long stretch of time. Her honey-sweet scent invades my senses. I bask in the smell, the feel of her at rest on my chest. Everything about the quiet moment feels right. No matter how much my brain says it's wrong, reminds me I need composure. The control to be clear-headed and cool if I'm ever to succeed in this family empire.

"How about we order room service and watch another Tarantino flick?" I ask.

She smiles. That pretty damn smile of hers I'm willing to murder a man over. "*Inglorious Basterds* is on Netflix."

"Put it on."

I will not fail at claiming my father's throne as my own. But Falynn is mine and there will be no compromises. I'm going to have it all.

13

Falynn
PLAYLIST: ♫ BAD AT LOVE - HALSEY ♪

"GIOVANNI SORRENTINO, the Cowardly Lion in his school's production of *The Wizard of Oz*? I doubt it." A cruel giggle bubbles out of me as I twist in the sheets and wrap a leg around his.

For his part, Gio is relaxed, lying on his back with one muscular arm folded behind his head. "Believe it, Honey. The 1997 production of *The Wizard of Oz* at Brighton Private School in New York."

"Pics or it didn't happen."

He raises one amused brow. "You first. Let me see that pretty smile, brace face."

I gasp in horror. "Are you kidding? I burnt every last photo with them. No evidence of such an atrocity exists today."

"Evidence cover-up, huh? Very mob-minded. You sure you're not in the family?"

"If I am, I must've gotten a lot more sun than everyone. It explains the tan."

"I love your skin color. It's beautiful, like—"

"*Honey?*" I provide with another giggle.

A rare Giovanni Sorrentino smile flits across his face and he reaches for me. His kiss is tender but demanding, his hands playful. They skim over my naked body, making me shudder. A wave of lust rolls over me. It pushes any other thought from my mind except for how Gio's large, dominating hands light a trail of fire on my skin.

It goes without saying, I'm already dripping wet. These luxury $200 panties don't stay dry for long these days. The sun hasn't even finished rising, and we've already indulged in each other twice. It seems Gio is as addicted to me as I am him.

He pulls away from our kiss and admires me, tucking loose curls behind my ear. "How did it happen?" he asks suddenly. "You winding up at gentleman's clubs?"

Though the question is serious, I'm still feeling playful. I shrug and trace the muscular outline of his perfect, shredded abs. "I left home before I even graduated high school. Moved in with a boyfriend at the time. Eventually followed him to Vegas. Tried out some waitressing jobs and a few other gigs. None of them worked out. Boyfriend was a fuckboy loser who left me. I started dancing."

"Just like that, huh?"

"I was always in dance growing up. It's one of my few talents."

"You sell yourself short. You're smart. Funny. A girl like you shouldn't be there."

"Hence me *trying* to go to college. As it turns out, it's not so easy to pay for."

"And your family?"

I scoff and roll onto my back, finally giving up my playful antics. "I come from dysfunction, Gio. No, seriously, if you look up the word on Dictionary.com, you'll find my family as a reference point. We could barely keep a roof over our heads. Dad left when I was two. Mom worked hard to make ends meet, but as it turns out, I inherited my thing for bad boys from her."

"What? She would bring around bad guys?"

"I lost count. Most of them violent. Or into street life. Or both." My throat itches as I consider if I should keep going; I've spent so long blocking out my teenage trauma, it almost feels like another life. "One of the guys…when we were alone…he forced himself. She didn't believe me. So I left."

Gio's entire body tenses up. Each one of the sculpted muscles tightens. A bloodthirsty fury darkens his features; I recognize the look from the night at Lovato's party, where he'd almost broken a guy's hand over me. I don't need him to say a word to know he's already thinking about tracking down Mom's old boyfriend and hurting him. Badly. Just for me.

"What happened to him?" he asks finally in a restrained tone.

"I'm not sure. I haven't spoken to my mom in years."

"I don't take kindly to men who abuse women…and *girls*. You were a girl."

The itch scratches some more in my throat. Maybe it wasn't such a good idea to tell my Mafia boyfriend, even if temporary, about the man who assaulted me. Then again, I spent a long time after leaving home angry at the world praying karma would ensure the asshole suffers. Those prayers went unanswered like all the others.

But a change of subject is needed. I stroke fingers through Gio's dark locks and offer a small smile. "What about you? How did you end up in 'the life'?"

"You know my father is Don, right? There was no other choice. It's a lifestyle."

"Don sounds so scary."

"My father's *not* a nice guy if that's what you're implying."

"And…and I'm going to meet him?"

"Maybe. He'll be at my uncle's homecoming."

"What about your mother?"

It's like a light switch. Gio's demeanor changes again, but this time, he's tuning out. His face hardens and he withdraws his arm from around me. He gets up off the bed, bare ass and all, and heads for the bathroom.

"No more time to waste," he says coldly, as if I'm a stranger. "Today's a big day. Grand opening of the casino."

He disappears into the bathroom. Even closes the damn door. I sit up, drag the sheets with me like a makeshift toga, and debate if I should be so bold to knock. Though our arrangement is still new, we've pretty much lost any pretense of privacy when alone—meaning we don't shut doors.

I tap lightly and wait. A tinkling noise from inside tells me he's taking a piss. After the whoosh of the flush, I knock again.

"Falynn, what is it?" He sounds agitated.

It's moments like these, where I'm dealing with the downsides of our setup, that I wonder if I'm in over my head. Last night, we fought over Gio's tardiness. Actually, it wasn't even about being late—it was that he hadn't thought of me enough to let me know, like he expected to drown in pussy the second he got home no matter how *I* felt.

"Did I do something wrong?" I hear myself asking. The voice is so timid-sounding it doesn't even seem like it's mine.

The door flies open and he's on the other side. I can't place the look on his face. It's not as hardened as before, but there's no emotion either. He's a blank canvas, like he's emotionally checked out. "No, you didn't do something wrong," he answers. "Why would you think that?"

I'm clinging to the toga sheets like a lifeline. It keeps my hands busy to fuss with the fabric. "I don't know. I asked about your mother and then you—"

"Said I've got no more time to waste. Today's the grand opening of Vittoria's casino. You know that."

"Right, it just seems like after I mentioned..." I draw in a breath and then shake my head. "Never mind. What do you need from me?"

"Spend the day as you like. Louis is at your disposal. Tonight, I need you dressed to the nines. You'll be on my arm for the casino's celebratory dinner at La Pergola. Can you do that, honey?"

The nickname sweetly rolls off his tongue. He's softened his tone for me, any trace of agitation gone. I smile and give a nod before he drops a quick kiss on my lips. Though I can't escape the nagging feeling *this* is as open as Giovanni Sorrentino gets.

He's said it himself. He's not an emotional man. He doesn't do vulnerability or closeness. As a man so prominent in the Sorrentino crime family, with countless enemies out there and an empire to run, can I blame him?

It's important to stay realistic. No matter what kind of feelings I've developed for him—and through the haze that's my constant lust for him, deeper feelings have started to form—I have to accept he's not the man I want him to be. He's a mafia prince, son of King Giuliano Sorrentino, and there's nothing and no one that's going to stand in his way of the throne.

Beyoncé and Nicki Minaj had me in mind when they recorded "Feelin' Myself" years ago. At least that's what I tell myself as I strut on the arm of Gio hours later. I've worn the sexiest dress of my life, a black backless Valentino with daring slits in the fabric, teasing plenty of boobage, legs, and ass. I spent an hour on my makeup, going for a matte finish and dramatic smokey eye. My natural chocolate curls have been straightened and smoothed into a topknot. I have a lot of faults, but I know when and how to turn on the sex appeal.

It was part of the job as a dancer at the Dollhouse.

Every man we pass stops and stares. Their eyes sweep up and down my body then face as I hold on to Gio and we approach the game floor.

The opening of the Vittoria has been a massive, record-breaking success. Though I wound up lounging by the penthouse pool for most of the day, I followed the Vittoria's opening on social media (with Louis close by, monitoring my activity). Giovanni had been right—the day was an incredibly busy one as co-owner and manager of Vegas's newest, hottest resort and casino.

There were hundreds of millions to be made. More money than I'd ever see in my lifetime.

But I had to do my part—be sexy and sultry on Gio's arm. We stop at a blackjack table, surrounded by a large crowd of people watching on in interest. Gio's the man of not only the hour, but the day.

He oversees the first blackjack table to play a round in the entire casino. I'm at his side, paying attention to the game. Dozens of others crowd around the players at the table, abuzz with chatter. Once the first game ends, Gio announces to the crowd that all tables and games are officially open to play.

I look up at the crowd. Hundreds of eyes are on us. A

strange sensation flutters in my stomach. The kind you get when someone menacing could be watching you. I peek over my bare shoulder and glance at the faceless strangers. None of them stand out as problematic. Besides, Gio's covered by his men. Robby, Louis, and others circle us like a wall of protection from anyone.

We're completely safe. *I'm* completely safe. I shouldn't feel in danger.

And yet I do. The uneasy, fluttery feeling continues as I scan the rest of the casino floor. I can't put my finger on it, but something's off about tonight. Let's just hope it's only the paranoia talking.

14

Giovanni
PLAYLIST: ♫ HEAVEN OR LAS VEGAS
- THE WEEKND ♪

"LET THE WINE FLOW, and the cards fall as they may!" Everett Johansson shouts to cheers around the dining room of La Pergola, the fine Italian restaurant in the casino. Glasses chink and dozens of sidebar conversations break out.

Dinner is served.

He returns to his seat on my left. On my right is Falynn, looking like a sexy doll. She's played her role perfectly tonight, milked the most out of being on my arm. Every man in the casino has eye-fucked her at least once.

So long as they don't touch, there's no problem. If even one puts his grubby paw on her, he's dead meat yesterday.

I can't concentrate during dinner. The food is delicious, some of the most authentic Italian food in the country—it was one of my hard lines when designing the Vittoria. I didn't want manufactured Americanized Italian, where you might as well take your ass to Olive Garden. I wanted legitimate, authentic Italiano with handmade pasta and freshly picked truffles.

Despite the meal being delicious, the only thing I'm

able to focus on is Falynn's scent. I feel like a fucking hound dog next to her, her scent permeating my senses even in public. It's like I've developed a superhuman sense of smell as far as she's concerned.

Her sweet, sweet scent makes me hard as fuck. If I had my way, I'd knock every glass and piece of silverware off the table, and take her right here, right now, in front of everyone. But that's not even the most frustrating part—she's composed as can be. She makes charming conversation with others at the table, including wandering-eye Johansson, who has a wife half his age at home, but still can't keep his shrimp dick in his pants. Go figure.

I'm supposed to be the cool and collected one, but tonight, Falynn is showing me up. I have to get her out of my system. Immediately.

With a clearing of my throat, I make an announcement to the table. "If you fine gentlemen and ladies will excuse me, I have business to tend to."

Polite murmurs ripple around the table. Johansson looks shocked, but says nothing. I stand up, Louis and C.J. along with me. Falynn stays seated.

"Falynn," I say, lips tight.

Her mouth dips into a startled frown. She's really been enjoying the dinner; probably because it's an opportunity for her to socialize. Even including her outings with Louis, she hasn't had much interaction with the outside world in the last two weeks.

I should feel guilty, but I don't. What can I say? I'm a selfish bastard. Always have been, always will be.

We take the private elevators to the management level. I order both Louis and C.J. to wait outside in the hall, grabbing Falynn's hand as I stride toward my office.

As soon as the door's shut, I'm on her. It catches her by surprise at first. Her back bounces off the wall as I grab her face and plant a deep kiss on that pretty, pouty mouth. Her lipstick is immediately smudged, but again, no fucks given here. She finally catches up with me once my tongue rubs against her own. Her arms go around my neck. She's on tiptoe, even with those high heels, trying to even our heights out. If I weren't so blinded by lust, I'd find it adorable, like I always do when I take in her diminutive size.

But I'm horny, and time is of the essence. Every minute, every second counts.

I move on to kissing her throat, my hands feeling her up. I squeeze her breasts then grip the swell of her hips and then palm her ass. But up against the door isn't conducive, so I pick her up and carry her to the desk. I don't think twice about knocking everything on top of it off.

Shame, really. After my tirade yesterday, the office was *just* refurbished today. Now there's broken shit scattered over the floor again. Only this time it was worth it. I place her on top of the desk with no effort at all—she really weighs about nothing—and then start on ripping this damn maddening dress of hers.

She surprises me when she stops my hands. "Gio," she says with the straightest face, "this is *Valentino*."

"Am I supposed to give a fuck? I'll rip it off with my teeth if I have to. Then buy you five more." My hands tug at the fabric, pushing it down, exposing those magnificent, full breasts. She teased them all night long in that low-cut, backless dress. The design is dangerous, one bad move away from a wardrobe malfunction where she flashes the casino.

I fill my hands with her breasts, tweaking a nipple. She arches into my touch and hangs her head back. The mounds of flesh and fat call my name and I'm too fucking hard and turned on to pass them up. I bend forward and take a tit into my mouth. I'm sloppy and aggressive about it, swirling my tongue along that hardening nipple. It turns into a pebbly bead I rake between my teeth, and yank on.

Falynn hitches a breath, her fingers in the tufted hair on my nape. She spreads her legs, allowing me to step even closer between them. Heat radiates not only between our bodies, but from her sex. That pretty pussy is already hot for me. I'll bet wet as hell too.

I find out for myself, shoving a hand under her dress. A deep groan reverberates in my chest. Wet and slick just like I like her. I test the waters, literally, strumming a thumb over her clit. She trembles and gushes some more. Her folds are nice and plump, *dripping*.

"You didn't wear panties again, Falynn," I scold her, sinking two fingers deep. "You've been on my arm all night with this pussy out in the open?"

She moans her answer, hands sliding over my broad chest.

"Answer me, Falynn."

"Yes," she breathes. Her honey-brown skin is glowing. She looks like a goddess perched on my desk, pouty lips parted, legs spread for me, breasts exposed with no shame. "I wanted to surprise you," she continues breathily. "Easy access."

"The only one who has easy access to this cunt is me. Look at me." With my free hand, I grip her chin and force her gaze to mine. I'm an intimidating man with a gaze I'm told is intense. I don't hold back glaring at her. My hand moves down to her neck, applying some pressure as I kiss her hard. "No other man gets to see, touch, or feel it except me. I *own* this cunt. She gets fucked when I say so. Are we clear?"

"Mhmmm."

I tighten my grip on her throat. "Yes or no answer, Falynn."

"Mmm," she purrs, "yes, Gio."

I kiss her again, tongue grazing hers. I haven't stopped working her with my fingers. The feel of her slick walls as they clench around me is unbelievable. I withdraw them for a taste and then let her suck the rest off.

"Honey, the sweetness between those thighs isn't for any *stronzo* off the street."

A lusty smile spreads on her lips. She kisses me this time, fingers back in my hair. But I have no more time to waste. It's been a long day and I need to relieve some stress and frustration. Between opening the casino, fighting Lovato and this turf war, and Falynn's naughty little ass distracting me, I'm walking a thin tightrope.

Yesterday, she asked about my mother. It caught me so off guard, I shutdown. I chilled into ice and reminded myself we're not a real relationship. Everything between us is fake. Just another transaction.

But what *is* real is Falynn's delectable curves and this pussy of hers I salivate for.

I shove aside the bottom portion of her dress 'til it's nothing but a scrap of fabric bunched at her waist. I don't even bother to take my pants off. Belt unbuckled, zipper down, dick out, I push her back onto the desk and drive my entire length into her. She gasps and arches, her legs falling wider apart.

Her nether lips are swollen and glossy, stretched around my dick. The sight is one of the most beautiful I've ever seen.

I waste no time going hard. I slam my hips into hers again, drawing another gasp from her. I'm well aware Louis and C.J. are in the hall outside. These walls aren't impenetrable—surely they've heard our dirty talk and whatever pants and moans we release now. But I don't give a fuck. It doesn't matter how much they hear; I'm the boss, and I make the rules.

Her pussy's hot, wet silk. She pulls at me, sucks me in with an unforgivingly tight grip. I revel in the feel, like it's the most luxurious pussy I've ever had. If this is the last one I'm in before I die, I'd go a happy man.

She holds on to my biceps to keep from sliding on the desk with each hard thrust I give her. Her eyes are darker than I've ever seen them, stuck on my face. They're deep with lust, a dark gleam I've never seen before.

I'm corrupting her every second we're together. It's a thought I've avoided, the more time we've spent together, the more caught up we are in this entanglement. But I'd be a lying man if I said the prospect of corrupting her doesn't thrill me. Molding her to fit this deadly sinful world of mine.

Our heavy pants are the only sounds other than the sloppy wet noise her pussy makes as I pump into her. I bend to leave biting kisses all over her breasts. My teeth scrape on her nipples. Any marks left will be a reminder of me. My imprint all over her as it should be.

She untucks my dress shirt and slips her hands underneath, dragging sharp nails across my abs. The scratchy feeling spurs me on, slamming into the depth of her. I play with her pussy as we pant and moan. Her clit pulses against my thumb. I'm rough rubbing it in tight circles.

It's enough to push her over the edge. She tightens up, head tipped back, and cries out as an orgasm rocks her. I keep up my fast movements, loving how her gushy, hot pussy grips me more desperately. I ride out her orgasm 'til my dick twitches and spills.

My seed empties inside her, making a mess once I pull out. Some trickles down her perineum. Another hot fucking image for the memory spank banks. I bend forward and collapse on top of her. It's easy to forget our weight difference; I can easily crush her, but she's out of it. As enveloped in pleasure as I am, she lies there in a breathless heap.

I grab her neck and give her a sloppy kiss. "For the rest of the night, you'll walk sideways, and everybody'll know it was me who fucked you this good."

She moans, twirling her tongue with mine. "I'd much prefer not to be able to walk at all."

"Later," I growl, nipping at her throat. "Go clean yourself up. Make yourself respectable again."

She smirks at the joke. "Same to you."

I laugh. I love it when she mouths off.

I take my time regrouping in my office. There's a knock at the door and I grunt to welcome them inside. It doesn't surprise me when Louis walks in looking like the cat that swallowed the fattest canary alive—no easy feat considering Louis is no small guy.

"How was that business you were tending to, Boss?"

I glare at him. "You grow balls all of a sudden, funny guy?"

He chuckles. "You both were so loud, the ground floor casino probably heard."

"Louis, I'm addicted," I admit with a shake of my head. I pick up my whiskey on the rocks and carry it over to the sofa. He follows suit, sitting across from me. "Damn kung fu grip pussy. It's better than any drug."

"Those are the worst ones—the girls who know how to work it."

"She does some shit with it I've never seen before.

Dozens of girls and not one like her. Some type of master-level Kegel shit."

"You know, Boss, Robby's concerned—"

"I've heard Robby's concerns. I've told him to shut the fuck up. I'm telling you the same."

"No need. I like the girl."

I cock a brow. "You what?"

"She's funny. Kinda silly like my kid sister, Nikki."

"Yeah, she is, isn't she?" I say, nodding in thought. "Very...bright. A *shine* about her."

A bright shine I shouldn't want to darken. I shouldn't want to corrupt her. But I do. I *will*.

"Listen, there's something else I wanted to bring to your attention. It's Lovato and his guys—they've been spotted in the casino."

"Who's been spotted? Specifics, Louis."

"Not Lovato himself, but a few of his associates. Some schmucks named Pauly and Lorenzo."

"And how the fuck were they allowed in?"

"Security at the front—"

"Didn't do their fucking jobs. Where are they at?"

"Kicked out on the curb somewhere. As soon as I got word, I tossed their asses."

I lean over and grip the fat on the back of his neck. It's an affectionate squeeze, showing my appreciation for his competence. "Good. Good. You're not half as dumb as you are fat. Anybody ever tell you that?"

Louis's ears turn red and he chuckles along. "Just wait 'til I'm done with my diet of celery and carrot sticks, Boss. I'll be trimmer than you."

We head back onto the casino floor. On a Friday night like this, the casino is thriving with life. We're the hottest spot in town. Guests crowd our table games and sip drinks in the lounges. They jiggle cups filled with coins by the slot machines and flirt brazenly with our cocktail waitresses dressed in their skimpy little skirts.

The place reeks of liquor, smoke, and money—three scents that make a businessman like me grin.

"I'd call it a success, Boss," Louis says at my side, arms folded. "What do you think?"

I'm surveying the floor, letting my eyes travel among the groups of customers. In the distance, a man in a leather jacket catches my eye at the last second. He moves too fast for a proper look at his mug, but his retreating form slips down a side hall. Something's up.

On alert, I nudge Louis. "You see that? Some fuckhead's lurking down the hall."

"The one leading to the private elevators? On it."

Louis troops over like the soldier he is, bulldozing through the crowd. I stand my ground, watching him every step of the way, my jaw clenched.

If Lovato wants to fuck with me tonight of all nights, he has another thing coming.

15

Falynn
PLAYLIST: ♫ TOXIC - 2WEI (BRITNEY SPEARS COVER) ♪

I STARE at myself in the mirror. "I really let him make a mess of me."

A laugh escapes me as I dig around in my makeup bag. It's never felt like more of a badge of honor than it does right now. Sex with Gio is explosive in the best way possible. It's carnal and primitive, without regard for anything else in the moment.

The more it goes on, the less I know how to wake up from the lust-fueled haze he puts me in. Even worse, that deep-rooted desire has transformed into real feelings. I *care* about Giovanni Sorrentino and his well-being. I want to be in his orbit and no one else's.

I reapply a fresh coat of my cherry-red lipstick as knuckles tap at the door. I already know who it is.

"Another sec, Robby!"

"Mr. Sorrentino wanted you to be quick. We're supposed to meet him on the casino floor."

"I know, I know," I huff.

After what happened in Gio's office, I carefully inspected my Valentino dress. The last thing I want is to be walking around in a designer dress with a splooge stain. It's bad enough I'm commando. Now every time air hits my pussy, all I can think about is lying on Gio's desk, taking his dick.

Robby makes a face when I finally emerge from the restroom. It's on the private floor with Gio and the other managers' offices. He escorts me to the elevators at the end of the hall and we ride down to the ground level.

Robby doesn't like me and he makes no effort to hide it. The feeling's mutual as he's my least favorite guy of Gio's main crew. Probably why Gio's hardly tasked him with watching over me.

We walk side by side more mismatched than the Odd Couple. We're on the floor for a couple seconds before another guy in the crew, Fozzi, approaches. He pulls Robby into conversation right away. Something about security and Lovato crew sightings. Blah, blah, blah.

My interest wanes. Now that I'm back on the floor, I'm getting ogled again by any man who passes me by. I forgot how sexy I look in this dress. I own it with a hand on my hip, shoulders aligned, breasts out. Hopefully Gio turns up soon…

It's as Robby and Fozzi gab away that my falsie starts bugging me. Damn fake eyelashes, always causing problems. I sigh and move to tap Robby on the shoulder. He's so engrossed in his talk with Fozzi, I don't even bother. I already know he'll bitch and moan if I ask him to escort me back to the restroom.

So I go by myself. I slink away, side-stepping off, letting guests passing by cover me. Neither Robby nor Fozzi notice a thing. They keep chatting away about security or whatever. I'm fast in my stilettos, weaving through people headed in every direction. I make it to the hall leading to the private elevators.

One quick ride upstairs, and I can fix this disrespectful eyelash. My thin heels click against the glossy marble floor when an arm wraps around me from behind. A hand follows, clamping over my mouth to silence my scream. I squirm and fight in the person's viselike grip, but it's no use. They're way stronger than me, drawing me deeper into the hall, out of sight.

Panic rings through me louder than an alarm bell. A stream of worst-case scenarios filter through my head. What the hell does this person want from me? Is he grabbing me to rob me? Is he going to rough me up? Even worse?

My heart slams against my rib cage as I fight as hard as I can against his hold. Finally, he lets go, leaving me to stagger more unsteadily than a damn baby deer. I whip around for a look at him and gasp.

Tan skin, a head of shiny black locks, a nose with the bump from being broken too many times... I'm dreaming. I have to be.

"Enzo?! You scared the shit out of me!" I sock him with as much strength as I have in the shoulder.

He grabs my wrist and holds me at bay. Something about him is different. He's got on a leather jacket and reeks of smoke. His pupils are dilated, eyes bugged out and black. "What the hell kinda slut getup you got on, Fal?"

"You have to be kidding me? You catch a charge and leave me with the bills. Your debts. You stopped taking my calls at the jail. The first thing out of your mouth after ghosting me for two months is to shame me about my dress?"

"I knew you'd start selling pussy as soon as I was gone—"

SMACK!

My palm burns from how hard I slap his piggish ass.

King of Vegas

Anger simmers inside me, prompting me to go for another hit. As my hand rains down, he catches my wrist a second time and then shoves me hard against the wall.

"You're acting bold as fuck right now. Must be your new investor giving you a big head. C'mere." He grabs my hand and yanks, causing me to almost lose balance on my stilettos. He doesn't let me recover before he's dragging me down the hall and toward the private elevators.

Try as I might to wiggle myself free, it doesn't work. Enzo is more than a head shorter than Gio, but he's probably about as strong. He's always dedicated a lot of time in the gym, bulking up his arms.

When we reach the elevators, he lets go of me so suddenly, I stumble. He gives me another shove and grits out, "Go ahead. Punch in the code or whatever. We're headed up."

"Enzo, what do you think you're doing?"

"Punch in the code, Fal. Don't make me say it a third time." His hand goes to the side of his waist, his leather jacket pushed back to reveal he's carrying a piece.

I swallow hard, dizziness rolling over me. With a small nod, I face the elevator and dial the code as Gio showed me. The doors jump apart and he jostles me inside, handling me like the police do him whenever he's stopped and frisked on the street.

"No need to be so rough!"

The doors close and he smashes a finger on the top button. He won't look at me.

"You asshole, I'm talking to you!" I scream.

I'm pissed off all over again. I can't hold back as I charge toward him. My fists beat against his chest as I channel my inner animal and snap and growl. It's pure hurt and resentment beneath the anger. This criminal fuckboy of an ex left me to fend for myself, never returning my calls, and forcing my hand—I never would've agreed to work the VIP room if he hadn't left me to drown.

For him to come back out of nowhere, then talk down on me as he manhandles me is the straw that breaks the camel's fucking back.

As I hit him again in the shoulder, I don't care that I'm not hurting him, or causing him any real damage. I don't even care what happens to me. A hot flash of anger blinds me, and my heart pounds in my ears. Everything else around me blurs into a nonfactor. I hit him again and then again, pushing him too.

He lets it go on for a second longer than I think he would. I'm sputtering out another erratic breath when he backhands me. The hit is so hard and so sudden, I fly to the other side of the elevator. I bounce off the wall and then slide to the ground in a heap. Shock paralyzes me, keeping me there as he stands over me.

This isn't the first time Enzo's hit me. But it doesn't make the flight, fight, or freeze reaction any less instant. As I did the first time, I freeze. It was a situation like this where I found out he was thousands in debt to loan sharks. We had a blowout argument loud enough to wake our apartment complex. I refused to shut up, so he'd backhanded me and made me. I'd crumpled into the corner in a damn near catatonic state. Like mother, like daughter…

"Will you fucking calm down, you dumbass?" he barks. "I'm *trying* to save you!"

I taste blood on the corner of my lip. I lick it off and glare up at him. Half of me wants to cry, the anguish and tears bubbling under the surface. The other half of me wants to stay strong, give him straight bitch face so he knows he hasn't gotten to me.

"You're always so stupid, Fal!" he rages when I say nothing. "You never listen to what I've gotta say! You ever think to ask what's going on? You ever think maybe shit goes down for a reason? Use your brain —*THINK!*"

I flinch out of instinct when he raises his voice again. He notices and heaves out a loud sigh.

"I'm sorry for smacking you. You know I don't like doing it. But you wouldn't listen. I'm saving you."

"By kidnapping me."

"You don't wanna be on the ground floor in the next five minutes. Trust me."

"How are you even here? How'd you get out of jail?"

"It's a complicated story. You know I was in deep on my debts. Turns out, the money I'd borrowed was Antonio Lovato's. He needed some street guys, so he cut me a deal. I work off my debts to him, he pays my court fees and bribes a judge to get me and some other guys off. He's building an army of us."

"An army of what?"

"Guys on the street. To protect his territories. You didn't get the message I left with Jerry? I'm not supposed to contact you directly."

My mind jumps back to my last shift at the Dollhouse. Jerry had mentioned an important message for me. I shake my head, trying to make sense of everything that's going on around me.

"If you're working for Lovato, then why are you in Gio's casino?"

Enzo sneers and then clenches a hand around my arm, forcing me onto my feet. We've reached the top floor of the casino. The elevator doors roll open and he drags me with him. We're walking down the long hall—the same one I walked down only an hour ago when Gio and I were heading off for our quickie.

"There's a war brewing, Fal. You shouldn't have gotten

caught up in this. You'll end up a casualty," he warns out of nowhere.

"Are you talking about between the Sorrentinos and Lovatos?"

My voice is cut off by a thousand other voices. Screams from the floors below tear into the night air, drowned out only by the louder, more abrasive crack of gunfire. *Somebody's* shooting up the place.

16

Giovanni
PLAYLIST: ♬ SOMEWHAT DAMAGED - NINE INCH NAILS ♪

THE GUNFIRE STARTS up out of nowhere. Louis is at my side when it goes off. We dive behind a nearby row of slot machines for cover. I don't have my piece on me—a rarity and the worst fucking time—but Louis clutches his gun and searches for the source of the trouble.

The casino has erupted into mayhem. People scream and scurry in every damn direction like ants when it comes time for the bug spray. The cracking and popping noise from the guns going off is so loud it could burst an eardrum. The smell of alcohol and money is overpowered by the gunfire, producing a stomach-churning rotten-egg stench.

"What the fuck's happening!" Louis shouts over the streaming bullets. He creeps out from behind the slot machine enough to fire return shots.

Sirens have now joined the fracas. The police are en route.

I grit my teeth hiding out behind the slot machines. I feel like a cowardly little bitch in hiding while the casino gets shot up. *My* fucking casino gets shot up!

I should be putting bullets between the eyes of every *cazzo* who was bold enough to cross me on my turf. There's no doubt Lovato's behind this stunt. He's thrown down the gauntlet and revealed he's not willing to play fair.

What he doesn't know is I can play dirtier than the dirtiest out there.

Louis retaliates some more, firing shot after shot. He lands a hit on one of the guys. By now the casino floor has been cleared. Everybody's either gone down, hid somewhere, or run off. I chance a look around the edge of the slot machine.

The fuckhead Louis shot is wearing a ski mask, but judging by his street clothes, he's low level. Just some dumb fuck Lovato and his crew must've recruited off the street. His partner has disappeared, probably ducked the hell out the way as soon as Louis landed a hit.

It hasn't even been a minute since the ordeal has popped off, but it feels like an eternity. Every second is a second hanging between life or death when you're involved in a shootout. A million different thoughts stream through my head.

As foolish as it sounds, more than a few of them are about Falynn. I haven't seen her since we fucked in my office. She'd gone to go clean up and was supposed to meet me out on the casino floor. The only reassurance I have is knowing Robby's with her. He might have his misgivings about her, but he's not stupid enough to let anything happen to her. It's *his* ass on the line if he does.

Still, I worry as my heart pounds faster. Everything about the night has gone to hell. The grand opening of the Vittoria Resort and Casino happens to be the grand closing too. At least 'til this clusterfuck gets sorted out.

"Cops are here, Boss," Louis mutters.

We shift for another look, but then a gun's hammer

clicks and we freeze. The cool barrel presses into the back of my neck. It's the other shooter. He's gone around the other side and come up behind us. I hold out both hands to show I'm unarmed and no threat.

But in my head, I'm already calculating how to get out of this bullshit.

Louis lifts his gun, taking aim at Lovato's guy. He's so mad, his pudgy face is flaming red. "Don't even try it, fucker."

"Get back," snaps the shooter.

"There's no need for anyone else to get hurt tonight," I say calmly. My voice is leveled. I'm steady as a surgeon on the outside. On the inside, I'm a burning firestorm of rage. I want to tear this fucker limb from limb as he screams in agony. "Put the gun down and we can all walk out of here living and breathing. Sound like a deal?"

He wavers. Even though he's behind me, I can sense him shaking. He's an amateur. Lovato's dumber than I thought if he's sending rookies to carry out hit jobs on his biggest rival. Probably so it doesn't get traced back to him and his main crew.

That second spent wavering is one second too long. Louis moves to pull his trigger at the same time the rookie switches aim to him. Both guns go off and both guys crash to the floor. I'm on the rookie fucker before he even touches the casino carpet. I wrest the gun out of his clenched grip and then hammer my fist into his ugly mug of a face.

Crunch!

His nose breaks and blood spills out. A little blood's never stopped me before. I slam my fist into his face more, beating it in 'til his eyes are swollen shut and I knock teeth loose. Even if I want to stop, I can't. The fury's pouring out of me by way of my fists. His head lolls to the side as he slips unconscious, but it only increases my bloodlust.

I press the barrel of his gun to his temple. Never mind that his face is bloodied and bruised. Never mind that Louis's bullet hit him square in the chest and the cocksucker's half dead anyway. Never mind that the police are already on the premises. I want to blow his brains out and watch them paint the carpet floor.

The police order everybody to throw their hands up, effectively saving him. They've flooded the casino floor in bulletproof vests, weapons drawn. Captain Rodrigo is on the scene, speaking through an airhorn, his voice carrying across the carnage.

He's another I've struck a deal with under the table. Cities are only as corrupt as their leadership, and Rodrigo is as crooked as they come. A little blackmail and bribery have gone a long way in winning over his cooperation; he turns the other cheek and I reestablish the Sorrentino reign in Vegas.

As far as the public knows, he works to serve and protect them. But, at the end of the day, he really answers to me, and the Sorrentino name.

Two cops run up on me and the bloodied rookie at my feet. Right away, they're trying to mishandle me. The smaller one forces the handgun from my grip and then twists my arms behind my back. The other checks on the rookie and...

Shit! Louis!

My gaze lands on his tank of a body limp on the floor. Blood trickles from his shoulder area. He's been hit, but his eyes are open. Thank fuck he survived!

The smaller cop steals my attention again by pinching his fingers into my forearms. My jaw clenches up in response and I growl, "Do you know who I am? You know what you're doing? Think smartly."

"Standard procedure, sir. Until we figure out who's responsible, everyone is apprehended—"

"Captain Rodrigo!" I shout in mock excitement. "Your officer is over here's getting a little rough. I told him it's not such a good idea. What do you think?"

Captain Rodrigo's bushy mustache bristles. He lowers his airhorn and stands blinking at us. For a second, he loses his voice, but he knows one thing for sure—I own his ass. He crosses me, I end him. Just like the mayor and all the other corrupt elite in this dirty town.

With a rough clearing of his throat, he motions for the small cop to release me. "What are you doing, Jenkins? Mr. Sorrentino owns the place! He wouldn't shoot up his own casino."

The small mouse cop reluctantly lets me go and I step forward, straightening out my suit like the cocky son of a bitch I am. Medics are on the scene and I bark an order at one of them to get Louis medical attention.

My brain's still frazzled. I don't know which direction to walk in. My precious casino is eaten up by thick smoke on night one. There are bullet holes everywhere. Guests cower in the corner. A few have pissed themselves. Louis is injured, and I don't know where the fuck Falynn or the rest of my guys are.

One thing's for sure, Lovato's not getting away with a stunt like this. I'll crush him 'til nothing remains but dust.

I'm speaking with Captain Rodrigo when Robby finds me. Robby and I might have our differences, but one thing about him is that he's as level-headed as I am. It's part of what makes him such a reliable right hand. In that moment as he rushes over, he looks a sloppy, panicked mess.

His normally beady eyes are large as he chokes out, "Boss!"

I look over and my stomach drops. He's alone. Which means he's not with Falynn. Which means…where the fuck is she? I'm halfway into roaring out the question, but he speaks first.

"Boss, I don't know what happened to her. She'd finished freshening up and then we came down here. I was talking to Fozzi. Next thing I know, she's gone. Next thing I know, all this gunfire starts up!"

The venom in my gaze causes Robby to stumble a couple steps back. Even Rodrigo looks alarmed.

"You mean to tell me," I say slowly, tone low and dangerous, "you lost sight of Falynn? You don't know where she is?"

Beads of sweat break out on Robby's forehead. He gives a reluctant nod. "She has to be around here somewhere. She couldn't've gotten—"

"YOU STUPID MOTHERFUCKER!" I rage out of nowhere. I shove him out of the way as I storm across the casino floor, glaring left and right for any sign of her. "She could be shot up and you're over here sweating like a little fucking bitch! I never thought my right hand could be this much of a failure!"

"Boss…Boss, I'm sorry!"

"Don't be sorry, be competent, dumb fuck! Find her now!"

Now I'm panicking as I look everywhere but there's not a trace of her. Anything could've happened. She could've run off, breaking our deal. She could've been shot by the stray bullets in the air. She could've been fucking abducted by Lovato's guys—it'd be an Achilles' heel situation to get payback on me. How would Lovato know that? How would he know to go after Falynn?

Only my most inner circle knows the extent of what's going on between us. Has somebody switched sides on me? Do I have a rat in my midst?

Falynn is found on the top floor of the casino. The private level where I'd taken her earlier when we screwed in my office. One look at her, I know something's up. She's up against the wall in the empty corridor like she doesn't know where she is. If I didn't know any better, I'd guess she's in some state of shock.

"Falynn!" I yell, jogging over.

Only then does she stir, snapping out of her trancelike state. But her eyes are wide and filled with shock. I grab her by the shoulders and give her a slight shake.

"Hey, you all right? Nobody hurt you, did they? Where've you been? How many times do I have to tell you to stick with my guys!"

Goddamn it.

I care about her too much. Even as I scold her, I'm aware I'm still in panic mode. My nerves are shot and I need a drink to calm them. It's been a hell of a night.

"Falynn?" I say when she stays silent.

"Gio…" She trails off. She swallows and shakes her head. "What happened down there?"

"Lovato's what happened. We'll talk about it in my penthouse. You sure you're okay?"

"Yeah…I'm…I'm fine."

My gaze narrows. "You've been up here this whole time?"

"I was using the restroom."

She's lying.

I know a liar when I see one. All the tells are there. Her breathing is shallow. Her body is tense. She won't meet my eyes and she keeps nibbling on her lip. And her *silence*—Falynn's silence always means something. Whether she's mad at me, content and relaxed, or plain hiding something, it always carries meaning.

But why would she lie to me? What could she have to lie about? How'd she gone off by herself in the first place?

I'm careful in how I eye her. My grip on her shoulder tightens. Bitterness trickles into me, cold and slithery. We might have our issues and our arrangement might've started off rocky, but I've come to trust her over the last two weeks. For her to stand here and lie to my face is unacceptable.

It's a betrayal I will never tolerate. If she's chosen to betray me, she's leaving me no other choice. She'll have to be dealt with.

17

Falynn
PLAYLIST: 🎵 NOTHING'S GONNA HURT YOU BABY - CIGARETTES AFTER SEX 🎵

THE DOOR SLAMS shut behind us. One glance at Gio, and I know I'm in deep. I'm in *huge* trouble.

He knows I was lying. Yet, as I kick off my stilettos and turn to face him, I can't bring myself to tell the truth. After everything that's happened tonight, my brain is a foggy mess. I'm still processing seeing Enzo let alone making sense of *how* and *why*. Let alone figuring out how tonight affects me and Gio.

He stalks toward me, eyes menacing and dark. "Falynn, I'm going to ask you one more time. One more chance to come clean."

I back away, bumping into the side of the sofa. "Come clean? About what?"

My voice is unlike my own. It's fraught with a shaky nervousness. I've never seen Gio this serious; even the night I stumbled upon him and his men disposing of Jerry's body. I had been on the brink of peeing myself, I'd been so scared, but tonight doesn't hold a candle. There's a predatory quality in how he moves, closing in on me. A frightening coldness on his handsome face, his bearded jaw set hard. He's the most intimidating man I've ever seen.

In this moment, he's every bit the dangerous, bloodthirsty Mafia king he was born to be.

The devil incarnate. Right in front of me in the flesh.

"You know what," he says. He reaches out, and I flinch. His hand curves along my cheek, a light brush as if I'm delicate porcelain. "What's the matter? You're keeping secrets from me?"

"Gio…" I make a gasping sound like I'm insulted, but I'm still struggling with words.

"You weren't in on what happened tonight, were you?" he asks.

"Gio—"

"'Cause loyalty is a way of life in the family." He drops his hand from my cheek and moves toward the massive window overlooking the Strip. "When someone is trusted, and that trust is broken, there's consequences."

What consequences? What broken trust? Does he think I'm conspiring with Lovato? With law enforcement? None of it makes any sense.

I wrap my arms around myself. There's a sudden draft in the room and goosebumps spread over my golden-brown skin. "I'd never betray you. You know that. I'm not hiding anything."

"On your life?"

"Huh?"

"On your life, you'd never betray me?" He's staring out the window, his back to me.

But his reflection is in the glass. His face is stony and emotionless, like he's possessed by an unfathomable darkness.

I shudder and tighten my arms around myself. "Yes. I swear."

"Wrong answer."

He abandons the window. He crosses the space between us in a single stride. Before I can react, his nails are digging into the flesh of my upper arm. He's dragging me into the bedroom.

"You're lying to me, Falynn. For that I've gotta punish you."

My eyes widen. "Punish me…lying…Gio…but…"

He throws me onto the bed with no effort, then pounces like a beast. I try to push myself up, but he flips me onto my stomach. The Valentino dress I was so worried about ruining earlier is torn off my body. The rip of the fabric is so crass it hurts my ears. I move to roll over, blocked again by his brute power. He holds me flush on my stomach, now naked. His hands are on me immediately. He's gentle at first, large and warm palms smoothing down the length of my bare spine.

I'm already aware of where this is going, but it doesn't make the first slap sting any less. Gio smacks my ass with more raw strength than I'm ready for. His palm collides with my supple cheeks once, then twice, then a third and fourth time. I gasp and flinch, jerking against the movement to get up, but again, he holds me down.

The sting burns all over my backside. It's sharp and unforgiving and leaves me breathless. But as he spanks me again, he shoves his other hand between my thighs. His fingers graze my swollen labia. I'm moist, whether from the spanking or his touch, I don't even know anymore.

A current of tingles ripple through my pussy as I ache for him to continue.

"You're wet, Falynn. You must like being punished." He pushes his fingers into me.

I moan in answer. My ass still stings, but the pleasure from my pussy drowns out the pain. He seems to catch on.

I'm enjoying this way too much. He brings his palm down again, and again. *And again.*

Fire has exploded across my skin, making me shake. His fingers are still doing wonderful things inside me, massaging my walls, distracting me from the pain.

But as he slams his palm across my ass again, the pain soon shoots up to new levels. I whimper and am a second away from protesting when he stops altogether. He withdraws his fingers from inside me and uses both hands to massage my sore, burning ass cheeks.

"You shouldn't lie to me, Honey," he says in a soft tone. Somehow, it's more alarming than his rougher one. It makes it harder to know what to expect next. "I was worried about you. Do you know that? I almost flipped the fuck out."

I'm incapable of real speech. A silly squeak noise emits from my throat. The massage on my backside feels amazing. If he could just add his fingers back inside me, it'd be pure heaven...

"So," he says, his tone suddenly severe. "I'm giving you one last chance. What were you up to tonight?"

You'd think this is the part where I'd smarten up and answer. I'd find my voice and tell him all about Enzo and how he'd abducted me into the elevator. Believe me, there's a huge part of me that yearns to tell him every last detail. The part of me that's fallen for Gio, that wants to be in his fucked-up world.

And, yet, the words won't come out. Out of some weird, twisted sense of lingering loyalty to Enzo, I simply can't. I'm no snitch, and I know exactly what'll happen to him if I tell Gio. Enzo's already a dead man walking, but telling Gio? He won't last through the night. Call me stupid. Call me gullible. Call me a doormat.

I *can't* betray Enzo. We might be over, but a part of me

still cares about him. For as many fucked-up things as he's done to me, I'll always love him in some way…

When my silence answers Gio, he's had enough. He releases an angry growl and lifts me up by the waist. My body soars across the large, king-size mattress, landing on the other end. He shoves my face into the pillow at the same time his cock drives into me. I squeal, but the sound is muffled by the pillow. His thrusts are hard and punishing, designed to take everything and give nothing.

But what Gio doesn't know is that, while I may be protecting Enzo, he's not the man I want. Gio is the only man I crave, and I've already given him all of me. Every last piece of me is his to own, to dominate in any way he sees fit.

I *trust* him. Our twisted arrangement is one nobody else understands, but it's not for them to comprehend. It's our own dark little deal, where I've sold myself to the devil, and I'm loving every fucking minute of it.

The euphoric, orgasmic highs. The painful, gut-punching lows.

Moments like this, where lines blur, and they mix in the most delicious ways.

I knot fingers into the sheets and scream into the pillow, pushing back against Gio's brutal assault. He hasn't let go of my neck, holding me facedown as he drills into me. My pussy has never been more soaking wet. She clenches at his cock each time he hits a new depth, discovers a new angle that's never been explored before.

The fat tip of his thick cock bounces against the little ring that's my cervix.

"Oooffff…." I groan as dizzying stars shoot underneath my lids.

"Don't you ever fucking betray me, understand?" he growls, riding me. He grips the headboard and curls his heavy, muscular body over mine, our skin sticky and sweaty. He gives his hardest thrust yet to emphasize his point. I moan and snake a hand between my thighs to touch myself.

I've drooled all over this pillow, but I don't care. I turn my face and press my cheek into the feathery mound, watching the room float around me. I'm so dizzy and delirious, I'm capable only of babble.

His aggression pours out of him in every hard, forceful thrust. A lust so powerful it brings me to the brink of insanity consumes me. I want him to destroy me, break me down in my barest form. Then build me back up, treasure me as his most prized possession—the one that makes him lose control.

He'd destroy the world for me.

"You fucking belong to me and only me. Nobody else."

My hands ball up in the sheets as his brutal thrusts almost overwhelm me to tears. But once again, there's something about the pain that keeps me begging for more. I grind back against him, pleading for everything he's got —the pain, the pleasure, I want it all.

I'm seconds away from coming. I sneak a hand to my clit, in desperate need of release, but he forces it away. It's cruel, and a whimper bubbles out of my chest. As it turns out, since I've been so bad tonight, I don't get to come. He twists both of my arms behind my back with one of his titan-sized hands and uses the other to yank my head up by my hair.

His lips tickle my ear as he speaks, pistoning into me. "You want to come, Honey? Should've thought about that before you fucking lied."

Gio comes in the next second, spilling into me. He releases my arms and his grip on my hair, and I fall into the mound of pillows. My body buzzes, a conflicting contrast of both painful fire and pleasant tingles. I don't know whether I'm about to orgasm or seek out an ice pack.

He doesn't say a word to me as he pulls out. He slides off the bed and begins dressing. I don't move from where I'm lying. My whole body feels like liquid and my mind is in a fog. He dresses fast without sparing me a look. When he leaves, he says nothing. The door slams shut and I'm alone with my delirium.

Completely spent.

Gio's gone for hours. I'm a mess for hours. At first I lie in the bed, rolled up in sheets, and stare out the wall-to-wall window, watching the city lights glisten in the dark. At some point, I sit up and then drift to the window. I press my forehead against the warm glass and close my eyes, sorting out the loud noise in my head.

Between what happened with Gio and what went down with Enzo, I'm shell shocked. It's like I'm outside myself, helpless as I watch myself fall down a rabbit hole. On the other side is a world darker, more dangerous than I ever envisioned for myself.

The night I met Gio, a seed was planted inside me. Now a dark flower is blooming out of control, and I'm powerless to stop its thirst for more. Even as I stand here, I crave him. I want him to return and give me anything. Love. Affection. Punishment. It's all started to blur.

But how can I feel so strongly for a man who will never be mine? He's said it himself—he doesn't fall in love. He doesn't do relationships and happy endings. I'm the woman he intended to purchase for the night, and nothing more. When the situation got fucked up, he showed a little mercy and kept me for a few weeks. How have I deluded myself into thinking he cares about me?

I know how. Each warm touch and every passionate kiss. The stolen smiles and hard-earned laughter. The small moments where, even if brief, things between us feel real. Just like we're any other couple. I haven't imagined these things; they're as real as my flesh and bones.

A wistful sigh escapes my lungs. If he'd come back, we can talk it out.

Including Enzo.

The thought of him makes me cringe. I didn't even know Enzo was out of jail much less involved with Lovato's crew. When we were together, he hadn't shared details about his street dealings. I hadn't asked, using the logic, if I didn't know, I couldn't lie or snitch to the cops. It protected us both, but his reappearance tonight raises too many questions.

"There's a war brewing, Fal. You shouldn't have gotten caught up in this. You'll end up a casualty."

"Are you talking about between the Sorrentinos and Lovatos?"

My question was cut off by the pop and crackle eruption of gunfire. I screamed and he grabbed hold of me, hauling me down the empty corridor.

"Lovato's sending a message to your boyfriend. I'm supposed to be with the other two getting the job done, but I couldn't let you be in harm's way."

"Gio's in danger? Let go of me!"

"What's the matter with you? Who's the guy you really love—me or some Mafia bigshot?"

I shake my head and walk away from the window. I need a soak in the tub. The fresh lavender and frothy bubbles will relax me, rid my body of the pinched nerves. Then maybe I can clear my head and even get some sleep.

There's no telling when Gio will be back. Knowing

him, he'll be gone 'til dawn. He's not big on sleep, and a lot of shit popped off tonight. He probably has his hands full.

As the bathtub fills with soap and water, I dim the lights and put on chill music from one of the apps on the TV. I'm skimming my fingertips across the water, testing the temperature, when the penthouse door sounds.

Just when I thought Gio would stay gone for hours, he's back. His footsteps pad down the living area and through the bedroom. He appears in the bathroom doorway a second later. His face is hard to decipher—his classically handsome features blank. The vibe he gives off is nothing like before, though, no trace of menace to be felt anywhere.

Neither of us says anything for a long, drawn-out moment. Then, as I turn away and continue prep for my bath, he speaks.

"Let me."

I look up in confusion. He strolls into the bathroom, assuming command of my bath prep. He fills the tub with more liquid bubble bath and lights a few candles. He turns to me, the blue in his eyes as vibrant and electric as the first night in the club.

"Are you all right?" he asks, sliding a hand along the side of my neck. It travels upward, his warm palm cupping my cheek.

For the first time since our romp in his office, Gio gets a good look at my face. It's bare, washed clean of any makeup. His brow wrinkles. He brings his thumb to my mouth, running it along my lower lip. He stops at the corner, where my small cut from Enzo's hit is. I flinch and turn my head away.

"What is that, Falynn?" he asks in a testy tone.

"What's what?" I stick my hand in the bathtub filled

with frothy water to test it again. "It's hot enough I think—"

"The cut on your lip. Where did it come from?"

"Oh. That. I accidentally bit my lip earlier."

I swallow and force myself to meet his gaze. I'm not the best liar. I can't even stop blinking, for Christ's sake, but I stand there in my robe, hoping he doesn't continue this game of 21 Questions. He's doubted my loyalty enough for one night.

"You bit your lip," he repeats slowly. Suspicion drips from his smooth, deep tone. "Are you sure about that?"

"Yes..." My insides quake as much as I do on the outside. I turn my back to him and disrobe. The satiny fabric falls to my bare feet and I carefully step into the tub. "I'm exhausted, Gio. Can we not fight for now?"

He stares at me for an unnervingly long moment—so long it's obvious he doesn't buy my lie. But instead of interrogating me further, he seems to agree. We've fought enough for tonight. He moves closer and sits on the ledge of the garden tub.

"Just relax," he tells me. Any hardness about him is gone. He picks up a loofah and dips it into the soapy water before wringing it out and sliding it down my bare back. "It's been a long night."

18

Giovanni
PLAYLIST: 🎵 DRAGON - LVNDVN 🎵

SHE HAS a cut on her lip. A light bruise that develops on her cheek. Her voice trembles when I ask her about it.

I'm not stupid. I know the signs of a woman who's been smacked around—*my woman*. It takes everything I have in me to play it cool. If she's afraid to tell me or thinks she's protecting somebody, it doesn't matter. Whoever's responsible is dead. Bottom line.

For the rest of the night, we relax. I give Falynn a bath and then we lie in bed, quiet and in our heads. I can't begin to break down the shitstorm that's tonight, but at the top of the list is Falynn. She's number one.

Guilt is heavy in my stomach. Tonight I took out my aggression and frustration on her. I went too far trying to force the truth out of her. It can never happen again.

I whisper to her that I'm sorry. She's half asleep, tucked into my side. For all I know, she barely hears me, but I need to get the words out anyway. A man like me, who will soon take over the throne that is the Sorrentino crime family, never says sorry. It's a word that's not in my vocabulary—but for Falynn, it's one I'll make sure to learn for situations like these.

Fuck.

I never expected to care for the girl this much. Our encounter was supposed to be a one and done. For the night, some pussy, maybe a blow job, and it's over. She goes her way. I go mine.

How the hell did everything get this mixed up?

I *can't* let her go. I don't care what I promised her. That I told her this arrangement was only for a few weeks. Then she'd receive a huge payday, and a one-way ticket out of the country. Circumstances have changed. I'm not letting her go.

A cold, ruthless, power-hungry bastard like me has a heart after all.

And the only thing it wants is Falynn Marie Carter.

"We're throwing the book at 'em," Captain Rodrigo says the next afternoon at lunch. We're the only two seated at La Pergola.

After what happened last night, the casino portion of the resort is closed. The casino floor is officially a crime scene, but Rodrigo assures me it'll be sorted out quickly. Come a couple weeks from now, we'll have a grand reopening with heightened security, and show a *stronzo* like Lovato he ain't stopping us. No way, no how.

I sip from my Campari soda. "Throwing the book at them isn't enough, Captain. The man had my *casino* shot up…on opening night! We had three individuals injured, one an employee! This was an act of *war*."

Rodrigo gives a nervous laugh and dabs at his forehead with his cloth napkin. For being as crooked as he is, he's a coward. He doesn't like big moves. They draw too much attention, and his shadow petrifies him.

But it doesn't matter if he agrees. He'll comply.

"You understand why we have to retaliate," I say plainly, leaning back in my chair. "Lovato is in way over his head. He doesn't play by the rules. If he's willing to do what he did there's no telling what's next."

"I've told you, the two we have in custody—Montana and Daniels—aren't seeing daylight anytime soon. I've already spoken to Judge Williamson. The fix is in. They'll be doing three to five if not more."

"And the third?"

Rodrigo's brows connect. "What third?"

"We've been over this. There was a third gunman. Robby saw him. He was lurking near the hall leading to the private elevators. Then shit popped off." I didn't mention this is also the prick I'm certain Falynn encountered. He must've used her as a hostage and then taken off. I'd reviewed the security camera footage at every angle, but the cameras hadn't gotten a good enough shot of his face.

My guys are on it. I've tasked C.J. and Dominico with finding out who the grainy mystery man is.

"He'll join his friends," Rodrigo promises. "We'll get him a cell right next to them."

I shake my head. "Still not enough, Captain."

"What more do you need from me, Mr. Sorrentino? I'm afraid we've used my resources—"

"If I had word Lovato's cutting some shady deals at La Festa, would you be able to use more resources?"

A knowing glint shines in the crooked cop's eyes. "Depends how much of an incentive there is."

"The incentive is mutually beneficial for both of us, Captain. Have I ever led you astray?"

When Rodrigo leaves, his gut is rounder than before.

He makes sure to tell me how good the food is and that he'll be waiting on my call about Lovato. I stay seated at the table for a while longer. It's the first moment alone I've had since the shooting last night.

Everything's been on overdrive ever since. Even as Falynn and I lay in bed, my brain was buzzing. I couldn't relax. Barely got a wink of sleep between holding her and letting my feelings sink in.

First thing this morning it was business with Robby and the crew. Louis is still in the hospital, but if all goes well, he'll be a free man by sundown.

My phone rings. I know who it is without even glancing at the caller ID. Word's gotten back to Papa about the shooting at Vittoria, and he's calling to rip my head off. After assuring him just two days ago everything was good, this fuck shit happens!

It's humiliating.

The phone call's like a verbal spanking. Too much to deal with when I've already got enough on my plate as it is. Papa and his finger-wagging, tongue-lashing speeches about my failure can wait.

I press Decline, sending the call straight to voicemail.

"You are looking good enough to eat." I come up behind Falynn, slipping arms around her waist. She's wearing her curls pinned up, exposing the nape of her neck. The strip of skin is too tempting to pass up. I press my lips to the space between her shoulders and then work from there, kissing my way up 'til I reach the spot behind her ear that makes her shudder. "How am I supposed to keep my hands off you through dinner?"

Falynn leans against me, her tight little ass another

temptation. Why the fuck can't I get enough of this woman?

It's evening, and I promised to take her to dinner. Just the two of us (and my guys providing cover).

"Where are we going?" she asks, spritzing perfume on her pulse points.

I catch a whiff, the sweet scent making me drunk. My grip on her waist tightens. "Wherever you want to go, Honey. How about dinner at Ornella? The filet mignon is exceptional."

"Can I ask you a question?"

"Something tells me this might cause a headache. But go ahead." I give her hips a squeeze.

"Do you always eat at five-star establishments?"

"Is that a problem?"

She shrugs. "You're right about the food being exceptional."

"But…?"

"Sometimes those hole-in-the-wall joints have good food too."

Our eyes meet as she turns around in my arms. I smile like a dumb *cazzo* and say, "Is this your way of telling me you want to go to a mom-and-pop?"

She giggles, kissing me. "It'll be something different."

"I'll say. A lot cheaper. A lot…dingier."

"The food hits the spot at a lot of those types of places. They always have some little old mom or pop who oversees the kitchen. The food tastes more like ol'-fashioned home cooking."

"I could go for ol'-fashioned."

"Just saying."

"All right…all right, you've convinced me with that smile of yours…and fat ass."

Robby and Dominico are waiting for us in the hall

outside our penthouse. As Falynn makes friendly conversation with Dominico, I fall into step with Robby. Tension between us has been thick all day. He's barely met my eyes since last night when I chewed his ass out. Louis's injury only serves as a further divide between us.

He doesn't need to say a word to tell me how he feels. Like Papa, he feels I'm losing my focus. I'm wearing myself too thin with frivolous things and not the important stuff. If I were conducting business as usual, as calculated and shrewd as I normally am, last night's shootout never would've happened. It boils down to Falynn with him.

I know it does.

As soon as I mention there's a change of plans and we're headed into East Vegas, he grimaces. I stop him as we enter the private parking garage reserved for me, my crew, and any of the other investors. Only the best of the best cars fill up the spaces, row after row of Audis and Bentleys.

"Do you have a problem you'd like to discuss, Robby?"

"Boss, you're asking like I can tell you. You said—"

"Forget about what I said. I'm saying now, do you have a problem?"

"*East* Vegas after last night?"

"Yeah, so?"

"It's the ghetto! Why are we headed into carjack city after we were in a shootout not even twenty-four hours ago?"

"Listen, here," I say firmly, brows raised, "we're headed there 'cause I say so. And, shootout? Who gives a fuck? May I remind you of your vocation? You're sure as hell no elementary school teacher."

He grits his teeth. "If we were conducting business, I'd understand. But this is for…it's for nothing but a *date night*." He says it like it's a dirty word. To him, it is.

But I'm not backing down. I poke him in the chest with my index and pinky fingers. "If you want to go, Rob, go. You can get the fuck out of dodge any moment. Just don't be surprised if it comes back to bite you in the ass."

"Boss—"

"What's going to turn that frown on your ugly mug upside down, huh? Some pussy? Is that the problem? You've got a bad case of blue balls and you're mad at the world?"

By now, I'm speaking so loudly, my voice echoes through the empty parking garage. Falynn and Dominico have stopped outside our town car, staring over at us. I don't give a fuck, though, because humiliation is the point.

"Is that it, Rob?" I go on in a brash tone. "All you had to do was ask. I'll take you to the Dollhouse tonight. Buy you a girl with the biggest tits and ass imaginable—"

"That won't be necessary, Boss." His forehead shines red as he turns down my offer.

"You sure? Let me know because it's a stop along the way. Now if you're done being a jackass, get in your car and provide cover. What's it going to be?"

Robby moves to the driver's side of the car, giving me the answer I need. I pat him on the back as I pass him by.

"Good choice."

Falynn's pick for hole-in-the-wall home cooking is a restaurant called Sam's Smokehouse, located in East Vegas, what many refer to as carjack city. It's at the end of an outdated strip mall between the cash advance place and a tattoo shop. It's not where you'd usually find me when out for dinner, but she swears the food's that good.

We're the only ones dining in except for another couple

on the opposite side of the room. Not that there's more than five tables crammed into the place. The walls are an ugly mustard color with photographs from over the years hung up. The ceiling fans are going, circulating the savory scent of barbecue sauce. At the back end of the restaurant, there's a kitchen window where plates are passed through, and then a short hall off to the side with three doors. One for the kitchen, another for a unisex bathroom, and the last marked office.

An older woman with dark brown skin and a kind smile brings us menus and introduces herself as Hattie. She knows Falynn by name. Her eyes swivel to me and she says, "And you've got a fine man taking you out. I'm scared of you, honey."

Falynn gives an innocuous shrug. "I told Gio he hasn't lived 'til he's had Sam's hickory-smoked ribs."

"That'd be correct. They're good as sin. Worth the five pounds you gain." She winks before leaving us alone.

I glance over the menu. It's sticky and has graphics that look straight out of 1995. A single brow hiked, I ask, "Are you sure about this, Falynn?"

"The food is *ahhh-maaazing*. Trust me."

"Then tell me what to order." I fold the menu and slide it across the table.

Falynn eyes me with amusement, those chocolate-brown eyes shining. "All right, you need to know the tricks of the trade."

My brow climbs higher. "I'm intrigued. Go on."

"The regular smokehouse dry rub is okay, but if you're looking for flavor, you want to go with the smokehouse deluxe rack. Extra pepper. Mac and cheese on the side. Cornbread too."

"I'm wearing a six-hundred-dollar shirt. You know that, right?"

She giggles. "Aren't you always saying you can afford to buy a new one?"

"It's the principle. I expect to stain it with other people's blood. But barbecue sauce?"

"We'll have to get you a bib," she teases.

A tough, hard-as-nails guy like me should growl and scowl. Tell her she's real mistaken if she thinks for one second I'm donning a fucking bib to eat some ribs. But as the melodic sound of her laughter rings out, I find myself breaking into laughter with her.

I...I actually want more of this. Whatever this is between us.

Our food arrives, and sure enough, Hattie brings us bibs. Falynn puts hers on and then eyes me expectantly. With a sigh, pretending it's a chore, I do the same. When in Rome...

We dig in. Falynn wasn't lying when she said the food was "*ahhh-maaazing.*" It's better than amazing—it's one of the best meals I've ever had. The ribs are succulent and pack the perfect peppery punch. The mac and cheese is baked with a crispy layer on the top, fresh out of the oven. The cornbread is handmade by Hattie herself, as she boasts when we've licked up the last crumbs on our plates.

A five-pound gain was an understatement. I sit back in my chair, the fit of my pants noticeably tighter. I'll need to run a few miles and do a few hundred crunches to work this feast off.

Falynn's nose wrinkles in the most adorable way as she sits across the table and stares at me.

"What is it now?" I ask, baffled.

"Gio, I can't take you anywhere."

"What are you talking about—?"

Falynn interrupts me, reaching across the table. With her thumb, she wipes at the corner of my mouth. Some barbecue sauce leftover from the meal. I grab hold of her wrist and pull her from her side of the booth.

"Oh, you wanna be a wise guy, huh? You think you're so funny." I nip at her neck with my mouth. She struggles against my side with another laugh falling freely from her tongue. "How about I get barbecue sauce all over you. What are you going to do then?"

"Ew, Gio! Do *not* even think about it!"

I wrap an arm around her and drop a kiss on her cheek. "I'm going to ask Hattie for a bottle to go and we'll see tonight when I get you alone."

Falynn is breathless, but smiling ear to ear. "Actually…I don't know why, but that sounds kinda hot. I never knew I could be so turned on by barbecue sauce."

A wolfish laugh reverberates through me. Beautiful as hell. Sexy as sin. Smart and funny to no end. This girl's going to be the death of me.

19

Falynn
PLAYLIST: 🎵 BROKEN CLOCKS - SZA
♪

"ARE YOU SURE ABOUT THIS?"

Gio's eyes meet mine like I've told a joke. "We're on the plane, aren't we? We'll be taking off in a few minutes."

"Yeah, but...it doesn't mean I have to come with you to see them. I can wait while you go."

"Is this your way of saying you don't want to be the gorgeous woman on my arm?"

Gio teases the faintest grin, but I can hardly laugh. The sick feeling in my stomach is way too unpredictable. I don't get nervous often. Not even for performances. This is a different case altogether, though. I'm about to meet the rest of Gio's family—the Sorrentino *crime* family. On top of that, I'm not the best flier.

Pair the two together in one situation and this is the result—me a fidgety, quaky mess upon takeoff. No doubt the next seventy-two hours are going to be cruel and unusual.

The flight attendant strolls down the aisle of the private jet and only stops to ensure we're buckled in safely. I can't sit still. I squirm against the buckle of the seat belt and urge my heart to stop pounding so hard against my rib cage.

Don't panic. Calm down.

Gio must sense my oncoming meltdown, because he grabs hold of the hand in my lap. His fingers thread between mine, his touch engulfing me in warmth. When I glance over, he's already looking at me. His bright blue eyes reveal yet another superpower of theirs. One that doesn't involve making my panties wet: the ability to calm me down on sight. My pounding heartbeat slows down. My stomach stops squirming.

"Once we're in the air, I'll have the flight attendant bring you a drink," he says in his cool, composed, smooth as leather voice. "It'll calm you down."

His reassurance alone helps. It sets my nerves at ease. I lean closer, my head dropping to his shoulder. By the way he glances down at me, I can tell he's usually not the type to let a woman—or anyone—rest their head on him. The gesture's too affectionate for a dangerous, powerful man like him.

But he doesn't pull away. He strokes the back of my hand with his thumb, and lets me drift off curled against his side.

Traveling cross-country is such a whirlwind, the next few hours are nothing but a blur. It feels like the next time I open my eyes, it's hours into the night. I'm lying balled up on a bed as massive as the one in the Vittoria penthouse, but different in style and frame. It sits on a dais above the rest of the room with Roman columns on either side. The headboard curls in a sleek, modern curve of padded leather.

I blink and fight to untangle myself from the burrito I've rolled myself into using the bedsheets. Those are different too—black as onyx and the smoothest satin I've ever touched. The walls are as dark, painted black without a hanging portrait to their name. In fact, the entire room is empty, a large space without much personal touch.

That's when it hits me. It's Gio's bedroom. I'm in his main home.

As if reading my thoughts, a figure moves in the shadows. Sight still groggy, adjusting to the dark, I stare harder as it grows closer. The mattress shifts as it lowers its weight to the edge, sitting beside me.

Light from the nightstand table blinks on and illuminates Gio. He's never looked sexier, this muscular hunk of a man with his biceps poking out from under a cotton T-shirt and his thick head of hair pushed back against his scalp. But it's his eyes that stand out most in the dimly lit room—two intense sapphires piercing through the physical, peering straight into my soul.

An electric tingle surfs down my spine. I lick my lips and note how his gaze dips to watch. My throat is dry; it feels like a thousand years since I've had a drink of water, but I patch together a hoarse sentence.

"Are we late...what time...I must've fallen asleep—"

"Shh...it's okay." He gives me a soft, fleeting kiss, his warm palms sliding over my cheeks. His fingers find the wild curls framing my face, and he strokes them like they're delicate and precious. "You weren't feeling well after the flight. You've been getting some rest."

I close my eyes at the soothing sound and touch of him. The tingle down my spine transforms into tiny shocks throughout the rest of my body. He doesn't let go, curling me into his strong arms and kissing me again. At first more soft, fluttery kisses that are nothing more than a tease, and then kisses that are deeper, longer. Fueled by passion.

My lips part as my body surrenders to him. I'm his for the taking, in whatever manner he sees fit. Just the thought of him and those hands, his fat cock, arouses me. My pussy is already moist, begging for him with frantic throbs. I can hear myself breathe, a collection of sharp gasps and moans.

His fingers band around the nape of my neck and my head tilts back, offering him every inch of my throat. His mouth trails along the arc like I'm his to feast on. He sucks and licks, even nibbles with ravenous delight, sure to leave marks.

I'm so tuned into how warm and wet his mouth feels, I don't even notice he's unbuttoned my pajama top 'til it's too late. It's pushed off my shoulders and discarded. He fills his hands with my breasts. They fit perfectly into his large palms. He takes his time toying with them, tweaking my nipples, making them achingly hard.

"You're so tense," he whispers into my skin. His breath is a warm, wispy tickle. "Lie back, Honey. Let me relax you."

His hand dives down the front of my pajama shorts. He groans when his fingers touch my bare mons pubis and discovers, once again, I'm not wearing any panties. His fingers glide across the silky patch of intimate skin 'til he meets my pussy lips. They're unapologetically swollen and slicked with my juices, but that only encourages him more.

I listen to his orders and lie back. My head touches the pillow as he tugs off my pajama shorts and tosses them over his shoulder. I'm waiting with bated breath for his next move. Any grogginess has faded, replaced by adrenaline pulsing in my veins.

Gio spreads my thighs wide and dives in. Even his

breath on my pussy makes me tingle as I arch and grip the sheets. His tongue licks the juices from my folds and then dips inside for a deeper swipe. His fingers are soon to follow. First his thumb pressing over my clit, applying pressure to the throbbing nub. Then his others, prying me open, splaying my lips apart to reveal my soft, pink center.

"Look at this pretty pussy," he moans, lapping at me like I'm the sustenance keeping him alive. His deep baritone vibrates against my delicate core and sends another tingle pulsing through me. He pushes his tongue deeper, digging inside me and flicking at my clenching walls. "Prettiest pussy in the world. So pink, so wet, so fucking tight."

"Ohh…Gio…" I whimper in another thrash. "Please…just…just…ahhh…"

"Please, what?"

"Just…I need it…" My brain doesn't work as he laps at me.

Gio eats me out like I'm the finest delicacy in the world. His moans, groans, and heavy breaths are that of a man savoring the taste, every last drop of me, because none can, or will, go to waste if he can help it.

My whole body trembles, enraptured with the pleasure he inflicts on me. He gives another long sweep of his tongue before switching it out for his thick fingers. Two of them curled against my walls, seeking out my holy grail, the pads of his fingers finding the hidden treasure that's my G-spot. A frisson of shocks erupts from the magical button and percolates throughout the rest of me.

I'm out of control, unable to keep myself from writhing. My hips gyrate, pushing against his mouth and hand, begging for more. I'm a woman possessed by a man who seeks to drive me insane. He's halfway there as tears spring to my eyes and my mouth hangs open. I don't fight it, clutching desperately at the satin sheets, bracing for the explosion.

His mouth suckling at my clit, his fingers deep inside me, I'm ready to blow. I don't even fight it. My pussy flutters as my orgasm erupts like a ticking time bomb. I leak all over his face, but he never pauses, devouring my juices.

Heat flushes over my skin as I lie encapsulated in waves of tingling pleasure. My curls are a damp mess, spread around me on the pillow, and my chest heaves in a clumsy attempt to catch my breath. Gio rises onto his knees and looks down at me, his lips glossed with evidence of me. His tongue pokes out and licks his lips as he moves closer. He pushes my legs further apart and lowers his sweatpants. I'm too weak, too high to move, or even care. Not as long as my body pulsates in the aftershock of my orgasm.

His large cock flops out, already hard as the muscles on his sculpted body. How is it possible that, as soon as I set sights on it, I'm already throbbing with need again? My sex responds at once, desperate for him to fill the emptiness in me.

In a fluid motion, Gio makes it happen. He captures my lips in a hot kiss and sinks every inch of his thick cock into my sopping-wet pussy. All I can do is gasp and dig my nails into his biceps. I'm along for the ride as he fucks me into the night.

Gio's gone when I wake up the next morning. He's left me a note on the bedside table, a neatly scribbled message about conducting important business. He promises not to be long and that he'll return in time for a late breakfast with me. My face lights up as I realize I'm enough of a priority he's making sure to come back as soon as possible.

I lie back among the satiny pillows and sheets. I'm sore from last night. But it's a good kind of sore. The kind that's a reminder of him between my legs. Another sign he was here, inside me, marking me as his. I run a hand along my folds, with him in my mind, and moan at the memories of last night. Somehow, I want him again. Right now, soreness be damned.

It occurs to me I don't know anything about Gio's home. After the flight yesterday, I collapsed from a toxic cocktail of anxiety and nerves. Add in the three whiskey sours I had on the plane, and I hadn't given a thought to explore my surroundings.

But with Gio gone, I have free rein of the massive house—and I know it's massive even before setting foot outside his room. When the size of his bedroom is bigger than the one-bedroom apartment I shared with Enzo, it's sorta a given the rest of the house will be humongous too.

The double doors open to a wide hall with dark obsidian floors and white paneled walls. I pad down the hall with curious glances left and right. Many doors line the hall, along with the occasional piece of abstract artwork, each piece moodier than its predecessor. Gio definitely has a thing for dark, clean, almost sterile environments.

It sinks in that I'm in Mafia boss Giovanni Sorrentino's home *unsupervised*. How many federal agents would kill for the opportunity to poke around his private abode? For a chance to dig deep for something incriminating enough to take him down?

When I reach the end of the long, wide hall, I'm at the top of a grand staircase that curves along the wall as you descend. I hold on to the black iron railing with each step, feeling like some debutante making her entrance at a ball.

The foyer is another huge space, lit by the natural light from the doors and front windows.

As I make my way into the living room with vaulted ceilings and a generous view of the terrace outside, I discover I'm not so alone after all. Robby is seated on the white leather sofa, poring over some documents in his lap. He looks up when I enter, his beady eyes immediately narrowing with dislike.

I've had enough of it. Hands on my hips, I call him out. "You know, I'm not your biggest fan either."

"Good. Then you understand why I don't feel compelled to talk to you right now."

I suck at my teeth. "There is such a thing as manners."

He chortles. "Honey, you've got another thing coming if you're expecting manners from a Mafia guy."

"Where's Gio?" I ask instead. I've given up any hope of amicability with this asshole.

"Don't you worry. Gio'll be back when he's back."

I fold my arms and stride toward the glass door and windows overlooking the terrace. If I'm going to be trapped in Gio's house with my least favorite guy on his crew, I deserve to bask in any positive I can find—one being the gorgeous autumn day. Living in Vegas, it's easy to forget so many other parts of the country have real seasons.

Gio's lawn sprawls deep, lined by trees on either side. Their fall foliage is in full effect, vibrant oranges and golds you don't see in the desert. I'm not standing there long before voices enter the silent air. I recognize Gio's smooth baritone at once.

Robby rolls his eyes as I spin away from the window and dash through the living room. I'm so fast, I meet Gio in the foyer before he can set foot anywhere else. His arms open automatically to catch me launching myself at him. I don't need to look to know Robby's rolling his eyes a second time. Gio plants a hello kiss on my mouth and then peers at me like I'm the most baffling thing he's seen.

"What's the matter? What's got you so worked up?"

"I woke up and you were gone."

Robby's probably going for a third eye roll, but I don't give a fuck. He can kiss my apple-bottom ass.

"I'm back now, aren't I? We'll have breakfast on the terrace." Gio holds my hand as we move into the living room.

I was so excited to see him, I didn't register C.J. and Louis are with him. I smile at both, noting the sling Louis's arm is in.

"Does it hurt?"

He shrugs. "I've had worse. You try getting shot in the ankle and get back to me."

"I'm glad you're okay, Lou."

"It's appreciated, Miss Falynn."

When it's just me and Gio on the terrace, seated at a table with our breakfast, Gio teases me about the nickname.

"Lou? Since when are you giving my guys nicknames?"

I pick up a croissant and give a mysterious shrug. "Lou and I are cool. He says I—"

"Remind him of his kid sister, Nikki. So he's told me. I'm glad you two get along." Gio shoots me one of those subtle smirks of his, where his eyes do more of the talking than his lips ever do. The good-humored gleam in them paired with the cocked brow. Like everything else he does, it's unbelievably sexy, and takes my mind to X-rated places.

"You know who I don't get along with is—"

"Something tells me you're going to say Robby."

"Why'd you leave me with him? He's such an—"

"Asshole," Gio answers again for me.

"Are we playing Mad Libs and you didn't tell me?"

Gio chuckles. "I know you better than you think, Falynn. And you're right. Robby is an asshole. It's part of what makes him a good asset to our family. None of us are nice guys—not even *Lou*."

"But at least Lou and the others have manners. Robby...he gives me the stink eye any time he looks at me."

"All right, all right. I'll talk to him. Better?"

My smile from earlier returns, bright and grateful. I'm aware how it makes Gio soften up like no one else has the ability to do.

He drinks from his mimosa eyeing me like I'm a rare gem. "After breakfast, get dressed. Something nice but a little more conservative. Uncle Claro's welcome home party's going to be a long one."

Uncle Claro, his wife, Julianna, and their two teenage kids live in a mansion rivaling Gio's. Maybe bigger. It's a lot less about clean lines and polished vibes than it is about flexing their money. The home is adorned with gaudy gold accents and heavy furniture that looks right out of the '70s. But Claro and Julianna aren't exactly stylish themselves.

Claro welcomes us into his home in a velour tracksuit a size too small, smelling of a spicy cologne that probably cost an arm and a leg, but is repugnant just the same. Julianna is at his side wearing heavy gold jewelry on every part of the body possible. They both give us hugs and double kisses on the cheeks.

"You're some of the first ones here!" Claro exclaims in a loud, abrasive voice. He's balding and wrought with wrinkles, but his smile never leaves his face. He throws an arm around Gio, though he's about a head shorter, and walks at his nephew's side. "Nephew, every time I see you, you get more and more shredded. Whoever told you you need to look like some MMA fighter in our line of work?"

Unsure of where to go, I start to drift after them, but Julianna cuts in. She touches my arm and says, "Honey, it's so interesting to have you. Giovanni *never* brings women to meet the family."

My laugh's a nervous one. "Oh, really? I guess it's true what they say—there's a first time for everything."

"Well, we've always known he has a thing for the caramel kinda look. But I never thought he'd bring one home," she says with a smile that's meant to be friendly. It feels a lot less harmless and a lot more ignorant. As she walks with me to the kitchen—another room decorated with heavy wood and gold finishing—she adds on a compliment. "You're a gorgeous girl, of course. I see why he's gaga over you."

By the time Julianna launches into talk about how happy she is to have Claro home, I've tuned out. I don't have patience for Julianna's casual racism, and I'd prefer to stick with Gio for this family outing. My opening for an escape comes when more family arrives.

Cousins Alonzo and Marco show up with their wives and kids in tow. Julianna's distracted with greeting them, so I escape down the hall I'm hoping leads to a bathroom. I need to freshen up, ensure my flat-ironed hair has no flyaways, and check for any stains on my simple white dinner dress (Julianna forced some wine on me). After that I'll find Gio.

But I come across him a lot sooner than I expect, within footsteps down the hall. The door to what appears to be a den is cracked open. Gio's in there with Claro. I slow up enough to catch a couple words exchanged.

"You're playing a dangerous game, nephew."

"It's not any more dangerous than the money-laundering scheme you had going at your car washes."

"And I paid for. Fifteen years in the joint. You wanna join me? You wanna end up in the morgue?"

"Neither of those things concerns me."

"Oh, 'cause you too big and bad, is that right? Nothing and no one's gonna stop you, eh?" Claro huffs out a sardonic laugh and puffs on what sounds like a cigar. "You're so eager for that crown, you're gonna fuck it up along the way. Desperation is never a good look."

"Everything is handled."

"You said that about Vittoria's opening night. And look."

"Lovato will regret making such a move. I've already seen to it."

Claro laughs again. "You are your father's son. My brother may have succeeded, but it's different times, my nephew. The same power moves of the past don't work these days."

Their voices grow nearer and I skirt away from the door in fear they're on their way out. It's too risky to hover in the hall any longer and listen to their conversation. I keep going until I find the guest bathroom I'm looking for.

A glance in the mirror shows me I'm flyaway and stain-free, but I take my time anyway. I'm processing what I overheard between Gio and Claro. His uncle says times are different and Gio's playing a dangerous game. Is he talking about the war waged between him and Tony Lovato? Was Claro right when he said Gio is too desperate, too hungry for his father's throne?

Nothing and no one's gonna stop you…

It's true Gio is determined to rise up the ranks of his family at any cost. Though this isn't surprising given I've gotten to know Gio well over the last few weeks, it produces a sharp stabbing pain in my chest.

Maybe I've let my fantasies about a future with Gio get out of hand. I've let myself believe it's possible for us to be together when reality seems to point in the opposite direction. Gio and I are destined to part ways. We'll never work out.

His career in the family, taking over for his father, is what matters most to him. He's willing to sacrifice any and everything. Everyone. *Including* me.

On that glum note, I sigh and leave the bathroom. I'm passing the den again when a "pssst" catches my ear. I look up and find Claro in the doorway. He grabs my hand and pulls me into the room with him, closing the door once I'm inside.

"Claro, what—"

"You were listening in on us, weren't you, honey?" he asks outright.

I stammer. "Oh…not really…I was passing…I wouldn't…"

"Hey, it's okay, don't sweat. I'm not mad." He winks at me.

"You're not?"

"Course not. Maybe you can talk some sense into my hard-headed nephew. You're his girl, right?"

"Um, yeah…but I don't want to get involved—"

"Honey, you are involved. The second you walked in on his arm, you're in deep."

Residual nerves from yesterday make a fluttery return. I move toward the door. "I should go find Gio."

Claro blocks me with his wide frame, a strange gleam in his gaze. "You're real beautiful, honey. I'm sure you know that."

"Oh. Err. Thanks."

"I bet that's why Gio picked you. A real dime on his arm."

"I'm going to go." I step to go around him, but again, he blocks me. "Excuse me, Claro."

"I haven't had some young cooze in a long time. Since before I was locked up. How much?"

Revulsion churns in my stomach, making me want to puke. I take a large step back. "For what?"

"You know what. I know all 'bout you, Miss Falynn Marie Carter."

As he moves to close the gap between us, I scurry around him, wrench the door open, and flee down the hall. My heart's beating fast and I'm jittery, but I don't stop until I'm back in the bathroom. I twist the lock on the knob and lean against the wall, breathing in and out like I've run several miles.

The moment is so random, I don't know what to think. Claro knows my full name. He knows who I am. Did Gio tell him about our arrangement? Did he tell him how we met? How he'd hired me for the night?

Embarrassment and rage simmer through me at the same time. I fold my arms and tears gloss my eyes. I don't want to be here anymore. I want to go home. Not Gio's home. Not Gio's penthouse suite in the Vittoria Resort, but home—*my* home however craptastic it is with its cracked walls and out-of-service washer and dryer.

I'm done playing Giovanni Sorrentino's girlfriend.

20

Giovanni
PLAYLIST: ♬ TERRIBLE THING - AG ♪

"YOU SEEN FALYNN AROUND?"

Louis is at the bar along with C.J. Both guys shake their heads. "Nope, haven't seen her, Boss. Is something wrong?"

I don't answer them. I maneuver through the big room now filled with family chitchatting. Cousin Alonzo puts an arm around me and tries to talk sports, but I shrug him off and keep looking. Falynn's nowhere in sight.

Juliana said she hasn't seen her since earlier. The two shared a drink in the kitchen and chatted about something or another. Julianna swears it went well, and that she didn't say anything to upset Falynn. So then why has my woman gone missing?

Claro tries to snatch me up into his den for another talk, but his lecture can wait for a later time. It's more important that I find Falynn. As I wander down the hall on the main floor, once again it's evident how this girl has me wrapped around her finger. I'm seeking her out like some lost puppy dog!

Fuck, this is pathetic.

Relief pours over me the second I see her, easing up the tension in my muscles. She's coming out of the guest bathroom. I'm over here acting like a pussy-whipped jackass, and she's over here powdering her nose, or whatever it is women do on bathroom breaks.

Sliding an arm around her, I kiss her cheek. "Everything all right with you? You went MIA. I was about to send out a search party."

She *recoils* from my touch, but doesn't utter a word.

The hard lines on my face are back. I stop and glare. "What's the matter with you? Did I fuck something up and not know it?"

"Did you tell him?"

"Tell who what?"

"You know who! Did you tell him I'm some prostitute?!" she demands.

I look over my shoulder, left and right, in case anyone overhears. Her voice carries and the house is full. Nobody's around as far as I can tell, but this isn't a good spot for an argument—and it seems she's sure as hell set on having one. I grab her arm and pull her into the nearest room.

We wind up in Claro's game room. It's nothing but another tacky display of his wealth and connections. Nothing on the walls except sports memorabilia he's paid an arm and a leg for. Boxing gloves signed by Muhammad Ali himself. Photographs of him and Joe Montana at the 1984 Super Bowl. Also autographed. A VIP fan jersey awarded to him by Shaquille O'Neal years ago. La-Z-Boy leather recliners facing a gigantic HD smart TV and a kitchenette for making drinks and snacks on game days.

"Answer me!" Falynn says once inside.

"Let's get one thing straight. I answer what I want when I want, understand?" I put up a warning finger, holding on to my mantle as boss regardless of how I feel about her. "If you're talking about Claro, I didn't say a word about you—"

"He knew my whole name! He knew... he knew..." Her breath catches, and she stops mid-sentence. Suddenly, she looks like she's about to cry.

My alpha tough-guy shit goes out the window. I grab on to her hands to bring her closer. "What'd that piece of shit *stronzo* say? He do something stupid?"

"He *propositioned* me, Gio. Like I'm for sale."

I close my eyes and pinch the bridge of my nose. Claro's never had a way with women, despite what his delusions lead him to believe. If he's not smacking strippers on the ass and getting hauled out by security, he's catcalling women on the block, or screaming at Julianna about his mistresses.

Claro has old school views. Which means he treats women with little to no regard.

I'm no saint, and neither are most men. But I like to think I'd be smarter than bragging to the woman I've married that I'm fucking three other girls on the side.

"Did he touch you? Is that what happened?"

"Gio..."

"Tell me."

"I'm not telling you, because I know what you'll do. You'll go out there and break his hand... or some other body part. I don't think ruining your uncle's coming home celebration is a good impression, do you?"

"Impression? Who gives a fuck about impressions?"

"You do! Isn't that why you had me dress like this?" She gestures to the conservative (for Falynn and her amazing figure) dinner dress that still looks phenomenal on her, but doesn't hold a candle to anything else she's worn. She even toned down her makeup. "Isn't that why you prepped me about them? Why you kept saying I look good on your arm?"

"Falynn, what are we arguing about here? What is it you want from me?"

She folds her arms and shudders out a sigh. "Where is this going?"

"You know what this is."

Probably the wrong thing to say. Especially after telling me my uncle just propositioned her for sex. She reacts like the words sting as much as any slap across the face. The trace of light pink on her golden complexion no longer looks artificial from the makeup—it's natural as she flushes from emotion.

"How could I forget?" she says, her volume dropping. "Thanks, Gio. You always know how to make me feel cheap."

"That's not how I meant it, and you know it!"

"I can't do this."

She turns to go, but I grip her arms and stop her. "Falynn, look at me. Honey, *look* at me. Do you see me? You see how you've got me? You think any other woman's ever had me like this? Had me searching down halls for her? Had me about to deck my uncle in the fucking face for coming at her sideways? You are as far from cheap as a human being can get. You are worth the world and more."

Her fight leaves her. Her body softens, melting into mine. I cup her face in my large palms and our gazes connect. Peering into her beautifully deep brown eyes slows my heartbeat; it makes it flutter like the damn lovesick puppy I become when with Falynn.

I'm pretty sure I'm falling in love with the girl. Or as close to love as a cold, heartless bastard like me can get. So much for my beliefs that relationships are strictly transactional and the concept of love isn't real.

Our lips meet halfway in a slow, soft kiss. It sets everything right again. I'm breathing easy again, tasting the sweetness on her pillowy lips. Nobody's sweeter than Falynn. Every part of her is like a taste of honey.

"Are we good?" I ask, my head bent, our foreheads touching. I kiss her again for the hell of it. "Let's go back out there."

Papa arrives minutes before dinner flanked by his main guys... and Giancarlo. For as old and frail as Papa is, he carries a sense of authority. He's automatically the most powerful man in the room. Everyone's eyes are on him as he enters with the aid of his cane. He's shrunk even in the last month since I've seen him swimming in his dress shirt and slacks. But his eyes are ever the same, the bright blue stones only I inherited, not Giancarlo. It's the most obvious way to tell us apart, because otherwise, we're identical.

Giancarlo is powerful in his own right, matching me toe to toe. His dark eyes meet mine and we step to each other, gripping the other's arms before a brotherly embrace. Two rivals sharing the same DNA, same bloodline pretending for one night we wouldn't do whatever it takes for that crown atop Pa's head.

His grip on my arm tightens. Mine does the same. We draw apart after the embrace and let another second of tension crackle between us. Giancarlo's an easy read. The hunger is clear on his face, in the flare of his nostrils and clench of his jaw. In his near-black eyes that are so dark they reflect mine back at me. He blinks, and the moment is over, with him moving onto other family members.

His fiancée, Fiona, is like a songbird, pretty to look at and a voice that chirps. She follows him after a brief hello to me. No doubt she aspires to be the future queen to his king. The two remind everyone of Pa and our mother years back when Pa finally bit the bullet and chose a woman for his heirs.

I glance down at Falynn, and she gives my arm a squeeze—or as best she can with how thick and hard my forearm is. Though we might not be the most traditional pairing in every sense of the word, she's by my side too.

Dinner begins with a toast to Claro's freedom. He's at the front of the table, cheesing hard, showing off his yellow teeth. Pa is at the real head of the table, but barely speaks a word. His looks say enough; his mind is elsewhere.

Julianna and the wives went all out. The table is covered beginning to end in every favorite Italian dish known to man. Silverware and cutlery clink and clank as everybody moves to fill their plates.

I can hardly concentrate on my meal. Once again, it's a case of irritation scratching away at me. The mask I'd normally be able to wear at a family dinner is nowhere to be found. Where Falynn is concerned, there is no mask. Only the emotion I've learned to bury for years. I grit my teeth thinking about how upset Claro made her earlier.

On my left, Claro doesn't help the situation. He's already halfway drunk. He slops down more red wine, spilling some on the tablecloth. When Julianna tries to tell him to be careful, he waves a hand dismissing her and turns to Alonzo to tell him about the time he met Jack Nicholson.

"You're exaggerating," Alonzo says with an easy laugh. "There's no way."

"Exaggerating? What's that, you dimwit? My whole life's a movie. Watch it sometime," Claro slurs. He snorts, the snotty sound like nails on a chalkboard to my ears.

"Just 'cause you jackasses have boring existences, you think that's everybody! Not Claro—my shit's box office!"

"Claro," Julianna sighs.

"What? It's the truth, ain't it? Not everybody's like me! You know I got Steve Jobs on speed dial?"

"Steve Jobs died a decade ago. He's *gone*, Claro," Juliana says to laughs around the table.

Claro sways to a stand from his chair, empty wine glass in hand. "So is that figure of yours. Remember when you were a size two?"

The table's reaction is a mixture of oohs, ahhs, awkward laughs, and tears from Julianna. Claro takes it as a win, a smug smirk on his ugly mug as he moves for the kitchen.

"Don't mind me. I'm grabbing another bottle. It's a celebration, ain't it?"

As he passes our end of the table, his hand falls onto Falynn's shoulder. He gives it a soft pat I probably wouldn't have thought twice about had the situation earlier not occurred. But given my current mood, the irritation bubbling up inside me, seeing his grubby paw on her makes me snap.

I leap over my seat to gasps around the table, spearing into Claro from the side. The wine glass tumbles from his fingers and crashes to the floor. The crooked toothed fuck doesn't understand what's happening 'til I shove him against the wall. His egghead bounces off the wall, eyes wide and mouth agape. I press my forearm harder into his windpipe, cutting off his air.

"G-Gio," he sputters.

"Don't you touch her," I growl.

"What're you—GIO!" Claro struggles against my grip, but he's a weakling. Nothing but flab and more flab. Not an ounce of muscle in sight.

My arm digs harder against his throat. "Is that understood? Don't you even look at her—"

Pa's guys, Alonzo, Giancarlo, and a few others rise from their chairs to break up the commotion. Nobody dares touch me, though. Even Giancarlo, as he comes over, doesn't dare put his hands on me.

"He's turning red," Giancarlo says at my side. "Let Uncle go."

I'm not so sure I'm ready to let go. As I glare into Claro's saggy, ugly face, his eyes bulging out of his sockets, there's something pleasurable about seeing him squirm. After being inappropriate with Falynn, he deserves every second of it. If she hadn't gotten away, would he have stopped when she said so? Given Uncle and his history with women, I know the answer.

"Gio, don't," Falynn says. She's the only one bold enough to touch me. Her fingers slide over my forearm, giving the same squeeze from earlier. She's here. She's at my side. She's got my back.

I let him go. He chokes, his hand flying to his throat as he stumbles away. Julianna and a few others rush to check on him.

My breathing is out of control. The muscles in my jaw ache from clenching down so hard. I barely register anyone else in the room as I force my raging temper to shut down. I close my eyes and exhale a deep breath.

"Are you okay?" Falynn whispers.

"Giovanni, a talk," Papa says finally. Everyone's gazes dart between the head of the table where Pa hasn't moved a muscle, and where I am, standing by a knocked-over chair and the wall. Pa grips his cane and rises up. His guys accompany him toward the doorway leading to the hall. He doesn't even check if I'm following.

He knows I will. I have no other choice. I leave Falynn

and the others behind, following like a child about to get his butt spanked—and that's basically what's about to happen. We go into Claro's den, the door snapping shut. I don't know why Giancarlo's come along. Chew my ass out in private, I don't give a fuck. But invite my brother, my rival, to witness it go down?

It's crossing a line. Pure humiliation.

"Don't go telling me I shouldn't have touched him!" I snap. "If he wants to act like disrespectful trash, I'll treat him like it!"

Pa sits down on the sofa against the back wall, watching me pace around the room. The others remain standing, but nobody says anything. They let me pace back and forth as many times as I need to, the tick from the wall clock the only sound.

"Are you done?" Pa asks after what's nearly five minutes. "Is your temper tantrum out of your system, Giovanni?"

"I'm not saying a word."

"Reason being?"

I stop in my tracks, my expression hard. Pa understands from the way I flick my eyes left and right. He motions for the others to leave the room. His guys do so reluctantly, but he shoos them along. Giancarlo's last to go. He pauses as he passes me, a spark of tension charging between us. I return his stare without a word. My brother and I have our own set of issues that won't be solved any time soon.

But someday we'll be forced to. Just not right now. He continues on his way out without another look.

Door closed, father and son alone, Pa gestures for me to sit down. This time I listen, choosing the armchair farthest from where he sits.

"All this commotion you've caused," he wheezes,

admiring the twenty-four-karat-gold handle of his cane. "This is over the girl?"

"She has a name. You know she has a name."

"*Honey?*" A vague, cruel smirk flickers across Pa's wrinkled mouth.

"You told Claro about her."

"Did you think I wouldn't do my research? You let a girl who's witnessed your business activities roam free, and you think this isn't a concern?"

"None of your concern."

"Oh? Because you don't belong to my family? Are you no longer claiming Sorrentino?"

My eyes narrow. "'Til the day I die, Pa. You know that's not what I meant—my operation is my operation. I'm my own man. I can handle business on the west coast without your interference."

"Giovanni, in the past, I believed so. Now? Not so much."

"Have I not proven—"

"Falynn Marie Carter, age twenty-four, born and raised in Pomona, California. Moved to Las Vegas at nineteen. Worked many jobs. Never held one down longer than a year. Most dancing gigs at different clubs. Part-time student at UNLV. She and that ex of hers are two-hundred and sixty-seven thousand in debt," Pa rattles off in his smoky voice. "She's been involved with some doozies. Would you like me to list them by name?"

I make a sound of disgust in my throat, dismissing his claims with my hand. "Is any of this supposed to mean something to me? I know all that already. She's told me most of it herself."

"You can never make a wife out of a woman like her."

"Let's cut the shit, Pa. Because she's not Italian, is that right? Because she's Black?"

"Being Italian is our heritage. You know that. But what's *worse*, you've picked a girl from the gutter—somebody half of Vegas has seen, and God knows what else."

I bark out a loud laugh, heartbeat roaring in my ears. "Not my murderous, drug-handler, money-laundering criminal father judging anybody for what they've done. That's ironic, don't you think, Pa?"

"You're not thinking clearly."

"I'm thinking clearer than ever. You just don't like that it goes against what you want."

"A pussy-whipped man is a man unable to think straight. How many times have I told you this?"

I ignore the point he's making. Deep down, maybe it's true in the basest sense of the words. I'm addicted to Falynn, am no longer able to visualize my life without her. I've claimed every single part of her as mine. I'll stamp it on her plump, round ass if I have to. She belongs to me, and nobody else.

"You're going to have to make peace with it. I *like* the girl," I say after a pause.

"You're falling for a scammer. Pure gold-digging, promiscuous, money-hungry scammer. *And* she ain't even Italian!"

"I've had enough of this. We're done here." I stand up from the armchair, but Pa holds his hand up to signal I'm not going anywhere.

"We are *not* done. I haven't told you the men she's involved with."

A muscle in my jaw twitches. "Whatever angle you're working—"

"Her ex-boyfriend, the one she's told you about, Enzo."

"What about him?"

"You know what crew he runs with?"

I clench my hands into tight fists. My insides freeze into ice as instinct tells me where this is going. The gleam in Pa's eyes is too bright, the cruel smirk returning to his lips.

"I bet she's never told you. Enzo is short for Lorenzo Espinosa."

"That name means shit to me. Same as any other name."

"Does Lovato?" Pa asks, palms wrapped over the handle of his cane. His smirk spreads. "Lorenzo is one of Lovato's street guys. That charge he caught—the one Falynn told you about—was from the night they tried gunning down Everett Johansson in revenge for our partnership. Lorenzo was one of the guys hired to do it."

My brows push together. "Falynn knows nothing about that. He never kept her involved in anything he did."

"Maybe. Maybe not. But she knows his latest job. Shoot up the Vittoria Resort and Casino. That third guy you've been looking for? Guess who?"

Pa's info slams into me like a freight train. I scrub a hand over my face and breathe through the resistance in my lungs. Too many thoughts, too many questions swarm through my mind as the info sinks in.

Pa can't leave it be. He has to twist the knife. "He spoke to her that night, Giovanni. The time she went missing? You know who she was with. She was feeding info to the enemy, to Lorenzo, to *Lovato*."

"No..."

"The insider you've wondered about? It's the bitch in your bed."

"NO!" I roar. I'm heaving for breath, a panic rattling in my broad chest. I can't seem to calm down enough for my heart rate to return to normal, but at the moment, it doesn't even matter. I back away from Pa, seated on the sofa with his twisted smirk.

But I have no defense. Because… because there's a real possibility it's the truth. I play back every moment with Falynn. The good and the bad. The moments she's wormed her way into my good graces. The times she's broken my trust or tested my patience. Every last memory is thrown into question. Was her loyalty ever mine in the first place?

I took her against her will. She made the deal out of spite. Out of a sense of survival. She was always searching for an exit, always biding her time.

I should've known better. Instead I let myself become blinded by a pretty smile and tight pussy. I mistook it for love when it was never anything more than a transaction. I'd bought her, and she was providing a service. She was never supposed to have any worth.

But like a fool, I gave it to her. I let the bitch use me.

Intense pain throbs at my temples. I clench my eyes shut and rub away the pain to no avail. None of it is anything I want to deal with, but it doesn't matter what I want, or what causes me pain. If this is the reality, then it must be addressed. If Falynn is a traitor, if she defected to the other side, then I'll have to dispose of her myself.

For as many men as I've handled, for as many dark deeds as I've done, the thought makes me nauseous.

"Giovanni," Pa wheezes. With my lids shut, his smoky voice sounds from the dark corners of my mind. "You know what you've got to do."

21

Falynn
PLAYLIST: 🎵 BOYS LIKE YOU - TANERÉLLE ♪

"GOT A SECOND?" Robby asks.

Nobody else at the dinner table hears him. They're still buzzing about what happened earlier with Gio and Claro. As they sip espresso and nibble on cake, no one notices I scoot my chair back and follow Robby out of the room. He leads me through the house to the front door. When I stop and raise a brow, he guides me outside.

"We're gonna stand here for a chat." He offers me a cigarette, but I shake my head.

The night's cool and breezy, dark except for the lights from the house windows. Robby's silhouette looms against the shadowy background, almost blending in. The only feature of his I can distinguish is his hook nose in profile and the shift of his beady eyes as he stares at Claro and Juliana's front yard.

"Gio knows, Falynn."

The words stop my heart even if I have no clue what he means. I'm already jittery as feelings of guilt shake through me. "Knows? What does he know?"

Robby lights up his cigarette and takes his first drag.

"C'mon, Falynn, don't be stupid."

"I've never been stupid a day in my life, but you are right now if you think I'm into your games, Robby."

"Lorenzo Espinosa," he says. The weight of his gaze is heavy even in the dark.

My blood runs cold. "Wh-what about him?"

"See? There you go, being stupid. We both know you're no dum-dum, Falynn, so why are you acting like one?"

"Call me another name and—"

"What? You'll go run to Gio? Tattle on me like you did Claro?" His laugh is sharp and cold, biting into me on sound alone. "If you keep up this little innocent bird act, I'll run to him for you. Tell him all about how you're protecting *Enzo*."

"I'm not protecting anyone!"

"Then what happened opening night of the Vittoria? Where'd you disappear off to? With who?"

So *this* is what he's brought me out here for. Robby had been keeping an eye on me the night Lovato's guys shot up the casino, and I went missing. He hasn't mentioned it since, but I should've known an asshole like him resents me. When I disappeared, it made him look bad in Gio's eyes. He blames me.

But how does he know about Enzo? How does Gio?

"What do you want?" I ask tightly, folding my arms.

"You need to get outta here," Robby says, blowing smoke. He uses his fingers holding his cigarette to point at me in the shadows. "I'm only gonna give you this out once."

"An…an out?"

"Let me put it this way, Honey. You're fucking shit up big-time. You've got Gio's head—the wrong head—in all the wrong places. The thing is, he's never gonna hurt you.

He's a cold-blooded man, but he cares too much about you. Even if you've betrayed him, he can't have you blasted. He won't do it. I can tell."

"I've *never* betrayed Gio!"

"You realize it's your word versus Enzo's? How do you think it looks, you disappearing off with your ex? The same ex who's working for Lovato? Who shot up Gio's casino? Who looks like the bigger shithead here? You or him?"

"It doesn't matter. I'll explain to Gio what really happened—"

"Too late. Word's gotten around, Honey baby. Should've calculated those steps better. Now the story's been spun, and the target's on you. Whether you realize it or not, it's already in motion," he explains. A grin forms around the cigarette stuck between his lips. "Now, I'm gonna tell you how to get outta this. It's up to you if you take the out."

"But if you say Gio will never hurt me, then what do I have to be afraid of?"

Robby plucks the cigarette from his lips and laughs. "You sweet little innocent thing. Maybe you are really that dumb. Honey, you're in the middle of a Mafia war, or have you not been paying attention? I said *Gio* will never hurt you. Didn't say a damn thing about anybody else. Including Sorrentino Senior."

The coldness in my blood spreads into my lungs. I can't even breathe. I stand there without air, staring at Robby with wide eyes, unsure of what to do or say.

"*Including* me," he finishes, and he grins wider.

I take a step back and bump into Julianna's rose hedges.

"Didn't say I'd hurt you now. Just…if orders come down the pipeline, you understand." He flicks the cigarette butt into the ground and then stomps on it with the heel of his shoe. "But with this out, you get outta dodge. You stop sabotaging my boss, and shit can go back to normal."

It feels wrong. Every last part of it. I'm still not breathing, still can barely form a thought. I swallow against a lump in my throat and try to blink back some tears. My heart aches at the idea of what Robby's suggesting. How can I go through with this? I care about Gio too much. I can't imagine my life without him anymore.

But if what Robby says is true…am I dooming myself to an early grave? Am I dragging Gio along with me?

Robby's right about one thing. In recent weeks, Gio's become more reckless, less cool and calculated. The emotionally detached man he was when I met him is no more. Now he's passionate and volatile. It's affecting him and the work he does…

"If you're gonna go through with it," Robby says, interrupting my thoughts, "you've gotta understand, it needs to be tonight. Listen to me carefully."

Gio doesn't say a word the entire drive home. With him quiet, I'm quiet too. We go up to his room and get ready for bed. I shower, and he doesn't join me like he usually would. He's preoccupied with a phone call, but when I wander into the room, he cuts the talk short and tells the other person on the line he'll call back tomorrow.

I'm not talented at much. But one talent I've developed from my years of working in gentleman's clubs is how to read customers. I can pick up on when a man is in a bad mood, when he's feeling reckless with his money, and even when he's preoccupied with thoughts about his wife at home.

As I approach Gio, my strut slow with a sultry sway to my hips, I know right away he's closing himself off from me. I slide into his lap, the hem of my negligee riding up my thighs, and wrap my arms around his neck. He doesn't kiss me, doesn't even meet my gaze.

He keeps his attention on his phone. I go in, peppering kisses along his bearded jawline, moving downward to his throat. He loves when I play the minx role, but tonight no amount of teasing him, raking my nails down his chest, seems to do the trick.

What I don't expect is his rage. As I boldly start teasing his ear, small little nibbles like he usually likes, his grip tightens around my hips. He pushes me off him and snaps to his feet from the desk chair. I stumble from the strength of the push, startled for a second he'd kick me off so suddenly, so forcefully.

He gives me his back, but I don't care. Nobody treats me like I'm some nuisance. If he doesn't want me touching him, that's fine. I'm not going to be disrespected, though.

"If you're pissed, then say you're pissed!"

That does it. He turns around for a look at me.

The second Gio's gaze connects with mine, I know I've done it. His eyes electrify, sending a frisson of tingles through my body. I watch as the vibrant blue of his irises darkens into a deeper shade. His expression is a chiseled one as sharp as stone as he's never looked taller. He towers over me, a muscular mass of raw power and strength, of sin and darkness.

"Well…" I trail off, losing half my nerve. I put a hand on my hip. "Are you?"

I have no insight into what he's thinking. The thoughts running through his head as he pins me with his intense stare. A long, seemingly never-ending second passes by with us squaring off on opposite ends. Finally, he releases a low chuckle and shakes his head.

"What?" I ask, puzzled. "What's so funny?"

He starts for the door, but I'm not letting him go that easily. We need to sort out whatever the hell is going on. Obviously, what Robby said is true—or at least partially true. I follow him, dogging his footsteps 'til I'm within reach. I give his back a hard shove. Given our strength difference, one of my hard shoves barely makes a dent; it doesn't even cause a single misstep.

But he does stop walking. He glances at me from over his shoulder. The reaction's not enough, so I do it again. I rush forward and shove him as rough as I can a second time. Then I'm zooming in for a third, ready to keep shoving him 'til he pays attention. He catches me on my next attempt. His large hands snap closed around my arms with such force, for a second I'm lifted off the ground. He lets go of me just as suddenly, and I wobble a few steps back.

"What the fuck is wrong with you?" he asks in a tone that's low and dangerous.

"I'm wondering the same! If you've got something on your mind, why don't you tell me?"

"You want to know?"

"Yeah, I wanna know!"

"No, you don't—"

"TELL ME!" I scream, losing a handle on my temper. It doesn't matter how petite I am, how he outweighs and outsizes me two to one. Right now, I'm as fucking ferocious as any other raging animal in the animal kingdom, snarling and snapping.

Gio doesn't grant my request. He spends another long moment staring at me, his gaze unyielding and intense, and then he strides toward me. With his long legs, he closes the gap between us in less than a second. I don't have time to react. His hand flies out and he grips my throat, pushing me backward. I hit the wall, my spine colliding hard against it.

Before I can process what's happening, he kisses me. He smashes his lips to mine, his grip tightening around my throat. Air cut off and head spinning, I'm submerged into a pool of desire as soon as I taste his warm lips. It burns through my body like a wildfire, setting me aflame.

My sex throbs as I gasp against his mouth for air. But he shows no mercy, his grip on my throat tightening. The tips of my toes leave the ground in my struggle to regain some control. He doesn't allow it, his mouth traveling to my ear. He nips and tugs and whispers, "Tell me who you belong to."

"You," I gasp.

His lips return to mine, hard and fierce. His tongue probes its way into my mouth, asserting dominance against mine. Dizziness rolls over me in waves, battling the desire that's taken over. I'm seeing stars behind my lids and aching in my core for even the possibility of him deep inside.

My sputters for air mix with moans of arousal. I don't need to feel between my thighs to know I'm already slick and sweet. Just how he likes it. Just how he makes me at the slightest, smallest touch. Wet as fuck by his demand.

He releases my throat from his powerful grip and then drags his mouth over the column of sore skin. It might even bruise, but in the moment, as my pussy throbs harder than my heartbeat, I can't say I give a single fuck.

"Say it again," he growls. His fingers find themselves entrenched in my curls and he pulls, yanking my head back so more of my throat is exposed. "Tell me again who you belong to."

I moan, my eyes fluttering under my closed lids. His other hand pushes down the strap of my negligee and gropes my breast. He rolls my nipple between his fingers, pinching harder than usual. Pain lances through me as I pant to catch my breath, but he doesn't stop. He pinches again, a reminder he's waiting for my answer.

"You, only you," I tell him in a breathless whisper. "Only ever you."

"You swear on your life…on everything?"

I still under his touch. For as fog-brained as I am in the moment, Robby's words play back in my head. Though I know I'd never betray Gio, the story's already been spun in a different direction. I'm already being looked at sideways. I've already become the traitor. The bad guy in the eyes of his father and the family.

"Answer me," Gio demands. For the first time, there's a sense of desperation edging into his growl. He *needs* to hear it from me.

But my sore throat goes dry, and like the night he interrogated me about Enzo, I don't answer him. I stand still, limp against the wall, and let silence speak for me.

Gio's temper returns in full swing. A growl rumbles from his chest and he clenches his hands around my arms, yanking me away from the wall. I'm thrown onto the bed, bouncing for a second upon landing. He's on top of me, prying my legs apart with his knee, capturing my lips in a hard kiss.

His hand cups over my warm, wet pussy and I squirm underneath him. Just a touch. Just a single finger. Anything would feel like heaven right now. If only he'd have mercy…

"You won't answer me, Falynn," he breathes, breaking our kiss. He withdraws his hand from my needy pussy and starts unbuckling his belt. "It's too late now."

"Gio…I'm yours…" I whine, but it's not enough.

He's not listening. He's tuned out from me, his face cold and unresponsive. I lie there and watch him undress, pulling off his undershirt and discarding his pants. The belt clangs as it hits the floor. Even now, I ogle the many ridges of his six pack and the hard lines of his sculpted chest. My gaze dips to the V indention at his pelvis, the arrow pointing to the thick, veiny cock that never fails to make my mouth water.

I'm so captivated, I barely notice he rips my negligee from my body. The satiny fabric tears away, now a rag for disposal. He plants his mouth over mine, smacking his cock against my wet slit. I can feel my folds swell in anticipation, my aching clit quiver in want as he bumps it with the head of his penis.

I moan and buck my hips, but he doesn't give me more. The tease is the point.

He breaks away and lifts my legs, tossing them over his shoulders. He comes in close, his eyes intensely on mine. His length spears deep into me on the first thrust. I claw at his shoulders to hold on, but there's no fighting against the power he exerts. He slams into me, forcing a gasp from my lungs.

When my lids lower to close, he grabs my face and forces me to hold his gaze. He wants me to watch every moment as he fucks me, breaks me in half, destroys me. The dark flicker in his eyes finally makes sense—it's rage.

Gio wants to punish me. He wants to make me hurt.

I *want* him to make me hurt. Make me hurt in the best, most pleasurable way possible.

He shows no mercy. His hips are like a machine, slamming into mine. He drills into me, filling me up before he retreats. His cock pulls all the way out and then dives all the way back to the hilt. He develops a hard and fast rhythm that's like an intense rollercoaster ride of highs and lows.

I can do nothing but claw at him. My nails sink into his skin, drawing lines of blood in some twisted form of retaliation. I'm marking him up the same way he's marking me up. The scratches are reminders for later when I'm gone. So he can look in the mirror and know I was here.

My body writhes uncontrollably as he sinks into me. The harder he thrusts, his cock burying itself over and over again inside me, the more my pussy gushes. My walls tremble around him, clenching at him for more.

He goes so deep, I don't know if I'm feeling pleasure or pain. I can't tell anymore as they blend into one. The sensation inside me builds as a collection of tiny shocks. I point my toes from over his shoulders and scream.

He clamps his hand around my throat and his hips slam into me so hard, his balls smack my ass. I sputter as, for the second time tonight, my air is cut off. He doesn't miss a beat, fucking me with his gaze still piercing mine.

I squeeze tighter around him, knowing it'll drive him crazy. More twisted retaliation. As he cuts off my air, his grip on my throat, I'm clenching my walls, choking his dick. Neither of us are going to last long. Our bodies grow desperate, pushing each other to the limit.

I'm light-headed. I'm breathless. Darkness tinges the edges of my vision. The orgasm building finally explodes through my body in pings and zings. The thousand little shocks tingle, forcing me to shudder and then go numb.

My mouth hangs open as, for a few blissful seconds, I feel like I've ascended earth into heaven. Gio lets go of my throat and replaces his hand with his mouth. His muscular form is curled over me as he gives me his most powered thrusts yet. He rams into me like a bull, his mouth on my throat. His kisses are sloppy, turning into love bites.

He reaches his breaking point in a flood of hot cum. It fills me up as he buries himself deep. We don't move for a long time, lost in the aftermath of what can only be described as an angry fuck. Finally, he lifts himself off me, and I breathe for what feels like the first time in a half hour. I reach for him, but he doesn't touch me. He doesn't even *look* at me. He slides off the bed and walks butt naked to the bathroom. The light blinks on and the door slams shut.

I lie back and stare up at the ceiling, knowing now more than ever what I have to do.

Gio suffers from insomnia. It's one of the first things I learned about him. Another thing I've learned about him over the last month is that if there's one way to put him to sleep, it's sex before bed. It knocks him out better than any nighttime medication.

As he sleeps soundly, I lie awake caught up in my thoughts. The room is pitch-black and silent except for the soft hum of his breathing. It's after 3 a.m., and I've been working up the nerve to do what I have to do for over an hour. I have to go now. Before it gets light out. If I wait 'til dawn, it'll only be that much harder.

Robby's instructions were clear.

I glance to my side where he's lying. Gio sleeps on his back. Most nights, he drapes an arm around me, preferring for our bodies to be touching. Tonight, after we fucked, was the last time he touched me. His king-size bed is large enough for the two of us to lie on opposite sides and not even come close to each other.

A shudder racks through my body. I don't want to do what I'm about to do, but what other choice do I have?

The more I mull over my talk with Robby, the more the pieces of the puzzle fit. Gio was angry with me tonight because he's learned about my alleged betrayal. It doesn't matter that I haven't given Enzo any info on him, in the Mafia any suspicion is bad suspicion. I'll never be trusted again.

Even if Gio takes up for me, if he defends me, I'm screwing him over too. Not only has he become more reckless since we've been involved, he's willing to fight his own family for me. The same family that's willing to stop at nothing to keep power—including hurt me, and probably Gio too if it came to it.

He's already escalated the rivalry between the Sorrentinos and Lovatos. His father is already unhappy with him. Now Claro, second in command who's freshly out of jail, is too. Lovato has vowed to stop at nothing for claim over Vegas. The whole situation is a fucked-up mess.

And *I've* caused most of it.

I have to go. Now.

I check Gio's still sound asleep before I slip out from under the sheets. I tiptoe across the large, shadowy room and pause at the door for another glance at him. One last goodbye look. It's too dark to see his features, but my heart aches at the thought this is the last time I'll ever see him. The only man I've ever truly seen myself with. The only one I hoped would really last. The one I've come to love.

The most difficult second comes when I turn away. I twist the doorknob and slink out of the room. If everything Robby says is true, I'll have a plane ticket and cash waiting for me. Gio will hopefully move on, and maybe I will too.

As I escape his home, my broken heart pounds, but with each beat, it tells me I'm doing the right thing. This is for the best.

22

Giovanni
PLAYLIST: ♫ LIE TO ME - BLACK ATLASS ♪

SHE LEFT IN THE NIGHT. I woke to an empty bed, an empty house except for my guys on guard. She disappeared like she never existed, and for once, I'm blindsided. I searched the house high and low for her. Robby and Dominico were the two on guard last night. Neither recall seeing anything.

At first, I'm spitting fire. I rage at them, screaming in their faces. I tear pieces of art off the walls and smash vases on the ground. I turn my once neat and sleek four-point-five million dollar mansion into a hurricane of broken glass and furniture. In my bedroom, I wrench open her suitcase and dig through its contents for any sign. Even the slightest clue.

An hour into my rampage, Robby approaches with caution. He and Dominico stayed out of my way, putting our resources to use in an attempt to find her. She's on no flights departing the city. No sightings at any bus terminals or train stations. Our connect with the local police even says there's not a trace of her anywhere.

She truly vanished into nothing.

Robby clears his throat as I bandage my bloody hand with a silk scarf of hers. "Boss, don't you think you should calm down?"

"You're sounding like you don't grasp the severity of the situation," I spit back. I round on him with a fiery glare. "Tell me you get how this is of utmost importance."

"Of course I do. Nobody disappears like a bump in the night."

I stalk closer, jaw clenched. "No. Nobody does. Which makes me wonder how? How does an amateur—a woman like Falynn with no experience at such things—disappear out of a guarded, heavily surveilled mob boss's home?"

The insinuation hangs in the air between us. I eye Robby with suspicion as I circle him, a lethal dose of fury pumping in my veins. Right now everybody's a target as my temper unleashes itself. Everybody's a *suspect*.

"In fact," I continue in a low tone, "if memory serves me right, this isn't the first time you and Dom have fucked up watching Falynn. Lovato's party. The opening night of the Vittoria."

"Gio, you're not thinking straight."

"Don't fucking tell me whether or not I'm thinking straight!"

My roar bounces off the walls, but it's not enough. I release another rumble of frustration and then stride forward to rip a lamp off the nearby desk. It shatters into a thousand pieces as I smash it to the ground.

"Find Falynn!" I bellow, veins strained in my neck. "Or I'm finding myself a new crew!"

I don't bother dismissing the failure of an asshole. I storm out of the room myself, snatching my keys off the console table as I go. Dominico tries to stop me downstairs, but when I jerk my shoulder back at his touch, he flinches away.

"Don't follow," I warn. "You two are to dedicate all of your time to finding her. I'll be back."

How could she leave me? We had problems. There's no doubt about that. Last night was another fucked-up rendition of our conflict resolution. Hate sex the sequel to the sequel to the sequel. At this point, I've lost count. I hadn't been able to bring myself to look at her after returning from dinner with my family.

Pa's words were still seared in my brain. The conflicting feelings warred inside me. Falynn had heated some of my cold, black heart with her warmth. But the tight knot that was my gut instinct said Pa's warning was legitimate. Falynn had lied to me, kept her whereabouts the night of the casino's grand opening a mystery. Had she also known her ex ran with Lovato's crew?

The night I met her, she had seduced me from the stage at the Dollhouse. With a body rocking the most incredible tight curves, I hadn't been able to take my eyes off her. She had owned that stage with her sultry moves and insane sexual energy. When her heavy-lidded eyes met mine, the connection sparked a jolt in my spine—and a heavy tug in my loins.

I knew I was going to handpick her for the night. She was going to be mine.

But she'd wound up curiously in Jerry's office. Falynn claimed it was an accident. I had believed her. Now I'm not so sure. Could Pa be right? Was she part of an inside job with Lorenzo? Were they working for Lovato?

I slam on the gas, hitting the highway in my convertible. The scenery blurs the faster I go, weaving between any cars I come across. Driving recklessly has always calmed my nerves. Even before Falynn entered the picture and uprooted my hold on my emotions, I had always sought speed to quiet the rage.

There's something about driving so fast you almost lose control that makes you feel *more* in control.

Years ago, after our mother had been murdered, Giancarlo had stolen Pa's keys to his Ferrari. We'd hit the windy roads a few miles outside our upscale gated community that shielded us from the rest of the world. We drove for hours, racing other cars, ripping through neighboring towns like we owned the place. We laughed and laughed as we ate up the most fun we'd had in months.

Then we lost control. We smashed through the front of a gas station convenience store. The damage we caused came out to over two million dollars. Nobody was hurt, including ourselves. We were lucky to be alive, but it was a lesson early on.

Never lose control. Never let emotions lead. Hold on to control with every ounce of strength you've got.

It's a lesson I've lived by for my whole life. One I'd developed into a skill 'til I met Falynn.

Pa's guards try to stop me, but there's no keeping me out. I push past them and force my way through the double doors leading into his office. Pa sits with his nurse as she counts out his medicine. She smiles up at me, thinking this is a friendly visit. Once she spots the grimace on my face, the smile drops off and she goes back to counting pills.

"We need to talk," I announce without preamble.

Pa grunts, keeping his gaze on the nurse's slender fingers. He's not interested in a word I have to say. I'll *make* him interested.

"You," I snarl, pointing to the nurse, "out."

She scurries like a mouse chased by a broom. I round on Pa.

"What'd you do to her?"

"Nurse Katie? I didn't do a thing except ask for my medication."

"You know who I'm talking about! What'd you do to Falynn?"

Pa makes a *tsk* noise with his tongue. "Why are you set on that girl? You've been a fool over her, Giovanni."

"Did you take her, huh? Kidnap her last night? Is that what happened?"

"I promise you, I have nothing to do with the girl."

"Then where is she? She disappears hours after your warning, and you don't think that's suspicious?"

The same smirk from last night lights up Pa's wrinkly, evil face. "*Think*, Giovanni. Use that fucking brain. Ever consider maybe your paramour found out I told you?"

My glare sharpens. "What's that supposed to mean?"

"You've been had. The girl skipped town because she's guilty. She left because she had to. Before she got got."

"No need to worry, boss. This place is more secure than Guantanamo Bay," Louis says. He's still in his sling, though decidedly more mobile. He ends our tour of Vittoria's casino floor where it began, right in front of the cash cages. "There'll be no funny business come opening night."

I survey the floor from where we stand, wearing a neutral expression. "You've done well. How's the shoulder?"

"Better. Doc says I'll be clobbering *cazzo* fuckers in no time. And your hand?"

A second passes by before I understand the question.

My gaze lowers to my bandaged hand, wrapped up in gauze after receiving five stitches. They're a reminder of me flipping my shit only a couple days ago when I discovered Falyn was missing. I stuff both hands in the pockets of my trousers and give a noncommittal shrug.

"A few stitches are nothing. Have you spoken to C.J.? What's he found out?"

"He's supposed to be calling you later. Says he has some intel on Lovato's whereabouts."

"Good work. Both of you. Keep it up."

I leave him where he is, strolling away at a languid pace. I walk the perimeter of the casino floor, watching the renovations like a man browsing a museum. So far, everything is falling into place with our grand reopening. Come soon enough, the Vittoria will be back in full swing even better than our first go.

Lovato isn't going to sabotage me a second time. As it stands, he has a debt to pay. The price is his head. I'm done with playing games. The little tit-for-tat battles we've been engaged in over the past few weeks have grown boring. The night Lovato shot up the Vittoria, he escalated shit to a level there's no coming back from.

This turf war over Sin City isn't over 'til it's his head perched on my mantle. Better than any trophy, it'll cement my place as the new king of the Sorrentino family. It doesn't matter if Pa is still alive and breathing. If Claro's been released from Club Fed. I'm the rightful heir, and I've run out of patience. It's time I ascend the fucking throne.

With Falyn gone, I've never thought clearer. The blackness in my heart has swept in deeper and darker than ever before. The monstrous rage is still there, but once again, the monster is back in its cage. It's controlled now by the calmer, cooler, more calculated side of me. The side that knows how to get results ruling with an iron fist, but doing so smartly. Gone is the reckless, emotional mess I was when I was under *her* spell.

The first place I stopped when flying back into Vegas was Falynn's old apartment. I brought Robby along with me, and we cased the joint. It wasn't hard to force our way in. There was already an eviction notice tacked to the door. Robby's lock-picking skills were far advanced for the flimsy locks.

Falynn hadn't been exaggerating about her living conditions. If I were still in an emotional state, seeing the lawn chairs for furniture and the cracks in the walls would've stoked a hot flame of anger in me. Just knowing that piece of shit Lorenzo had her living here. But I closed myself off from that level of fury. Instead I glanced around the squalid apartment, kicking aside piles of clothes.

Robby searched kitchen drawers, turning them inside out. "Nothing of importance. Looks like she hasn't even been back here for weeks. Probably since the night she met you."

"No, it doesn't look like it," I agreed. A photo hanging on the fridge caught my gaze. I removed the pineapple magnet and held up the photo for a closer look. It was of Falynn and another woman smiling and toasting with cocktails at some casino bar. Falynn looked as gorgeous as ever, but the woman next to her held my attention more for one reason alone. "This woman—her friend Tasha. What's the latest on her?"

"Don't know. We haven't kept tabs. Why?"

"Because, if Falynn is in touch with anyone, it'd be her."

The loud warble of a slot machine draws me back to the present. I shake away the recent memory of Falynn's apartment and look around the game floor. The sound comes from a maintenance man who's testing the slot to ensure it's in working condition. He greets me with a respectful, "Afternoon, Mr. Sorrentino."

I give him a nod, but the truth is, I'm still distracted. Before I can devote the rest of my attention to the casino's reopening and my war with Lovato, there's one last loose end that needs to be tied up.

Tonight. And it involves a trip to the Dollhouse.

23

Falynn
PLAYLIST: ♫ #1 CRUSH - GARBAGE ♪

ONE MONTH LATER...

Mom was wrong about a lot of things growing up. She was wrong about the men she picked. She was wrong about the unsafe environment she put me in. She was wrong the time she refused to believe me when her boyfriend took advantage of me. But there was one thing she got right. One kernel of truth she clued me in on from a young age.

Life comes at you fast.

Sometimes, so fast you barely know what's happened. You blink and next thing you know, everything around you has changed.

It's one of those nights as I pull into my assigned parking space. I flick off my headlights and switch off the ignition and blow a sigh of relief I'm finally home. Even if it's a place I've only called home for the last three and a half weeks.

The parking lot is empty and silent. Every window in the high-rise apartment building is dark. With my giant tote bag slung over my shoulder and keys in hand, I hurry across the lot. I stop only once I've reached the elevators.

The elevator jostles me up to the eighth floor. My feet are aching and I'm counting down the seconds 'til I get to take this damn bra off. It's been another long night at Club Diamond, but I'm settling in more and more each shift. The elevator dings once it reaches my floor. I have my keys ready by the time I stop in front of my apartment.

I have a whole checklist of things to do as soon as I'm home.

Flick on the lights. Check. Lock the door. Check. *Verify* it's locked correctly, then set down my stuff on the kitchen island. Check and check. Kick off my shoes and unhook my bra. Another check and check. I'm on step seven, charge my phone, when it pings in my hand.

Missed call from an unknown number. I've been getting a lot of those lately. The number's only been mine for a couple weeks. When I called up the phone company and asked about the weird calls, they assured me it's residual contacts from the last person who had the number.

I'm not so sure I believe them.

These days, the slightest thing out of the ordinary makes me jump. The knots in my stomach, which are always present now, twist into a tighter ball. Can you blame me? It seems like I'm fated to be the woman on the ID channel that you hear about. You *know* the one—she ran away from some psycho ex, tried to start a new life, and then ended up dead anyway.

Except my ex happens to be a high-ranking member of the Sorrentino crime family.

Which is about ten times worse.

I inhale a calming breath and shake away the paranoia. Robby promised me a life of solitude. A completely new start. While the amount of funds he gave me doesn't compare to what I anticipate Gio was offering, it's been enough to snag me a nice apartment and a car for getting around Miami.

Why Miami, you ask?

I don't know. Robby told me to leave the country. He gave me a fake ID, passport, and all the other documents I needed for a new identity. But after escaping Gio's, as I sat at the airport and awaited my one-way flight to Montenegro, I couldn't do it. What was I going to do once I got there? Who did I know? How would I survive once Robby's cash ran thin?

So, instead, I bought a ticket to Miami. The fake documents for my new identity have come in handy renting a place and even getting a job. I couldn't not have one. Not if I wanted to keep most of the money Robby gave me as a nest egg for a rainy day. Besides, Miami has plenty of strip clubs, and it's the only vocation I have real experience in besides waitressing.

I connect my phone to the charger and move down the hall into my bedroom. Between settling in and starting at Club Diamond, I haven't had much time to decorate, but I've managed to put a personal touch here and there, mostly in the soft pink and white color scheme.

A shower and a change into pajamas later, I emerge a lot less on edge. Then I move to check on my phone and see another missed call from an unknown number. My belly roils like I've missed a step going down the stairs. The hardest part of this new life is the hours dead in the night. When I return from my shift at Club Diamond and before I'm able to fall asleep. A few times I've stayed out all night just to avoid the odd hour.

Right now, as unnerved as I am, I crave a voice. Something familiar that can set me at ease. The problem is, when you abandon your old life, you're not supposed to contact anyone you knew. I've made good on that promise.

'Til now.

I rack my brain for options. The only reasonable one is Tasha. It's Wednesday night, and I'm three hours ahead, which means she's probably starting her shift soon.

Just this once.

It takes a couple minutes, but I call up the Dollhouse using a Google Voice number (in an attempt to protect my own), and I ask the girl working the phones for Tasha. She pops her gum and tells me to hold on a second.

"Hello?"

"Tasha?"

There's an uncertain pause. "This can't be…Falynn?"

"Shh, don't say my name," I warn quietly. "No one can know I'm calling you."

"What the fuck, girl? Where've you been? You know your place has been—"

"I know! Just….chill, okay?"

"Chill?! Girl, *fuck* chill!" Tasha blurts in her high-pitched voice. "You disappear for weeks without a word. I'm thinking you've wound up in some psycho's hands and you're chopped up in a hundred pieces. Then you call and tell me to chill."

"Keep being loud and I'll hang up! I called because I wanted to chat."

"Are you okay? Are you hurt? Do you need me to—"

"I'm fine. I just…I had to get out of town."

Tasha makes a growly sound from her throat. "It's that Sorrentino you got mixed up with! I told you the night Jerry disappeared—you do your job, get the cash, and you dip! You *don't* date the guy."

"Sorta didn't happen like that, but think what you want."

"Look, not trying to sound judgmental. Did you know he came by the club looking for you?"

The hairs on the back of my neck rise. "He...he did?"

"And your neighbor, you know, Ms. Erickson? She says she saw him and some of his men at your place."

I don't say anything for a long moment. It's not that I find it surprising Gio would look for me, but that even the topic of him brings back a flood of memories. *Feelings* I've tried my damnedest to suppress. A deep craving that's growing by the day.

No worse than in times like these. In the after hours of the night.

"You still there?" Tasha asks.

"Please tell me you didn't tell him anything."

"Of course not. It wasn't a lie anyway. You haven't told me shit."

"Well...if he comes by again, make sure you don't."

"But, wait, what about you? When are you coming back?"

"I have to go, Tash. Thanks for keeping me company."

Before she can protest, I hang up. Calling Tasha is a risk I can never take again.

In the silence, a soft thud echoes from down the hall. I don't move right away, taking another second to make sure I heard the noise. When it sounds again, I flick on the hallway light and peer into the distance.

That's another thing about starting a new life. You hear plenty of bumps in the night.

I go investigate, leaving the safety of my bedroom. The living room is empty, and so is the kitchen. The door is locked. The windows too. Nothing is out of place.

But my spirit is still unsettled. I return to my bedroom and lock that door as well. Worst-case scenario, I have a baseball bat I keep within reach of my bed.

As I slip under the covers, I'm wide awake. Ironically enough, I'm suffering from insomnia just like Gio. Once he's on my mind, I can't stop thinking about him. Lying in the dark, eyes on the ceiling, I wonder what he's doing right now.

Does he miss me? Is he hurt I left him? Or is he unbelievably angry and bitter? Maybe all of the above.

If I ever see him again, there'll be hell to pay. Consequences and punishments. And, yet, my craving only grows stronger. The need for him intensifies until it feels like it'll consume me. A sense of helpless desperation floods through me as I know it's impossible.

I'll probably never see him again.

My core throbs in protest. It's been weeks and the tension down below feels like a female case of blue balls. How do you go from constant mind-blowing sex to nothing at all? I haven't even looked twice at another man since Gio and I'm an exotic dancer.

I slide my hand down the front of my panties. I'm so sensitive, so eager for human touch, as soon as the tips of my fingers graze my folds, I'm flushed. Heat burns across my skin like it's Gio's touch, and I close my eyes to pretend it is. My lips part into a tiny O as I continue, pressing my fingers on the little nub hidden underneath my hood.

A ping of instant pleasure pulses through me. Gio loved teasing me like this, rubbing my clit with the pad of his thumb. He'd stick two of his thick fingers inside me and pump them in and out, alternating in rhythm. As I try to mimic his touch, I clench my eyes shut and a soft moan falls from my lips.

"Ohh…Gio…"

But no one answers me. The touch is my own. The orgasm I'm working toward eludes me. My hand stills on my pussy, and I open my eyes to the dark ceiling.

For a second, it felt so real. But it was only my imagination. Just like last time.

I think I'm going insane.

Club Diamond is similar to the Dollhouse in terms of clientele. It's one of the ritzier gentleman's clubs in the South Beach area. Most of our customers have plenty of cash to blow, which is good news for the girls dancing.

The first night I started at the Dollhouse, I met Tasha, and we became fast friends. I've been at Club Diamond for almost a month now and haven't had nearly as much luck. The girls are cattier, less friendly. I'm the new girl and I'm damn good at what I do, so I get it. Stiffer competition, fewer tips to go around.

But I'll be damned if I let them intimidate me. As I sit in front of the vanity mirror and prep for tonight's performance, I catch the dirty glare a girl named Kylie gives me. I smirk in response, vaguely reminded of Skye at the Dollhouse. I wonder how Skye's doing anyway, and if her attitude is still as stank as ever.

I finish with my lipstick and move on to my wig. I've already gathered my curls under a wig cap. Tonight I'm wearing a long blue-black one with layered waves. The dark shade against my golden complexion makes it pop that much more. New life. New job. New wig?

The smirk on my face spreads as I hear the stage manager call my name. I'm up next. The finishing touch is my heels, which are always a confidence booster. I strut toward the stage as my name is announced through the club.

The men in the audience whistle and cheer. Though shadows fill the club, the special bulbs on stage cast a sparkle-like effect, using some technology designed to mimic diamonds.

As the bass-heavy beat starts up, I grip the pole and twirl around in a basic spin. I'm wearing a nude-colored bra and thong set with jewels sewn into the fabric. It's an illusion I'm already nude, covered in diamonds, before my set even begins.

The beat drops and so do I, falling into a wide middle split. I bounce up and down, isolating cheek movement in my ass. It's a basic stripper move, but it always drives the guys insane. Already bills are being tossed onto the stage. In a fluid motion, I swoop my legs together and push myself up, bottom first.

Hand on the pole, I do a few more spins, and then the real tricks begin. I climb up the pole in another quick motion, flipping upside down with my legs spread. Another sharp whip of my body, and I'm right side up. I arc my knee around the pole, my other leg pointed straight downward, and let my hands go. My body flows around the cool metal pole as fluidly as any liquid.

It's as I slip into my next trick that I spare a fleeting glance at the audience. The club is too dark to make out much except for the number of men filling seats, but the section in the center is what grabs my attention. It's Club Diamond's VIP section, where the highest of high rollers sit.

Déjà vu pours over me as slow and warm as the honey I'm nicknamed after.

I'd recognize him anywhere. Even in the darkest room. Even when *blind*.

Giovanni and his crew are seated in the VIP section. In the center seat, right in the middle like the night I first laid eyes on him, is Gio. With the shadows engulfing the club and cigar smoke hazing the air, his face is obscured, but I *know* it's him. The way he reclines into the leather cushion, his arm relaxed along the back. One leg crossed over his knee. One hand loosely holding a glass of what's probably whiskey. He's strong and broad, taking up as much space as possible with no consideration to anyone else.

The most powerful man in the room. In the world. *My world.*

If I was giving a hundred percent before, I'm giving a thousand now. Desire pulses through my body, taking control of my performance. I hold on to the pole and whip my hair fast to more whistles and catcalls. My hips undulate in rhythm with the dark beat, heavy-lidded gaze set on the audience.

The gentlemen seated don't know who it's for. I can be staring at any one of them. In reality, there's only one man who has my attention. He's the only one I'm dancing for. The only man I crave.

I curl my body along the pole in a flawless figure eight, head tilted so that my hair swings along my back. I don't need a mirror to know the look on my face is pure sex. The guys in the audience all have their eyes unblinkingly on me, on the edge of their seats. Probably hard as hell.

Gio must sense it too. His thick fingers clench around his glass of whiskey. He's *jealous*.

Something about that spurs me on. I dance harder. My body isn't my own as I gyrate and work the stage. Never once do I take my eyes off the man who owns my heart and every other part of me.

There'll be hell to pay tonight, and I can't wait. Because, at this point, any piece of Gio feels like a win.

The music ends and men shower me with more cash. I'm barely paying attention as I sneak another look at the VIP section, the lights as low and the cigar smoke as thick as ever. Part of me wants to jump off the stage and run into his arms.

I resist by the skin of my teeth, strutting off the stage with adrenaline still hot like fire in my veins.

"I made two g's up there just now," Kylie announces in a singsong voice. She breezes into the dressing room and then stops short. Her stink eye is back. "Who's that from?"

I look up from the two dozen roses on my dressing table. I've been sitting here for the last five minutes in awe. I should've known to expect something extravagant from Gio, but the roses surprise me anyway.

Does this mean he's open to reconciliation? Is he no longer pissed?

"Well?" Kylie demands.

I shrug. "I...I don't know. They were here for me after my set."

"You've got a big admirer."

A smile comes to my face. "Yeah, I do."

"Did you bother reading the note?"

That snaps me out of my temporary love spell. I glance at the huge bouquet of roses again and that's when I notice it. Tucked into the vase is a little note card with my name scrawled across the front. I snatch it up and practically tear it open.

"What's it say?" Kylie asks, but I ignore her.

Meet me in the red VIP room in fifteen.

. . .

My heart skips a beat. The red VIP room is on the second floor of the club. Fifteen minutes ago must have dwindled down by now. Especially after I sat here for several minutes in a daze. I jump to my feet and rush out of the room. Kylie calls after me, but I don't have the time or patience to bother listening to a word she says.

I'm on autopilot maneuvering through the club. Twice other customers try to stop me. One of them a guy who has become a regular over the last month. I barely mutter an apology before I keep going, climbing the winding steps upstairs. The thrill is buzzing through me so deeply, I forget to knock when I reach the red VIP room.

I turn the knob and rush straight inside. I stop within a few footsteps. The room is empty. Nobody's here. I turn over the note again and skim the message, making sure I read it properly. Maybe I'm early after all.

That thought is still on my mind when the door swings open. Several men walk in. I whip around with my brows knitting together as I recognize none of them.

Except for two.

Tony Lovato stands as a towering presence in the red VIP room, his dark eyes glittering as he gives me a once-over. At his side, looking sharper in designer threads than I've ever seen him, is Enzo. He grins.

"Hello, Falynn. So glad you decided to join us."

24

Giovanni
PLAYLIST: 🎵 WORST BEHAVIOR - DRAKE 🎵

EVERYBODY WHO MATTERS IS at the Vittoria tonight. The security is tighter. The crowd's bigger. The media coverage is flashier. Fireworks shoot off and dazzle the late evening sky with colorful sparks. We pop open a celebratory champagne bottle, signifying the Vittoria's "cherry" popped a second time. The doors to the main entrance fly open to thunderous applause.

The table games and slot machines are packed within seconds. So are the bars. Those with reservations for La Pergola head toward the upscale restaurant.

I stand on the second-level grand balcony overlooking the main casino floor and watch everyone's movements in the form of dollar signs. That's what it boils down to at the end of the day. Every last customer means more money. More success. More profit.

There's no stopping the Vittoria now. We'll be on our way to one of the highest-grossing resorts and casinos in no time. It'll serve as further proof why *I'm* the rightful successor to Pa's empire. I've rebuilt the Sorrentino name on the west coast by my hand and my hand alone.

Once Lovato is officially out of the way in a few hours, the path will be clear. The west coast belongs to us.

I bring my flute of celebratory champagne to my lips and swallow a small mouthful. The fizzy liquid tastes sweeter on a night like this. The true taste of victory.

Robby approaches on my left. "I'd say it's a pretty good kickoff for it being a reopening."

"Pretty good? It blows the original out the water. You see how many news outlets are here?"

"And police."

"For a reason," I say with a brow raised. "Rodrigo gave us full backing for tonight. There'll be no incidents."

"And no police on the streets."

"Which works in *our* favor. How's the hit for tonight coming along?"

Robby lets a hesitant beat pass. "I'm not so confident we'll get him, Boss."

"I don't like the sound of that, Robby. Are you developing cold feet?"

"It's not that. Don't you think it's too sudden? Lovato's expecting it."

"Says who?"

"How can he not be?"

My gaze cuts over to him, hardened and shrewd. "Have you heard something on the street and not told me?"

"No, Boss. Of course not. You know I would."

"Good. Then give C.J. and the rest the go-ahead," I say coolly, swallowing another sip of champagne. "Lovato goes tonight."

The noise at the roulette table in the high roller's club is enough to pop an eardrum. Everett Johansson tries to compete with the loud noises, leaning closer with his Bengay peppermint stench. He has a piece of spinach in his dentures leftover from dinner at La Pergola, and he doesn't seem to notice the girls a third his age are running his black Amex up, a tab in the thousands.

"Fine job," he rasps with a proud glance around. "Reminds me of when the Sands first did their grand reopening."

My brows jump high as I blow cigar smoke in perfect ringlets. "The Sands, huh? Jesus Christ, Everett, that's a Vegas throwback."

"Nineteen sixty-four."

"My father was still in puberty. How about we stick to the twenty-first century?"

He grins, showing off his spinach leaf. "When you've been around as long as me and your pop, you realize there's nothing new in this world. Take note."

"Don't sell me on how exciting life is all at once, Everett."

"Wouldn't dream of it, sonny boy. Some decades down the line you'll realize old coot Everett Johansson was right. Take that fine piece of female flesh maxing out my black card." He points his gaunt chin in the direction of the bar, where a hot blonde and her friend—both in skimpy thot outfits—toast their latest round of drinks. "You think she's the first bimbo to spend my money like she breathes air? More like there's been so many gold-digging broads, I've lost count! That's what four marriages, countless mistresses, and plenty of hot young things surmount to. They're all the same. I expect nothing less."

I humor Everett with a nod and half of a smirk, hiding

behind more puffs from my cigar. Even a cold bastard like me doesn't have the heart to tell him his existence sounds pitiful as hell. Four marriages are pointless. So are the mistresses and the hot young things after his money. If it's the same result, why keep wasting the energy?

Now for something special, the reward might justify the risk. Otherwise, what's the point?

Falynn floats to mind. Funny how a man's outlook can change. If you asked me even a couple months ago, I probably would've sounded a lot like Everett. But the idea of a carousel of bimbos and gold diggers sounds like hell when I can have heaven.

Everett waves his blonde plaything over. She links arms with her friend and they totter over in their tall stilettos. Both are attractive if the porn star special is your thing—bleach blonde, bright eyes, overly tanned skin and bolt-on tits. Hell, in the past, I probably would've fucked them both to celebrate Vittoria's success.

But as they giggle their hellos, and Everett grins at me, I'm not feeling it. The only pussy I want to sink into is Falynn's. After a taste of the purest honey, I can't go back to the artificial shit. The high spirits I've been feeling from Vittoria's reopening dissipate. Suddenly, the solitude of my office on the top floor calls me.

"I'll see you around, Everett," I say with a nod. He calls after me, but I don't stop and answer. As far as I'm concerned, the celebrations are over.

Robby knocks on my office door and pokes his head inside. "Boss? Do you got a second?"

I grunt from where I'm seated, legs kicked up on my

desk. I've spent the last hour sipping on whiskey, surrounded by a lingering haze of cigar smoke. I've got the security screens up, a panel of television windows that are remote-control operated and reveal themselves when I press the button that slides back the walls.

"You okay?" Robby asks when he gets a look at me.

I'm sure I look a mess. My polished suit and slicked hair are no more. My eyes are red from exhaustion, and I don't need to glance in the mirror to know I'm almost pasty enough to give C.J. a run for his money. As much as I don't want to admit it, these past few weeks I've been deteriorating.

Sure, my cool and calculated mind has returned, but everything else? It's gone to hell. I'm not sleeping. I'm not eating. Not keeping up with my physique. Damn sure not getting any action, which means my balls are about to bust.

All because Falynn is gone. Even if I'll never admit it aloud.

Robby closes the door behind him. "The hit didn't pan out."

I quirk a brow. "You mean, you failed."

"Yes."

"You've been doing that a lot lately, Robby."

"Boss, I tried to tell you Lovato was a step ahead. He wasn't at the location we thought he'd be—turns out he's outta town on business."

"Get the fuck out of my face."

"But, Boss—"

"The only time I'm going to tell you." Cigar puffing smoke, I trail my fingertips over the glock lying on top of my desk.

Robby takes half a step back. I never get to find out if he's trying to play Russian roulette with his life, because in the next second, the door bursts open and C.J. hurries in panting.

"Boss, I ran up here! Lovato is on your main line."

"Lovato?"

C.J. nods, drinking in air. "He's calling from an unknown number. He…he wants to talk to you. He sounds like he's in a good mood."

My harsh glare is still on Robby as I drop my legs and sit up from my reclining position. I pick up my desk phone and press the button for the main line. C.J. wasn't kidding about Lovato being in high spirits. His reedy voice drips with fucking joy.

"Giovanni," he says. "How's the reopening of the Vittoria going?"

"Fuck off, Antonio."

"Still lacking manners, I see. You should really check that."

"Or else, what? Who's going to make me? You?"

"I've never had a problem making you before," Lovato says cockily. "I did make you shut down your casino for a whole extra month, didn't I?"

"What is this? You're calling me to talk shit? You're big and bad now? After you just skipped town like a little bitch?"

I can hear the grin in Lovato's voice. "I didn't leave town because of you, Giovanni. I left town for you."

"Whatever makes a shrimp-dick *stronzo* like you feel better at night. Just know, this isn't over. I'll be waiting for you when you decide to man up and show your face in my city again. You better be sleeping with one eye open."

"Something tells me I'll sleep *very* soundly tonight."

"With a Vienna sausage that small? I doubt it. We're done here."

"Before you go, Giovanni, I have a message to pass." Lovato pauses for a second, dragging it out with pure delight. The muffled sound of a woman's whimper is in the background, but Lovato's cruel laugh drowns it out. "Your girl says hello."

25

Falynn
PLAYLIST: ♪ WAR OF HEARTS - RUELLE ♪

I'M LOST the next time I open my eyes. I'm slumped in a seat in a narrow room with portholes for windows. When I try to move, a seat belt holds me in place. My body feels like it's floating through air, but then it sinks in. I'm not moving, the ground is. The entire room. Blurry vision fading, I glance around again, and then gasp.

I'm on a private jet! Who knows where. And with who…

"Ahh, princess is up," comes Antonio Lovato's fast-talking New Yorker accent. He strolls over holding a glass of what smells sour and lemony like a gin and tonic. "How are you doing, doll? Hope you don't mind we gave you a little…sedative."

As I look up into Lovato's gleaming, lecherous eyes, a shudder runs through my body. I've never felt more like a helpless lamb. He's eyeing me like I'm some slab of meat he's about to devour. It's then that I remember I'm half naked—or was. I jump in my seat, bucking against the seat belt, and my arms fly up to cover myself.

Apparently, as I slept on the flight, someone had

covered me with a thermal blanket. I hike that up my chest, my skin warm with embarrassment.

Lovato's lips twitch into a slightly wider grin. "You can cover up as much as you want, but it's not like it's anything we haven't seen. You put on quite a show up on that stage. Very, very hot."

My face falls into my hands. I can't even begin to make sense of what the hell is going on. The last moments at Club Diamond play in my head. I had gone on stage and saw Gio—at least who I *thought* was Gio—and then danced my ass off. He had sent two dozen roses to my dressing room and invited me to the red VIP room.

But no one had been there…until Lovato showed up.

And Enzo. *Enzo!*

Heart banging hard in my chest, I jerk up and scan the plane. "Enzo! He's here!"

Lovato cackles. "Is that gonna change anything? You think he's your knight in shining armor?"

"What do you want with me?"

The question falls from my lips in a whisper. I don't understand why I'm on Lovato's private jet, or why he was at Club Diamond watching me perform. I met the man once a few weeks ago at the dinner party Gio brought me to. Is this some kind of payback against Gio?

"I got off the phone with your other knight in shining armor," Lovato says, watching me closely for a reaction. "I told him you said hello."

"This is about Gio? You're going to kill me to get back at him?"

"I told him the conditions. If he takes me up on my offer, maybe you'll live."

The breath stalls in my lungs, and I gasp on my next inhale. My eyes are large as I look up into his cruel, amused face. "Please, I don't want anything to do with this—"

"Too late. You should've thought about that before you crawled into bed with my rival." Lovato sneers, raising his gin and tonic for another taste. He rolls his eyes up and down my body again. "But I might have a taste of you myself first. The way you shook that ass tonight." He does a chef's kiss gesture with his free hand, his glee at my fear palpable.

I don't bother dissuading him. He's a piece of shit with his mind made up. There's no use wasting my energy when I can wait for a chance to speak with Enzo. I glance around the cabin of the private jet. It's not as spacious as Gio's, but still luxurious with its plush leather seating and mini bar.

Enzo's huddled in the far end of the cabin with a few of Lovato's other men. As if sensing my gaze on him, he looks up at me. In the two years since I've met Enzo, I've never seen him in tailored clothes let alone any attire considered professional. But standing with Lovato's men, Enzo blends in, wearing a button-down shirt and dress pants when normally he wore sagging jeans and giant ball jerseys. Even his hair has changed. It's tapered and short on the sides.

Another version of me would've been attracted. A past me—the one whose stomach still fluttered when she saw Enzo's square face and dark eyes. Seeing him now, even dressed up, does nothing for me. If anything, my chest tightens with dread as he walks over. I can already tell by his expression, his body language that he isn't on my side.

He waits 'til Lovato is talking with one of his other guys before he addresses me.

"You've got yourself in deep shit now, Fal," he lectures.

I swear under my breath. "Is that what you have to say to me after kidnapping me?!"

"Your boyfriend kidnapped you, didn't he?"

"Ex-boyfriend, and it wasn't like that. But that's beside the point! Enzo…what are you doing? How could you?" My voice breaks off, tears coming fast.

"Don't turn on the waterworks. That shit doesn't work on me anymore."

"You're going to let him kill me?"

Enzo's eyes darken and he snaps forward, grabbing hold of my chin. "Don't expect sympathy now. It only took you a couple months to move onto selling your pussy to the highest bidder. You disgust me, Fal."

"I was doing what I had to do after you left me with *your* mess! Do you think they stopped coming by to collect after you got arrested? You put me in the situation I was in to even think about doing it!"

"Don't bullshit me. It's always been who you are." He eyes me like my presence revolts him to his core. "But I still tried to help you out. I told you to stop fucking around, didn't I? I warned you that night of the shooting. You *chose* to be a dumb bitch and chase after him. You think you would be in deep now if you didn't let him dick you down deep before? The *only* reason Lovato's snatched you is 'cause you're a bargaining chip!"

The heaviness in my chest increases. It feels like an anchor is pressing down on me, making me sound like I'm choking when I try to speak. "I would've never betrayed you, Enzo. I can't believe you're doing this to me."

"I'm no longer just a street guy," he brags, letting go of my chin. He stands up straighter and tugs on the collar of his shirt. "They're inducting me in as a solider. A real part of the crew."

I can't stomach looking at him anymore. I turn my

head, the disgust too overwhelming. As I sit here tearing up, pleading for my life, Enzo is bragging about being inducted into the fucking Lovato crime family. It's such a cruel joke, I can't help wondering if there's any possibility I'm dreaming.

I'm screwed. I'm *dead*.

Lovato will kill me to get a rise out of Gio. Nothing I say or do will change the fact that I'm collateral damage as these men war with each other. After years of hoping, dreaming of a stable life for myself, I'll never get the chance at such happiness. It's already over.

Enzo's still eying me, a bitter glint that lights up his dark brown eyes. "Your only hope, Fal, is your boyfriend shows up and takes the offer."

"Show up where? What offer?"

He sighs as if my questions are an inconvenience. "We're headed back to Vegas. This ends tonight. Either Sorrentino shows up unarmed and alone to La Festa, or you're getting a bullet in the brain."

"What will Lovato do to him if he does show up?"

"It's a surrender, a white flag. The turf war would be over, because it'd be a bullet in *his* brain."

I scoff, a pang of satisfaction hitting me as I taunt him. "You think the Sorrentino family won't retaliate? You kill Gio, you're all dead. His father—"

"Is a breath away from dying. Face it, Fal. You picked the losing side." Enzo moves to walk away, but then stops. "Oh, and don't even bother thinking your boyfriend will show up for you. You abandoned him, remember? Giovanni Sorrentino isn't going to risk his empire for your life." He comes in close, his lips next to my ear. "You mean nothing to him. And to me."

The brutal words sting, but I don't show any emotion. I sit still, forcing my face neutral, and let Enzo stroll off with a cackle. On the inside, I'm a mess. The weight pressing down on my chest has only increased, tight and heavy. My throat burns every time I swallow and the tears keep pressing against my eyeballs for release.

I shudder out an unsteady sigh and glance out the dark porthole window. Never in a million years did I think my life would end like this.

26

Giovanni
PLAYLIST: 🎵 BURN IT DOWN- LINKIN PARK 🎵

"FALYNN."

Her name tumbles past my lips in a shocked whisper. The other line has gone dead. Lovato's hung up, but I haven't moved a muscle, listening to the beep of the dial tone over and over again.

The bastard's got Falynn. I try to process that horrifying revelation, but my brain refuses to cooperate. How in the fuck has he gotten his hands on her? And, more importantly, what is he planning?

Scratch that. I know exactly what he's planning. Falynn is going to be used to destroy me.

Finally, an opponent has out-calculated me. It's a move I didn't see coming. A move that opens the floodgates for a thousand other questions, like how'd Antonio Lovato know things between me and Falynn had been serious?

She's not the first woman I've had on my arm at events. She's one of a million. How could he have guessed she's the only one I'd developed feelings for?

"Boss?" C.J. says nervously. "What now?"

"Go keep watch on the casino floor and await further

orders. Give him a moment." Robby jerks his head in the direction of the hall.

C.J. hovers uncertainly for a second. When I don't say anything to contradict Robby's order, he listens. The door snicks shut and Robby turns to me. I'm so damn out of it, I don't care that he's eyeballing me as I sit at my desk in speechless shock.

If Lovato lays a finger on her…

My hands clench into tight fists. It's only a hint of what's going on inside me—the rage roars to life in my veins. It courses through every part of me 'til it turns me from the calm and collected businessman Mafia king I am to something else altogether. Something not even human anymore.

A beast ready to fucking tear Antonio Lovato limb from limb.

Robby waits by the window, looking out the glass as the Strip sparkles in the night. He's patient enough to give me several minutes before putting out some feelers.

"We can't let him get to us."

The words pierce the silence out of nowhere. At first I'm certain they weren't even said at all. Then I glance over to the window and find Robby staring expectantly back, his face pale with a ghostly glow that's almost feverish. There's a new look in his dark eyes, a certainty what he says is the only answer.

My brow furrows. "You picked a dangerous time to start telling jokes."

"Boss, I'm serious. Lovato's got the girl because he wants to force your hand. But if you don't give in to the threat, then there's nothing for him to dangle. It's no longer the trump card he thinks it is."

"And Falynn?"

"None of our concern."

The anger coursing through me explodes. With a rumble louder than thunder, in a raw flex of power, I rise up and flip my executive desk over. The large hunk of luxury wood crashes down and shakes the floor. The laptop, landline phone, paperweight, and all the other useless shit on top tumbles right beside it, broken into pieces. I don't stop there, tearing down the gigantic Las Vegas canvas hanging on the wall behind me. It rips in half over my bent knee, and then I fling the halves across the room. One nearly hits Robby, but he ducks.

I come out from the wreckage I've caused and barrel toward him in a couple short, quick steps. He flinches as I close in, assuming I'm about to deck him. It's a good instinctual reaction—my fists itch to break his face for even suggesting what he has.

I hold back, my gaze dark. Our faces are almost close enough to touch. "Falynn," I say in my lowest, scarily calm tone, "is my biggest concern. Don't you ever fucking suggest otherwise."

He hesitates so long, I assume he's dropping it. He's weighed the pros and cons and decided it's not worth incurring my wrath. Particularly when the two of us stand a foot away from a giant window eight stories high. But, for the second time tonight, I've miscalculated.

"She *left* you," he says after his pause. He speaks the simple sentence plainly, like he's stating the fucking weather, telling me there's seventy percent chance of rain. "What I'm saying is, Boss, she made her choice. Now she's gotta deal with the consequen—"

My fist connects with Robby's nose. The crunch of bone is a satisfying sound to my ears given how livid I am. Blood spurts from his nostrils and he stumbles back, banging into the glass wall. It's not like that ugly, hooked schnoz of his was ever a prize. I'm doing him a favor.

No mercy.

I don't stop there, snatching him up by the shirt collar and dragging him toward me like he weighs nothing. "How many warnings have I given you? What did I tell you about speaking about her? Yet you continue to defy me. What's not sticking for you? Do I need to smash your fucking head through the window? Will that make you understand?"

Robby coughs up some blood. A few droplets spray onto the front of my Dolce & Gabbana dress shirt. But I only shake him some more, producing a rattling noise from his loose teeth. He spits one of those up too. The brutal impact of my fist is undeniable. The swelling starts up immediately along the center of his face, his nose more of a disaster than even his worst day.

I release him and move away for his own sake. If I hold on to him another second, I'm swinging again. I'm using him as a punching bag, as an outlet for the rage destroying me from the inside out. With my back to him, I force a couple hard breaths into my lungs.

"Get the fuck out," I pant. "Now. I don't want to see you for the rest of the week."

"Boss—"

"WE'RE DONE HERE!"

I expect the sound of his feet plodding as he scrambles to go. But Robby doesn't move an inch. He stays where he is, dripping blood on the carpet. He wipes the mess up with his shirtsleeve to no avail. His nose is too much of a leaky faucet. Then he laughs.

The fucker *laughs*.

My head snaps in his direction, my eyes narrowed. I don't know what to make of it. If Robby's gone off his rocker. Maybe I've knocked some screws loose in that brain of his. He must be delirious, out of his fucking mind if he thinks—

"This," he says, spitting more blood, "is why you'll lose."

"What did you just say?"

The left corner of his lip rises in a nasty grin, exposing his bloodstained teeth. "You don't even realize it's already over. You've *already* lost."

The boldness behind his statement is so unexpected, my anger is on hold. It gives way for the shock rippling through me. I take a step closer, staring at him with eyes narrowing further and further into slits.

"What are you talking about, Robby?"

As I step toward him, he steps backward. But he does so with a cavalier air, like he knows even if I fuck him up, it doesn't change the bigger picture. Which is…

I stop in my tracks, my fists dropping to my sides. "You're the rat."

"Such an ugly word."

"You're an ugly son of a bitch. It fits."

Robby sputters another bloody laugh. "Boss, don't do me like that. I've given you how many years of service? I've pledged my life to you."

The shock fades and anger returns in another burning flash. I advance, but he retreats like the bitch *stronzo* he is, putting a sofa between us. A grin curls onto my lips as my gaze darkens, tracking him and his movements.

"Oh, so you're going to make me chase you down like game. That fits too."

"You know what else fits? That you've allowed some stripper to ruin your empire," he goads. "Some stupid bitch who has you pussy-whipped is your downfall! Another Sorrentino fuck-up for the history books! Just like your father."

"Sounding bitter, Robby. This about your father never being chosen by Don Grimaldi?"

"If he was, things would've been different. The family would've been prospering. We would've already had our empire established in every corner of the country. We wouldn't be playing catch-up to the fucking Lovatos like you and your incompetent father."

"Careful, or I might have to break more of your teeth. You haven't learned your lesson about talking shit."

"Keep reacting in anger, Gio. That's gotten you far!" He rounds another corner of the sofa as I stalk closer, putting more distance between us. "I used to think you were going to be different than your father—a smarter, more logical boss over the family. But you've done nothing but prove the opposite. So deep in stripper pussy you didn't even see the signs."

"You told Lovato about the hit tonight. You gave warning."

"I didn't just give warning. I sabotaged our crew when we tried to carry it out."

Anger grips me tighter, suffocating me. I trek closer, waiting for the right moment. "And the night of the opening. You helped Lovato's guys infiltrate the casino."

"I'm surprised you didn't notice. Your right hand constantly slipping up like that? But you weren't even suspicious."

"You were supposed to keep an eye on Falynn."

Robby laughs. "The girl's not worth my time, Gio. The only use she has is to fuck with you. Which I did when I convinced her to leave you."

Even in my burning-hot anger, a cold draft blows through my heart. I can't even imagine what he told her to get her to go. I grit my teeth and growl, "What the fuck did you say?"

"I may have embellished a little. I told her she was on

borrowed time. That you suspected she was a traitor. That you or your father would ax her in due time."

My mind jumps back to our last night together. Falynn had been convinced I was angry with her—and I was after my talk with Pa. But the way she had provoked me, shoved me, and yelled as if desperate for any clues as to how I felt, she had been at her wit's end, grasping at straws for a reason to stay.

I hadn't given her one. Instead I had fucked her, convinced I was taking out my aggression, and then I had turned my back to her. No wonder she left in the middle of the night. She probably thought she had no other choice.

I snap back to the present with a howl of fury. I launch myself across the couch, spearing into Robby at full speed. Our bodies are airborne for a brief second as we soar across the room. We land with a crash against the glass entertainment center. Shards go flying in every direction, but we're too busy wrestling for control.

For being a gangly sack of bones with a broken nose, Robby's got fight in him. I admit to underestimating him as we grapple, and he proves to be slippery and limber as fuck. More than once he escapes my hold, forcing me to lock my arm around his throat in a chokehold.

"You fucking dipshit. You were supposed to be my right hand…my best friend!"

He grunts struggling against my stronghold. Blood is everywhere. His. Mine. We're stumbling over shards from the broken entertainment center. He manages to get his fingers wrapped around a jagged piece and jams it into my thigh.

I roar in answer, losing part of my footing. Arm still clenched around his neck, I bring him along with me as I collide with the wall.

"I was your right hand! Your best friend!" he spits.

"Then you got stupid! Why play for the losing team when I can win?"

"You think Lovato'll have you after you've proved you're a rat?"

He juts his pointy elbow into my stomach, finding nothing but hard-packed muscle. "He promised me power! My own crew on this coast! My own operation! More than you've ever given me!"

"And you call me a dumb fuck, dumb fuck!" I let go of his neck and swing another fist, knuckles banging into his chin in an uppercut. He sails backward, landing like a crash test dummy. I'm on him straightaway, throwing out left and right hooks, beating his bloody face in.

I almost notice his retaliation a second too late. His arm splays out at his side, stretching for something under the shards of glass. The gun that had been on my desk had knocked to the floor along with everything else. His fingers wrap around the handle and then the trigger. He moves his arm to turn the barrel toward me, but I've already grabbed the first item within reach.

As Robby's finger shifts to pull the trigger, I slice his throat with the shard of glass that was once lodged in my thigh. Blood spurts everywhere, spraying my face. Even my mouth. Robby goes still, his eyes open wide, the gun clattering onto the floor.

For a long time, I don't move. I've killed many times before. But taking the life of your best friend is another level. It takes something deeper out of you, leaving unsettled nerves in the aftermath. I struggle to catch my breath as reality sinks in. Robby was the rat. Robby's now dead. *I killed him.*

And Falynn needs me.

The door bangs open and Louis huffs and puffs

running inside. Horror strikes his face as he surveys the rubble.

"I heard glass breaking from the level below and came as fast as I could. What in the hell, Boss? Robby's...dead?"

"Robby was the rat." I rise onto legs that aren't so steady. I walk it out, tearing off my shirt and using it to wipe blood from my face. "He gave me no other choice. Have Fozzi dispose of him."

"Robby...the rat..." Louis mutters in shock. He shakes his head and swears under his breath.

"We've got no time to waste. Lovato knew about the hit. Robby told him. He called earlier and wants me to meet him at La Festa in," I say, glancing at my watch, "twenty minutes. I've got no choice. He's got Falynn."

"Kid sister?" Louis's shock vanishes, replaced with outrage. He gestures to the guns in his holster. "What are we waiting for? We've got a casino to crash!"

"I'm supposed to go alone, but can I count on you and the others to provide backup?"

"Boss, I'm ready to go in guns blazing myself if Miss Falynn's in trouble."

"Good. Call my pilot, tell him we're doing the chopper tonight. Grab Dominico. We're going to need his marksmen skills."

I mop more blood from my face and then check on the stab wound in my thigh. Luckily, the glass didn't go too deep. I clean it as best as I can and discard the damp, stained shirt. Louis and I fall into step with each other as we stride out the office, and I shoot him a sideways glance. "Louis?"

"Yeah, Boss?"

"Sorry I called you fat a few weeks ago."

Louis grins. "Enjoy it while you can. Next month, I'm doing Weight Watchers."

27

Falynn
PLAYLIST: 🎵 27 HOURS - BANKS 🎵

"YOU HAVE TWO OPTIONS," Antonio Lovato says, his lecherous grin spread wide. "Option one, I blow you away with a bullet in the brain."

My breath catches in my throat and I try to move back, but the henchman holding me only digs his nasty fingers deeper into my arms, pinching my skin.

"Option two, you blow me with that pretty mouth of yours."

His men break out into grunts of laughter. Except for Enzo. He hasn't taken his eyes off me, but his face is a blank slate, lacking even a hint of emotion.

We've been standing on the rooftop of La Festa for the last fifteen minutes. Gio's deadline has come and gone. The desert winds have blown through, powerful in the October night, with nothing but a flat landscape to cross.

The cool air forces a shiver out of me. It glides over my skin and makes me numb. A part of me is grateful. The number I am, the less pain stabs at my heart. At least I can stand here and feel nothing, as the man I've fallen for doesn't show up. The sinking realization that he's left me to die…

But can I blame him? I knew from the get-go nothing matters more to Gio than the Sorrentino crime empire. He'd kill his own family if it meant he ascends the throne and wears the crown. His *blood*.

Me? I'm just the toy who entertained him for a few weeks.

It was never serious on his part.

Damn. I had really let myself fall hard for him. Rule number one in the sex worker handbook: never fall for your client. Definitely never fall harder than he falls for you.

Yet the only thing I've done, even over the last few weeks we've been apart, is fantasize about Gio. Remember his touch and the rare smiles. The way he studies me and makes me feel safe. Even the dumb things like how the first thing he does when coming home is take off his watch, or how he teases me when he calls me Honey.

The wind is no longer enough to keep me numb. My heart shatters into a million pieces as I stand there with Lovato and his men, and a few tears trickle to freedom. Lovato being the cruel asshole he is uses it as more ammo against me.

"Never had one cry *before* they blow me and gag on my dick. Why am I more turned on at the thought?" Lovato cackles, grabbing his junk.

The crude joke wrenches me out of my pit of despair. My gaze chills as I shoot him my coldest glare, captive or not. "Fuck you."

"Yeah, honey, that's sorta the idea. I fuck that pouty little mouth."

"I'd rather walk barefoot on glass."

The laugh ringing through his crew drops off. Everyone's face hardens up as they await his reaction. Lovato doesn't move, staring at me with more interest than he has all night.

"You got some spice to you, eh? No wonder Giovanni's smitten. But, unfortunately, an ultimatum is an ultimatum. Your man didn't show. Which means if you're not gonna get down on those knees, then there's no use for you." Lovato reaches into the inside of his suit jacket and withdraws a loaded gun as casually as someone reaching for a wallet. He aims the pistol at me and says, "Shame, I've gotta do it. You are a looker. But *così è la vita*—such is life. *Arrivederci*, gorgeous."

I clench my eyes shut and flinch in the henchman's arms, bracing myself for the bang of a gunshot and my last moments of life.

Instead, something else happens.

"NO!" Enzo screams at the last second as Lovato moves to pull the trigger.

Shock cascades over me, paralyzing me to the spot. I don't even open my eyes for the first few seconds after Enzo's interruption. It feels too unreal, like I should already have a bullet hole in me, halfway dying.

Lovato's caught equally off guard. He holds the pistol skyward and cocks his head in Enzo's direction. "No, what, Lorenzo? Speak your fucking mind, rookie."

Everyone's attention falls onto Enzo. He falters for half a second, as if losing his nerve, but then he steps forward with his chest puffed out and a stiff expression on his face.

"Well?" Lovato prompts.

"Sorrentino's too pussy to show. But what if she had another use?"

Lovato glances over at me, salacious glint alive again. "I already told her what other use she has."

"She's a dancer. A good one. You saw her tonight. Think about how many stacks she can make you."

"I have plenty of dancers."

"She can make you money with other services on the side. What do you think she was up to at the Dollhouse?"

Lies. I shift my glare to Enzo as he spins this story on the spot. Enzo knows I've never escorted when I worked at the Dollhouse. Even if we barely had enough to pay our bills and he fell in deep with the loan sharks; I hadn't gotten desperate 'til he was locked up and I was alone. Cue that night I witnessed Gio's men disposing of Jerry's dead body.

But Lovato doesn't know that. He slowly smirks. "This is your ex girl, is that right?"

Enzo nods. "My main bitch. She made me a lot of money doing what she did."

Huh? Wait, is he insinuating he was my pimp?! Outrage erupts through my body and I struggle against the henchman still holding me in his viselike grip. I'm about to curse Enzo out for not only lying about my past, but offering me up for sexual services when Lovato decides without me.

He shakes his head. "I'm not convinced. You think I don't know you're playing Captain Save-a-Hoe, rookie? I let you into my crew and this is how you repay me? Fellas."

It's all he has to say before four of his guys flip on Enzo. They circle him, blocking off any means of an exit. Enzo tries to push through one of them, but they shove him back into the center and then the hits start. They knock Enzo to the ground, punching and kicking him without mercy.

Lovato watches, at first entertained by the flying fists and pained groans. Eventually, he grows bored and turns his back on the beating, redirecting his attention onto me.

I'm still preoccupied with Enzo lying on the rooftop being stomped on. It doesn't feel good to see him jumped by a group of guys, but I can't bring myself to scream for him. Even protest or fight against the henchman's clutches. The betrayal burns too deeply at this point. Enzo is partially at fault for why I'm being held captive by Lovato; he sold me and our relationship out for a taste of power. How can I ever forgive him?

"All right, enough horsing around. Time for you to bite the bullet, honey." He moves to aim his pistol at me again, but he's interrupted a second time.

A sudden and severe blast of wind blows through. It takes us only a split second to realize what's the cause—from far above our heads descends an unmarked, black helicopter. Its blades spin in dizzyingly fast circles as the chopper eclipses us.

My heart stills in my chest. It can't possibly be who I think it is…

A henchman standing over Enzo drops to the ground. He's dead before he even realizes it. Another guy, this time one right beside Lovato, is picked off with a bullet landing clean in his neck. He hits the ground as a limp body spurting blood. Lovato jumps back as if it's him who was shot.

"What are you waiting for? Return fire!" he shouts.

But it's too late. Two more of the men beating Enzo are taken out. The guard at the door to the rooftop is next. I'm snapping my head left and right, watching the men drop like flies when a gust of strong air zips past me. The nasty fingernails digging holes into my skin loosen and the henchman gripping me flops backward with a hard thud.

I scream and throw my arms over my head as I realize what's just happened. The sniper fired a bullet within inches of me and landed his shot. If he hadn't been exactly on point…

My stomach roils at the sheer insanity of it. Before I can process what to do next, Lovato's diving for me. He latches on to me, stretching as much of my smaller form in front of him. He's using me as a human shield!

I fight against him, but as usual, I can't overpower him, no matter how hard I try. I buck my head back and attempt to stomp on his feet. Even go for his groin area. Lovato holds me tight and starts sidestepping toward the door leading inside. His ragged breath blows onto the side of my face and bile rises inside me.

The helicopter touches the rooftop at last, its blades still spinning. Dominico sits near the edge of the open side door with a sniper rifle, his eye pressed into the scope. At his side is Gio. A wave of relief washes over me, leaving me lightheaded as soon as I see him. He hops out of the open side door, more fearsome and deadly than I've ever seen him look. His broad and powerful build automatically dominates the rooftop, his face hardened into a murderous rage.

"Shoot me and you shoot the girl!" Lovato shouts, a nervous tremor in his throat. He jabs his pistol into my temple. "You kill me, you kill her! I'll do it. I'll pull the mother fucking trigger."

His warning seems to work. Gio motions for Dominico to lower his rifle, but he never takes his eyes off of us.

"This is already over," he says, his voice a barely contained growl. "You won't be making it out of tonight alive. Your casino is being infiltrated as we speak by my men. Let Falynn go and we'll handle this the way it should be—one on one."

"You've cheated, Giovanni," Lovato huffs as he backs us toward the door leading inside. His fingers dig so hard into my flesh I'm sure he's breaking skin. "You were supposed to show up alone. Instead, you've come in a chopper with some sniper? You've killed several of my guys? Well, go ahead and shoot me if you want! Your girl's dead."

"LET HER GO!" Gio barks. The last of his self-control shatters as he whips out his gun and aims it directly at us.

Lovato spits out a laugh. "I don't think so. You wouldn't risk it…or you would've already had your sniper guy take me out. What's wrong? Do you actually care about this girl? Funny how that means I'm the one really in control, doesn't it?" He hugs me close, pressing his cheek against mine from behind. "Why don't me and you go have some private time, eh, gorgeous? You owe me that blowjob. If your boyfriend follows, you die."

He backs us the rest of the way to the door. I can't stop my body from shaking or tears from wetting my eyes. Gio is so close and yet so far. What if this really is the last time I'll see him? I haven't even gotten a chance to say a word to him, tell him how much I've missed him.

We step through the doorway into the stairwell. Lovato waits for the door to swing shut behind us before he unwraps his arm from my middle. He grabs my hand instead and makes a run for it. I scream and twist and fight to rip myself away from his hold, but he only yanks me harder.

"Keep up!" he snarls. "Soon as I alert the rest of my guys, your boyfriend's done and so are you!"

After stumbling down two staircases, he shoves a door open on a landing. We rush through some kind of private dimly lit corridor before I realize we're making our way back into the casino portion of La Festa.

The familiar ringing sounds of the casino reach my

ears. Lovato pivots around another corner and then clambers to an abrupt stop. Lying face down on the floor in a pool of his own blood is another one of Lovato's guys. He's directly in the path to the last door in the corridor.

"FUCK!" Lovato screams. "He's taking out all my guys!"

In an unmistakable act of panic, Lovato flees for the stairwell again. The last thing he expects is to rush onto the landing and encounter Gio on a staircase two flights above us.

"FUCK!" he yells again. He aims his pistol upward and opens fire, missing both shots.

"GIO!" I scream before I'm whisked off once more like a rag doll. I throw a panicked glance over my shoulder in time to see Gio leaping down rows of stairs.

Lovato only pushes us faster. We tumble down the steps and then launch ourselves down the next set. Gio's thunderous footsteps echo only a flight above us as he closes Lovato's lead.

If this comes down to pure physicality, Lovato's toast. Gio's faster, stronger, and hungrier. He knows this, which is why he twists around and fires some more warning shots.

When we reach the next landing, we escape through the door. We stumble onto the main casino floor, surrounded by patrons running in every direction. We're standing in the middle of a mob shootout.

Gunfire cracks, and the abrasive sound vibrates right through me. I'm so lost in the chaos, my brain can't process the danger. The bullets whizzing by and the horrified chorus of screams are too much all at once.

Lovato drags us deeper into the chaos. The game tables blur. People stampede by. At some point, I squeeze my eyes shut and run blind. I don't know what's going on 'til we flounder our way across concrete and into the casino parking lot.

"Keys!" Lovato roars before he shoots a man next to an SUV. The man crumples over, his arm flopping to his side.

Lovato snatches the keys and shoves me across the driver's side. I'm struggling to untwist myself in the passenger seat as he starts the engine and swings out of the parking space.

He slams the gas. The SUV's tires screech. We shoot forward as Gio bursts through the doors leading into the parking garage. I stick my arms out the window to flag him down and alert him to our vehicle speeding off. "GIO!"

"Shut the fuck up!"

Lovato's open palm collides with my cheek. He digs his fingers into my hair and yanks my head back. He steers with his other arm, spinning the wheel hard. The SUV crashes onto Las Vegas Boulevard and nearly collides with a taxi driving by.

Something inside me snaps. I've had enough of men putting their hands on me in recent weeks. His smack is one too many.

I claw at his face without care that he's driving.

"Bitch!" he screams, trying to pull his face away from me. He loses control of the wheel while fighting me off.

The SUV slides between lanes, cutting off cars. We jump a construction barricade separating the two sides of traffic. Horns blare as we veer toward cars speeding the opposite way.

Lovato's fist connects with my brow. The hit's hard enough to get me off him as I fall back into my seat and pain explodes on my face. He clasps both hands on the wheel and weaves against the blinding headlights of oncoming cars.

"You stupid bitch, you're gonna get us killed!"

I'm still reeling from his hit. Slumped in the passenger seat, my face throbs as I squint out the window at the city lights whizzing by.

"The asshole's following us!" Lovato exclaims, checking the rearview. His voice shakes with mingled horror and shock. "He's cutting through traffic!"

I gather every ounce of strength I have to push myself up in the seat and look behind us.

Lovato's right.

A black sports car speeds toward us, weaving wildly between lanes. I recognize the driving immediately—it's Gio showcasing more of his reckless speed demon skills. He's gaining on us by the second.

Lovato spins the SUV around another street corner and narrowly misses a group of tourists crossing the street on their way to the old Strip. Their terrified screams trail behind us even after we're gone.

We jump onto the next freeway entrance, so close to the side railing, the SUV doors spark against the metal.

I'm beyond terror at this point. My heart's speeding as fast as we're driving and I'm cold with sweat, but it's impossible to pinpoint what's causing these reactions—every moment of the last hour has been equally traumatizing and dangerous.

Gio fires at our tires. The first two shots are misses. The third lands on our back left. Lovato releases a string of cuss words and struggles with the wheel as we ascend the freeway on-ramp.

He doesn't recover in time. He slams the brakes, but it's too late to slow our momentum. We veer straight into a row of orange construction barrels. The barrels roll over and under the SUV. We jerk inside as the tires crush the barrels below. The ones on top smash the windshield and dent the roof above.

Finally, we come to an abrupt stop on the shoulder of the freeway. Smoke plumes from the engine and glass shards cover the dash and our seats. I have several nicks and scrapes and my neck hurts from the whiplash movements of the SUV.

Lovato's worse off. He's caught glass in his face and he's banged up his knee in the collision. An agonized grunt leaves him as he picks a shard from his cheek.

"Get out of the car, Antonio. It's over!" comes Gio's commanding voice.

An uncertain second passes by in which distant sirens and the soughing wind are the only sounds playing.

Lovato snatches me up by a fistful of hair and drags me out of the SUV with him. I'm back to being a shield. His hot and rancid breath blows on me once more and I turn my head away in disgust.

The first chance I get, I'm kneeing him in the balls.

We sway on the spot as he holds me intimately to his body. "I've already told you. I'm not going down alone. We're all in this deathtrap together. So go ahead and shoot —I'm blowing your girl's brains out."

I twist in his hold, but his arm merely tightens around me.

Gio aims his gun at Lovato, his hand as steady as a surgeon. "This is between me and you, Antonio. Face me like a man."

"Keep the manhood bullshit for your fragile ego. I don't need to fight fair to feel like a man. I'm a mother fucking king." His arm travels up my body and curls around my neck. His nasty smile returns. "See, this? This is what kings do—crush skulls and snap necks. Even pretty ones."

"Get your fucking hands off her," Gio warns, edging closer with his gun still drawn.

"I'd hate to snap it, but this is war, Giovanni. Who ever heard of playing fair?" A sick laugh rumbles out of him. He motions to Gio's gun with his own. "Put it down and kick it toward me or I kill her right now."

Gio hesitates, a long and drawn out moment passing. He complies and drops his gun, giving it a kick with his shoe. It skids across the tarmac in our direction.

"Good," Lovato says. "Now put your hands up on your head. No funny movements or she's dead."

I can't take another second of this. I'm tired of struggling in his hold and watching on as he uses me as a bargaining chip. It's time to finally make a move.

I stomp my foot down on Lovato's and snap my head back. My skull collides hard with his chin and earns a pained howl out of him. The fight worsens from there. He backhands me with zero hesitation, sharp pain smarting across my cheek.

Gio rams into him and knocks him back into the side of the SUV. I stagger out of the way and fall hard to the ground.

All pretenses are abandoned. They grapple against the car, throwing and dodging punches.

My heart booms in my chest as I watch helplessly on the sidelines. I'm halfway considering trying to break them up, but the pistol lying feet away catches my eye. It's Lovato's gun that he dropped when Gio speared into him.

I glance back at them and then rush over, picking up the sleek metal weapon in my hands and straightening my arms in front of me. As Gio and Lovato thrash like two titans, I know I have to do something.

Lovato gains an advantage, jerking his elbow into Gio's face. Gio stumbles and loses balance. Before he can push himself back up, Lovato kicks him hard in his side. He erupts in the same cruel laughter that's become agonizingly familiar to me tonight. I can't stand another second. I can't let him hurt Gio or get away with this.

My finger curls around the trigger, and I squeeze hard. The pistol bangs and my wrists snap back painfully. The bullet drives into the center of Lovato's spine. His scream is bloodcurdling as he staggers aimlessly. I squeeze the trigger again. The second bullet hits him in the back of his shoulder. The third on the side of his neck. He slumps over, folding into himself in a thickening pool of blood. The laughter's still on his face the second his eyes go cold and he dies.

I'm shaking, my grip tight on the pistol. I've never shot anyone before, let alone killed anyone. My breath leaves my lungs in sharp gasps as I stare wide-eyed at his dead body.

Gio spits a mouthful of blood out, steps over Lovato's body, and deftly slides the pistol from my hands. He stows it in the holster strapped to his waist and then pulls off his jacket, wrapping it around me. His lips touch my brow.

"Let's get out of here," he whispers into my skin. "My guys and the cops Rodrigo's sending should show up any second to handle the mess."

28

Giovanni
PLAYLIST: ♪ WORSHIP - AMBER RUN ♪

THE WAR IS WON.

The sun rises above the distant mountain skyline, bathing Vegas's desert landscape in golden warmth. I watch from the giant window of my penthouse suite at the Vittoria. Still dressed in last night's clothes, shirt stained with blood and dust, I can't help but allow for a rare smile.

Dawn means a new day is here. A new era for not only myself, but for the Sorrentino family, and for Las Vegas. I'm the new king looking down on the town I rule over. Today the city of sin. Tomorrow the rest of the world.

There's much to be done. Now that the Vittoria is operating in full swing, it's time to move in on Lovato's territory. With him dead, his soldiers are bound to scurry back to the east coast, running home to Don Lovato to lick their wounds. But it's the street guys who'll be up for grabs —the guys like Falynn's ex, Lorenzo, whose loyalty depends on the best offer made.

As for Lorenzo Espinosa himself, I made sure C.J. knew he was to survive last night's confrontation. I have separate plans for him—plans I've kept from Falynn in case the urge for mercy strikes her. No man puts his hands on my woman and keeps all ten fingers.

A knock on the door interrupts my thoughts. I glance in the bedroom, checking if Falynn is still asleep, and then cross the suite to the door. Louis stands on the other side with a cart of breakfast. I press a finger to my lips and let him inside.

"I figured she'd still be asleep," he says in a low tone. "But it'll be nice to wake up to breakfast."

"She'll be up soon enough. Then she'll eat everything on that cart." I move over to the door adjoining the bedroom with the rest of the penthouse and draw it to a gentle close. Falynn's been through hell over the past twenty-four hours. She needs as much rest as humanly possible.

As if reading my mind, Louis folds his gorilla arms over his chest and asks, "Boss, have you gotten a wink of sleep?"

No.

In the weeks of Falynn's absence, I have returned to my insomniac ways. I've been making due with two or three hours at most. With everything that went down last night, I can't power off my brain even if I want to. Even Falynn in my bed can't put me to rest right now. My brain's too alert, too overactive with a million thoughts about my growing empire, Lovato's downfall, and what this means for the future.

"You should get some rest. Take the day off," Louis says.

"I have an empire to run. You think I get days off from that?"

"Just saying. A chill day lounging by the pool with your lady sounds good, doesn't it?"

Like heaven.

Falynn and I haven't had any time alone. She barely spoke to me last night before she collapsed in the bed.

I think she's traumatized. Not that I can blame her. For the second time in two months, she was kidnapped by a mobster. Though seeing how she trembled, something tells me Lovato had been a lot less considerate and a lot more cruel than I had been. He had been seconds away from killing her. And when push came to shove, and the opportunity presented itself, Falynn had killed him. She's never taken a life before.

For someone as pure as she is, I worry it's darkened her soul. Being with me *will* darken her soul.

I'm a *capo* in one of the world's most powerful crime families. If we're to be together, danger and darkness will always be a part of our lives. It's part of the sacrifice you make for a position of absolute power. Can Falynn be happy in my world? Can she even survive it?

My mother had taken a gamble, and she hadn't lived to win that bet. She paid the price for it being with my father. In turn, her passing left two young boys—me and Giancarlo—motherless and closed off to emotion. I'd been sure any relationship I have would mimic my parents, because what other possibility is there in this lifestyle?

But I've learned it can be different with Falynn. I can have her and rule the throne I was born to inherit. I can have it all.

My phone goes off in the breast pocket of my shirt. The dried blood and gunk from last night have left it looking a mess. I really should light it on fire and toss it. Also, shower. I need one badly.

"Hello," I say, bringing the phone to my ear.

"Son," wheezes Papa, "you have been a busy man."

I meet Louis's eye. He stares back with his brows hiked up. He knows who it is and that this call is important.

We're either going to find out our actions last night were approved of, or that we've seriously fucked up. It's not lost on me that any developments on the west coast have repercussions for the east coast. The Lovatos are still power players in New York and Jersey.

"I take it you heard."

"How could I not? Coast to coast, the streets are talking."

"You know that from your nursing facility?" I add a humorous tint to the words, hoping it'll lighten the vibe of the conversation.

"A smart old man knows there's value to the streets regardless of his age or location," Pa says wisely. "Besides, you know you *cazzos* made the national news? Rodrigo put quite the spin on the situation. The La Festa shootout has been blamed on a street gang. Very risky moves you made last night."

Here it comes. The tongue-lashing. The blame game. The profanity-filled rant. I roll my eyes toward the giant window, where the sun has finished rising and hangs high in the sky.

"It was messy. Too messy, Giovanni."

"Pa, what choice—"

"But effective," he finishes throatily. "You eliminated the Lovatos' operation on the west coast. It'll take them a long time to rebuild."

"And in that time, we'll grow stronger."

I can hear Pa's cracked lips breaking into a small smile. "You're thinking long-term strategy. You'll need to keep that up for the war."

"War?"

"You may have won a battle in Vegas, but you've murdered Vincent Lovato's only son. The war's only just beginning. Prepare for it to be a long one."

My grip on my iPhone tightens. "Are you saying…"

"It's you, Giovanni. It's always been you. But I had to test you. I had to make sure you wanted it. I sent you to Vegas in hopes you'd do what I did fifty years ago and conquer the town. You've done it even faster than I ever did," he explains. Phlegm catches in his throat and he dissolves into a fit of coughing.

"Pa, slow down on your words. Are you okay?"

For a couple seconds, there's rustling sounds over the phone, and then what sounds like the gulp of a drink being taken. He returns to the phone with his voice slightly raspier, but recovered from his coughs.

"I'm not okay, Giovanni. That's why you must know this now. That you are to lead the family in my death."

The news is what I've spent my whole life working toward, but hearing it from Pa himself shocks me to the core. I stop in place and stare out the window, not really paying attention to the mountain skyline. Instead I'm in my head, with another million thoughts filling it up. This really is real—I'm going to be the next Don Sorrentino.

"It's an honor to be chosen to uphold our legacy, Papa."

"Don't thank me. Make it count, Giovanni."

When we hang up, the shock still pings through my body. Louis hasn't taken his eyes off me.

"Did he just…" He cuts himself off mid-sentence.

I tuck my phone back into my pocket and nod. "It's me."

"I knew it! Some of the guys weren't so sure between you and Giancarlo, but I always knew it'd be you."

"But my father's right when he says this is only the beginning. The Lovatos won't react well to what's happened."

"All the more reason you need today off," Louis says.

He chuckles at the skeptical look on my face. "Boss, don't you think you're gonna regret it later when you're head honcho, knee-deep in business? Better take some time off now."

He's right. After everything that's happened over the past couple of months, and with the revelation I am succeeding Pa, a small break is needed. If not for relaxation purposes, for the sake of my overall sanity.

And for Falynn. A slow smile spreads onto my lips. "*Lou*," I say, "maybe you're right."

Falynn moans seconds before waking up. Her eyes flutter open and she half rolls for a glance around the room. I'm sitting on the edge of the bed stroking my fingers through her curls. Last night when we returned to the penthouse, she'd stripped off a provocative outfit I assume was from her performance at a club and then collapsed naked in bed.

She does this thing where she wraps herself in the sheets like a burrito. The first time I saw her do it, I was baffled, but sitting here now, watching her eyes light with comprehension, I'm taken with these little quirks of hers. I brush more curls away from her face and drop a kiss on her brow.

"You're finally awake."

She squints. "It's not even morning anymore, is it?"

"A few minutes before noon."

"I could've slept through an atomic bomb."

"I believe you. You barely made it to the bed."

She lifts her arm and smells her armpit in typical Falynn fashion. "Gross. I need a shower. I need to wash off all of last night's dirt and blood…" She shudders.

"You and I both. It's been a long twenty-four hours."

"Gio…" The sheet loosens as she sits up and curls her legs. She doesn't meet my eyes, choosing to stare at the thread count in the sheet. "I really thought I was going to die. I…I really thought you weren't showing up."

"Hey," I say, tilting her chin up. Our eyes connect for the first time in a long time, sending my heartbeat into a frenzy. Falynn's expressive eyes always make my chest radiate with warmth. "I told you I'd never let any harm come to you, didn't I?"

"I thought I'd never see you again."

"But we made it. We're both here. Our hearts are still beating, aren't they?" My palms slide over the curves of her cheeks, holding her lovely face in my hands. Fucking hell, she truly is the most beautiful woman I've ever laid eyes on—even after twenty-four hours of hell, with her hair a tousled mess and dried blood staining her skin. *That's* love.

"I'm sorry I left you. I was scared, and…and I didn't know what to do."

"Robby told me what he did. That he poisoned your mind with paranoia. You did what you had to do. You're a survivor. I love that about you."

Her eyes soften looking into mine. "You do?"

"Of course I do. You ready for some alone time? Me and you. Relaxing."

"That's not a word I thought was in your vocabulary."

I grip her hand and pull her up, starting for the bathroom. "It is now. C'mon, we both need a shower. We smell like shit."

29

Falynn
PLAYLIST: ♩ KISS IT BETTER - RIHANNA ♪

"WHY DOES CHOCOLATE MOUSSE TASTE SOOO good?" I spoon-feed myself another mouthful. The creamy texture passes over my taste buds in a burst of chocolaty goodness. I moan along in delight, forgetting I'm not alone. When I open my eyes, my spoon still upside down on my tongue, I remember the second I look across the candlelit table.

Gio smirks as he watches me. He sips from his wine, a much more dignified eater than I am.

I'm definitely the bigger foodie around these parts.

I lick my spoon some more and fold my legs under me in my seat. I'm in nothing but a bathrobe with my damp curls gathered on top of my head and skin fresh and bare from our hot, steamy shower.

We're on the penthouse balcony overlooking the night's twinkling cityscape. It'll be just the two of us for the rest of the night—Gio told his men to give us uninterrupted one-on-one time. Once our dinner and dessert were served, they left us to our own devices.

To say we need this is an understatement.

After everything that's happened as of late, we've spent more time apart than together. But we've found our way back to each other, and even though the future's still uncertain, I can't help the giddy feeling bubbling in my chest.

It feels so good to be reunited with Gio. I never would've guessed what they say is true—absence does make the heart grow fonder.

"Do you ever get full?" he asks when I steal his mousse next. There's a hint of amusement in his cool, deep voice. He pries the spoon and fancy dessert bowl from my hands and then pulls me up to my feet. He brings me in close, his heavy-lidded gaze studying my face. "Your appetite's almost as big as the one I have for you."

My laugh's playful as I nestle deeper into his embrace. "Gio, are you saying watching me eat turns you on? That's the *last* kink I'd expect from you."

He nips at my neck and squeezes my sides, forcing another laugh out of me. "I'll eat you and then fuck the shit out of you for talking so much smack."

"You love when I do."

"I love shutting you up with my cock." He grabs my face and teases a kiss. "You know the deal's off, right?"

"Mmm. Does this mean there'll be a renegotiation with new terms?"

He raises a skeptical brow. "New terms? Like what?"

I can't help the little smile tugging on my lips. "More fresh air, for starters. The penthouse is fancy and Louis is cool and everything, but I'd like to not be cooped up inside with him sixteen hours a day. The other eight being sleep."

A laugh rumbles out of him and he smashes his lips to mine again in a hard, quick kiss. "See," he says, stepping back with a spank to my ass, "this is the kind of smart mouth that gets you into trouble. You drop that robe and get on all fours and we'll get started with this *renegotiation*."

For a second, I'm undecided on whether I should listen to the growing pulse between my thighs or the nagging voice in my head. For once, I choose the latter.

I lose my playful air as I turn to the balcony railing and admire the warm, breezy night. The penthouse in the Vittoria offers one of Vegas's most panoramic views—a colorful, glittering grid of lights that I can stare at for hours if I'm not careful.

The Strip itself possesses a chaotic and thrilling energy that can be felt even from all the way up here.

It wasn't long ago I was one of the people many stories below. A small dot on a major street rushing off to my next destination. For me, this time of night, that usually meant a shift at the Dollhouse.

But so much has happened over the last two months. I can't return to the Falynn I once was. I'm changed, different now.

The future's uncharted, and I don't know what that means for Gio and me.

He senses my uncertainty because he comes over and drapes his arms over me from behind. We stand still and silent and stare out at the magnificent view, the night's breeze combing through our hair.

"I need to know, Gio," I say finally. "What's next?"

The question hangs in the air before he eases me around in his arms. His hand settles on the side of my neck, his thumb tracing the line of my jaw.

"I already told you the deal is off," he says, his voice lower and huskier than usual. "I won't let you go."

Gio kisses me, his tongue stroking between my lips. The instant his lips touch mine, I'm drawn into him and the hot, passionate energy he exudes. Worries fade and anxiety evaporates into nothing as I rise on tiptoe and surrender myself to him.

Though only the sounds of the rustling wind and city traffic reach my ears, so much is being spoken.

I feel it shiver down my spine and quicken my heart beat.

Gio's claiming me, putting to rest any doubt in the wake of his kiss. He's not ready for this to end, whatever unexpected, twisted, visceral connection we've discovered in each other. He can't let go any more than I can.

Our kiss deepens in a dizzying torrent of passion as I tease his tongue with my own and his hands slide into the plunging neckline of my Terry-cloth robe.

It slips off my shoulders, catching on my elbows. I shudder as he palms my breasts with comforting familiarity, his touch warm and rough all at the same time.

He tears his mouth from mine, his lids hooded and blue eyes darker. He's like a lion that's finally caught its prey and now considers how to devour it.

Every part of me relishes in being that prey.

"In case it's still unclear, you're mine," he growls, and then he scoops me up into his arms.

I yelp, barely registering what's happening before he's whisking me away, back inside the penthouse. He carries me into the bedroom and drops me into the center of the massive, king-size bed. I prop myself up by my elbows and lay back, drinking in the sight of this dominating and deadly Mafia king standing over me.

He's as dangerous as a wildfire, and yet all I want to do is burn with him.

Run this sinful city with him. Rule the world with him.

I watch as he unbuttons his pristine white dress shirt and reveals the sculpted perfection that is his torso. From the hard-packed muscle of his pectorals to the ridged wash of his abs and the bulges of his biceps, his body still leaves me speechless.

My pussy clenches on air as his large hands shift to his belt and next an even larger sight greets me—his mouth-watering cock points tall and proud, weightier than I remember—and that's saying something.

Need quakes in my belly at the same time as desire licks at me and flushes my skin. I bite my bottom lip and stifle a moan, reimagining what he feels like inside me.

It's been so long. Way too long.

He joins me on the bed, promptly wrenching the already open robe off of me.

That's the thing about Gio—when he's ready to feast, he wastes no time. Right now, is one of those times. He wants to fuck, and as my arousal slicks between my thighs, I want every hard, dominating stroke.

His firm hands grab a hold of my hips and his long, heavy length brushes against me. He crushes his lips to mine with such force his kiss almost knocks the air from my lungs. He's losing the last semblance of control over himself as his fingers dig into my hip and he strokes his cock.

I take over for him, curling my smaller hand around his deliciously hot and velvety shaft. I'd suck his dick like a lollipop every day for the rest of my life if he'd let me. I'll have to remember to give him the nastiest of soul-sucking blowjobs later.

We kiss and tease each other 'til we can't hold on any longer. Gio pins me to the mattress using his larger, muscled body, and nudges my thighs open with his knee. He sinks into me, covering my body with his as he comes in close and kisses my neck and face.

A strained groan rumbles from his broad chest and vibrates against my skin. He kisses my throat some more and holds still as best as he can as I adjust to the feel and girth of him.

So thick. So full.

When he can no longer stand it, he drags his hips back and then thrusts forward. He bottoms out, filling me up to my startled whimper. I clutch at his arms and band my legs around him as he builds into a slow but deep-stroking rhythm.

His perfect abs ripple, practicing the restraint not to go faster. He's trying to make this last, indulge in our passionate lovemaking for once. He kisses me as deep as his cock slips into me. His tongue flicks against mine, our bodies tangled up as one.

It feels so right it's beyond words.

Our relationship hasn't been easy. Just two months ago I was broke and desperate, certain a mysterious man in the VIP section was nothing more than my mark that night. What unfolded has become the wildest turn of events in my life.

But through the danger and thrills and carnal passion, I've survived. I've discovered a new side of myself as I fall deeper in love with a powerful and deadly Mafia king.

Last night, I took a life. What's even more surprising is that I don't regret it. Antonio Lovato had to be stopped. He posed a danger not only to Gio's empire, but to our relationship.

In Gio's world, there's no black and white. Only gray. The ambiguity that exists in every situation. Murder is wrong, but sometimes the person is right. In this life, sometimes it's the only way.

And it's the world I want to be a part of. His dark, sinful world I can no longer imagine my life without.

I know that more than ever as we make love.

Gio switches our position with deft ease. He rolls onto his back and lifts me up over him. I gladly trap him between my thighs, and in an impressive collaborative effort, we slide his cock back into my slick, waiting pussy. I sink with a moan and shudder, squeezing his hot and thick cock as best I can.

I plant my hands on his chest and begin rocking my hips. My body's a sizzling live wire of growing pleasure. It zings through me, starting from my pussy, and coursing through the rest of me. I lose all inhibition and arch my back, head tilted toward the ceiling. I gyrate my hips, rocking harder, taking him in full.

Gio helps guide me. One large hand encircles my hips, and he slams me down on his fat cock. His other grabs the back of my neck and wrenches my mouth to his. His fingers find their way into my hair and he unwinds my topknot.

My wild curls unfurl, cascading to freedom about my shoulders. He plays with them, twining ringlets around his fingers, as he holds me in place and his cock hits new depths. The fat tip presses into my G-spot 'til an orgasm sweeps in and seizes me.

My mouth falls open and I can no longer move.

Hot pleasure sears through me, breaking me out in a feverish dew. I tuck my face deep into the crook of Gio's neck as tremors rock my body right down to my pinky toes. He lifts me up only to ram me back down. My wet and swollen pussy envelops his cock, still tingling with aftershocks of my orgasm.

So close to his own release, he slams me harder, his hips bucking up to meet mine. I'm so delirious, dizzied by my pleasure, it doesn't even register he's coming 'til I feel the warmth of his seed flooding me. Our bodies rock against each other before eventually tapering off in a breathless, sweaty finish.

He lays us back on the mountain of pillows with no consideration for the mess we've made. Our sheets are wrinkled, and the room smells of sex, but as we nestle close, it's an environment I'd die a happy woman in.

Just like this. Just us.

I rest my head on his chest, my body boneless. My lids fall halfway, a satisfied sigh rolling out of me. Gio holds me close, his arm slung over my hip. His fingers still play in my curls, tender strokes that elicit tingles across my scalp and down my spine.

It's nothing but content silence for minutes, and then…

"I meant what I said earlier," he says, speaking with more clarity post-nut. "The deal's off. I can't let you go, Falynn."

"We can talk about dating. Maybe… maybe…" I trail off before the 'r' word makes an appearance. Gio's been clear about not doing relationships.

His muscly arm only tightens around me. "No dating," he says in his calm yet commanding voice. "I don't need to date you to know I want you."

"Are you saying you want to be together… for real? Like a real relationship?"

Please say that's what you're saying. Please.

He pauses long enough for my hope to fall. But I learn a second later what he's really doing is collecting his thoughts.

"You asked about my mother before. Weeks ago. Do you remember?"

I do. We'd been lying in bed just like this, trading silly stories about our childhoods. I'd told him about my braces and he'd told me about his brief stint in a school play. He'd asked me about my family, but when I'd asked about his—his mother—he'd shut down. He'd gone into cold, callous Mafia boss mode.

"You don't have to tell me about her if you don't want."

"No. It's time. I want to share it with you." His breath rumbles from his lungs as he inhales then exhales, the rest of his body feeling harder and more like flesh-covered steel than ever. "When my brother Giancarlo and I were boys, our parents' relationship was a complicated one. My father was many years older than my mother. He never loved her. She probably never loved him either. But she loved us.

"That I knew. Even at a young age, growing up in the lifestyle we did. She was the only bright spot I remember—always so warm, so affectionate. She had a great sense of humor. My father never appreciated her. He made it known it was a marriage of convenience. Just something transactional. She gave him heirs. He gave her expensive jewelry and an enormous mansion. And when she died, it was of no importance to him."

A concerned frown twists onto my face as I tip my head up for a glance at him. His expression is unreadable, but his eyes tell a different story. They're a dark and stormy blue, pained.

"He didn't let us grieve her for long. He wiped our home of all traces of her. Their transaction was over. She'd served her purpose. I didn't understand this," he explains with another heavy breath. "I didn't understand how he could be so cruel, but soon I would. He taught Giancarlo, and me, to be coldhearted bastards just like him. Told us love, feelings are a weakness for men like us. Kings don't have hearts. It's how they're able to rule."

I ache for him. Even the strain in his voice stirs emotion inside of me. Deep empathy that pricks my eyes and makes me want to cry for the boy he once was.

"Giancarlo and I were home when it happened… when she was murdered. But we weren't allowed to express anything about it. We learned to forget it, and her. I've become the man my father molded me to be, which is a man who loves nothing but the power I hold. I've succeeded for many years. Then I met you."

My heart stills in my chest as suddenly the silence between his words feels poignant. Intuition whispers inside me, telling me where this is going, but disbelief won't let me truly absorb what he's saying.

"I told myself I'd have you only for a night, then it was a few weeks. Now I can't lie anymore. What can I say? I've fallen in love with you, my sweet honey Falynn."

A short gasp escapes me before I tilt my head and kiss his bearded jawline and then his neck, pressing my face into it and inhaling his warm, intoxicating masculine scent. It symbolizes safety and security for me, and most of all—

"Gio… I love you too," I whisper. "I just want to be with you… for real."

"You will be, Honey. You'll be at my side." His hand sweeps up my naked spine and makes me shiver. He pulls me up and captures my lips in a tender kiss, his fingers deep in my curls.

My smile happens organically even as we kiss. It's beyond my control as it finally sinks in. I have what I've always dreamed of. Security. Safety. A man who loves me, flaws and all. One who would scorch the earth if need be for me.

And I him.

So this is happiness.

30

Giovanni
PLAYLIST: ♪ NO CHURCH IN THE WILD - JAY-Z & KANYE WEST FEATURING FRANK OCEAN & THE DREAM ♪

"YOU DIDN'T THINK I forgot about you, did you?"

Lorenzo Espinosa squints against the bright light shining in his face. He's tied to a chair in a secret padded room of the casino. His wounds are still fresh from the standoff with Lovato. According to C.J., who's been on duty watching him, he's spent most of the last twenty-four hours sobbing and begging for mercy.

Unfortunately for him, I'm not a forgiving man.

This fucker not only helped shoot up my casino and worked as a street guy for Lovato, but he's put his hands on Falynn. He kidnapped her and almost stood by and watched her murder.

He's the man who failed her in the first place—if it hadn't been for his failure, she'd never have put herself up for sale that night at the Dollhouse. But even though his failure is my victory, his very existence disgusts me.

He needs to be taken care of.

I step farther into the padded room, emerging from the deep shadows, entering the spotlight where Lorenzo's seated. He blinks up at me, tears wetting the corners of his eyes.

"Mr. S-Sorrentino," he stutters. He's shaking in his chair, his knees bouncing. "P-please... I... I'm nobody important... just a street guy."

"Relax, Enzo. That's what your friends call you, right?" I ask calmly, circling him. "That's what Falynn calls you, isn't it?"

He chokes on his own breath. I stand by and wait as he coughs and tries to gulp down a better breath of air, but his nerves best him again. He's pathetic, barely able to breathe.

A grown ass man ready to grovel like the coward he is.

"Listen... you have to listen..." he pleads. Even his voice wavers. "If... if this is about Falynn... I don't want the bitch. You can have her. She's all yours. W-we were never that serious. I had plenty of other chicks on the side—"

Blood squirts from his mouth as I deck him hard in the jaw. The brass knuckles clutched in my fist knock two teeth loose, and those go flying too. They scatter on the concrete floor beneath our feet. I glance down at them and then back up at him as he breaks down in pained, bloody-mouthed sobs.

"You dropped something," I say, tapping his cracked teeth on the floor with my shoe. I stomp on them, pulverizing them into even smaller pieces.

Lorenzo howls out a pathetic cry of pain. A soft tinkle noise joins the sounds of his cries. The crotch of his pants darken by several shades. He's just pissed himself. Blood pours out of his mouth as he bows his head and begins mumbling a prayer.

"Don't be a fucking pussy. Look me in the eye!" I growl, clenching my fist in his hair and yanking his head up. His eyes bulge, meeting mine, his ugly face covered in snot, blood, and tears. A hot, intense rage I've kept under wraps surges free, tensing up my body. My muscles flex on their own, even my cheek twitching. "You're fucking disgusting," I spit. "You don't deserve to live, do you? What use are you?"

"P-please," he begs, "I'll do anything… anything you want!"

"You wet yourself like a little bitch. You should be begging me to end it."

"No…no!"

He devolves into more hysterical sobs. I snap my fingers and C.J. steps forward with the power drill and bits I've requested.

"I'll work for you. I'll be… I can be one of your new street guys."

"Do you think it's wise to call Falynn out of her name?" I ask him casually, inserting the drill bit into place. I power on the drill and adjust the torque to my liking. "Do you know she was so loyal to you she refused to rat you out? It almost cost her her life, Enzo. Yet here you are, calling her a bitch."

"I didn't mean it!" he screams. He eyes the power drill with naked terror.

"I think you did. Did you always treat her so poorly? Did it make you feel like a big, bad man when you smacked her? Now here you are pissing yourself like a child wets the bed. You don't have an ounce of pride, and that's why you don't deserve to live."

"HELP! SOMEBODY HELP!"

"Nobody's coming, Enzo. But if it makes you feel better to scream at the top of your lungs, be my guest. It's music to my ears."

Enzo continues screaming, spraying blood and spit. I

advance, the power drill's loud buzz filling the room. The sound's contained thanks to the ingeniously padded walls. Thousands of people wander the Vittoria Resort and Casino, none the wiser, a few floors below a man's about to lose his life… and every part of his body first.

Falynn doesn't know what's about to go down. Even though she's taken a life, she's still too pure. She'd forgive him. Beg me to let this piece of shit go. She can never know of what I'm about to do.

But this is for her. A bloody, violent ode of my love for her.

Let it be known: I'll slaughter every last *cazzo* who ever dares bring her harm.

"We're going to play a game, Enzo," I say. He's back to feeble sobs and slobbering snot slumped in his chair. "I'm thinking of a number between one and ten. Take your pick and choose wisely."

"S-seven."

"Not so good choice. That's seven holes."

Lorenzo erupts into fresh screams as the drill grinds toward his forearm strapped to the chair, but he goes unheard. The padded walls silence every last one of his screams.

The night's just getting started.

"That was a gruesome one, Boss," Louis says an hour and a half later.

I've used the private bathroom next to my casino office to shower and change. My bloody clothes have been disposed of, as have the extra baggage from our torture session in the secret room. It's already like it never happened.

Falynn's none the wiser.

"How was everything else?" I ask, buttoning my gold and onyx cufflinks.

"Falynn's almost ready. Johansson just arrived at La Pergola. Everything else around the resort and casino is running smoothly. Very festive vibe tonight."

"Good. Because it's an occasion to celebrate. We've won."

Louis smiles, his round face jovial. "Even quicker than I thought. The city's yours."

"This is just the beginning. I have plans for this city."

"Giancarlo has to know by now. That your father…" Louis trails off, his insinuation clear.

I pour myself a finger of bourbon and give a nod. "He knows. As does Claro. Neither are ecstatic about this turn of events, but how they feel is irrelevant. My father's made his choice."

"The best man got the job." Louis chuckles at his own comment like the big softie that he is. But a damn good soldier. My new right hand. "Which reminds me, boss, something came for you. Some kind of… card."

I'm too busy drinking my bourbon. Instead, I motion for him to continue. My mind's already on meeting Falynn at La Pergola for our dinner. I wonder what dress she'll wear tonight to drive me crazy. Perhaps we should skip dinner altogether, and go straight to the end of the night, where we're alone in the penthouse.

I can already taste her sweet honey nectar on my tongue.

Louis produces the card in question. It's a tiny unmarked envelope with an even tinier notecard. There's nothing on the card except the single word typed in the center in simple black ink:

. . .

Soon.

"What is this?" I ask impatiently, throwing Louis an expectant look. "Is this some kind of joke? Soon, what?"

Louis shrugs. "That's all it says. Fozzi mentioned it arrived anonymously earlier. You think it's Lovato Sr.?"

My interest wanes and I push the card and envelope into Louis's wide chest. "I don't care. Get rid of it. Any matter he wants to address, he can do so directly. There's more pressing matters tonight, like dinner."

"And dessert with Miss Falynn?" Louis grins slowly.

I laugh and clap a hand to his back as we head toward the door. "I've already told you, Lou. I'm addicted to the girl."

The casino thrives with life. Everywhere you look, there are crowds of customers milling toward the game tables, or strolling around our specialty shops. They stop by our bars and order drinks and they watch the sports games on our big screen TVs in our sports lounge. Our resort guests cross the lobby to the elevators, ready to retreat to their luxury hotel rooms after a long day spent touring the city.

I observe it all as I stride through my creation. The Vittoria Resort and Casino is a success because I made it that way. Every piece of the puzzle required to remodel this place and open it up with a fresh brand and image was due to me. My absolute determination to prove myself to my father.

That I could bring back glory to the Sorrentino name in the west. Just like old times.

I've succeeded. I've won the fight against Antonio

Lovato and his claim to the city. I've set myself up to rule not only Vegas, but soon the entire Sorrentino empire. I'm the King of Vegas, and in no time, I'll be King of Everything. The most powerful man in the world.

And Falynn Marie Carter will be at my side.

As I make my way through the casino, flanked by Louis and Dominico, heads turn and stare. I'm royalty, known by the city as its new king. Successful businessman, Giovanni Sorrentino, who arrived in Sin City months ago and already made it his.

But I relish in the attention, the reverence.

Everybody needs to know I'm on top. You don't mess with me, or you'll end up six feet under.

Falynn's beautiful face lights up the second she sees me. Tonight she's wearing a sexy red cocktail dress that pops against her brown skin and accentuates her cleavage and the rest of her curves.

I kiss her lips and grab her hand, leading us to our table. Johansson and the others already seated try to engage in conversation, but I'm much more interested in Falynn. Her sweet scent lingers around me as drinks are poured and the night feels endless.

She's what I've been missing. The heart I needed when mine was too black, too dark. Now that I have her, I'm unstoppable. A man who truly has it all, power and wealth, and the woman worth the world by my side.

The new King of Vegas.

TO BE CONTINUED…

Author's Note

Just want to thank you for giving King of Vegas a chance. It means so much to me!

This story was scary for me, because it's different than what I normally write. I like to think of it as Pretty Woman, but with a darker mafia twist. I was surprised by how much I enjoyed writing Falynn and Giovanni. I hope you enjoyed them too! Their story is far from over, and will continue in books 2 and 3!

If you have a free second, please drop a review for book 1. I would greatly appreciate it. :)

You can review on Amazon, Goodreads or Bookbub.

Soundtrack

1. 6 Inch - Beyoncé featuring The Weeknd
2. Blinding Lights - The Weeknd
3. Savages - Marina and The Diamonds
4. Catch Me - DXVN.
5. Human - Sevdaliza
6. Loyalty - Kendrick Lamar featuring Rihanna
7. In Time - FKA Twigs
8. Pryamids - Frank Ocean
9. Dreamers - K.Flay
10. Throne - Saint Mesa
11. Burning Desire - Lana Del Rey
12. The Beach - The Neighbourhood
13. Bad at Love - Halsey
14. Heaven or Las Vegas - The Weeknd
15. Toxic - 2WEI (Britney Spears Cover)
16. Somewhat Damaged - Nine Inch Nails
17. Nothing's Gonna Hurt You, Baby - Cigarettes After Sex
18. Dragon - LVNDVN
19. Broken Clocks - SZA
20. Terrible Thing - AG

21. Boys Like You - Tanerélle

22. Lie To Me - Black Atlass

23. #1 Crush - Garbage

24. Worst Behavior - Drake

25. War of Hearts - Ruelle

26. Burn it Down - Linkin Park

27. 27 Hours - Banks

28. Worship - Amber Run

29. Kiss It Better - Rihanna

30. No Church in the Wild - Jay-Z & Kanye West featuring Frank Ocean and The Dream

Listen to the soundtrack on Spotify!

Stay Connected

Sign up for Sienne's Newsletter

Follow Sienne's Author Page

Follow Sienne on TikTok

Follow Sienne on Instagram

Follow Sienne on Goodreads

Follow Sienne on Bookbub

Also by Sienne Vega

City of Sinners Series

Book 1 - King of Vegas

Book 2 - Queen of Hearts

Book 3 - Kingdom of Sin

Book 4 - Heart of Sin (Louis & Tasha Novella)

City of Sinners Special Edition Boxset

Gangsters & Roses Series

Book 0 - Forbidden Roses

Book 1 - Wicked Roses

Book 2 - Twisted Roses

Book 3 - Savage Roses

Book 4 - Devious Roses

Book 5 - Ruthless Roses

Gangsters & Roses Special Edition Boxset

The Steel Kings MC Series

Book 1 - No Mercy for Kings (COMING SOON)

About the Author

Sienne has a thing for dark and brooding alphas and the women who love them. She enjoys writing stories where lines are blurred, and the romance is dark and delicious. In her spare time, she unwinds with a nice glass of wine and Netflix binge.

For more info on Sienne and her books, visit siennevegaauthor.com.

Printed in Great Britain
by Amazon